PRAISE FOR LINNY MACK

"Linny Mack's debut novel, *Changing Tides*, is a **captivating tale** that explores the intricate dance between love, loss, and rebirth. With a narrative that will keep you on the **edge of your seat**, and an ending you won't see coming, this **story will break your heart** and piece it back together, one beautiful shard at a time."

–Buck Turner, bestselling author of *The Keeper of Stars*

"Mack's **striking debut shatters your heart** in fourteen different ways before masterfully piecing it all back together by the end. Cape May, Sophie, and Liam, will have a place in my heart forever."

–Lily Parker, author of *The Best Wrong Move*

"A **breathtaking debut**, *Changing Tides* is a masterclass in slow-burn romance, brimming with depth, heart, and hard-won healing. Featuring **beautifully drawn characters** in their 40s, it celebrates love not as a reckless leap but as a **courageous journey**—one where finding each other begins with first finding ourselves."

–Shaylin Gandhi, author of *When We Had Forever*

"This story of two broken people struggling to heal themselves grabbed hold of my heart and refused to let go. **An ode to fate and found families**, *Changing Tides* is a satisfying, slow-burn romance that will make you believe in second chances."

–Lindsay Hameroff, author of *Never Planned on You*

"Every page of Mack's debut was filled with the warmth and comfort of found family, the **bittersweet nostalgia** of childhood summers, and the yearning excitement of new love. Her characters have found a forever home in my heart!"

-Christy Schillig, author of *Wish You Weren't Here*

Changing Tides

Changing Tides

LINNY MACK

PAGE
&
VINE

Page & Vine
An Imprint of Meredith Wild LLC

Paperback ISBN: 978-1-964264-10-3

To my husband, whose World Series kind of love inspired me to write romance novels.
And to my seventh grade English teacher, who made me believe I could.

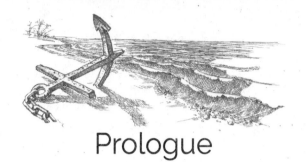

Prologue

Sophie

"Take all your worries to the beach and wave them goodbye..."

This is one of those surreal moments in life when the very thing I least expect to happen is, *in fact*, happening right before my eyes.

They don't hear me come in at first.

"What the hell is going on here?" I shake my head and blink my eyes, because I can't believe what I am actually seeing.

In response to my audible gasp, my *husband* and the woman jump apart, and she covers herself with a bed sheet. *My* bed sheet. I am too stunned to cry, but I know that if I look at James, the angry tears pricking the back of my eyes will start to fall. Before another word is spoken, the woman runs into my master bathroom, dragging the sheet with her, and slams the door behind her.

And here I am, on my thirty-eighth birthday, standing in the doorway of my bedroom, feeling heartbroken and betrayed. I had great intentions. I left work early; I thought I would come home and surprise James for my birthday. We hadn't made any plans. Instead, it appears I am getting a different kind of birthday surprise. As a marriage and family therapist, I think it's safe to say this is not how I saw my life turning out.

James fumbles over himself, throwing on clothes while I still have not moved from my place at the entrance to our most sacred space—a place that just this morning still felt sacred and now it feels tarnished. He tugs his shirt over his head and takes a step in my direction.

"Sophie." He chokes out my name.

I meet his regretful eyes and narrow my own, my sadness turning to rage. The rush of emotion surprises me like a strong gust of wind, knocking me off kilter. "It's my fucking *birthday*," I spit, seething with anger. I spin on my heel and immediately retreat to the guest room.

For the next ten days, my world is crashing down. James is apologetic. He weeps—guilt will do that to a person. He grovels. He says it was a one-time thing and tries everything to get me to talk to him, to work through it. Each day, I feel my resolve weakening. James is scared to lose me—he knows and I know it.

If I'm honest with myself, I'm scared to lose him too. Our marriage has been my entire life for the past thirteen years. To walk away now would be really hard. I have remained in the guest room, but I'm not sleeping or eating well. My self-care is in the toilet, even though I know what I should be doing to protect my well-being. To make matters worse, each night after work, James broaches the subject again.

"Sophie, please. We have to work through this. Isn't that your job? To help people through hard things? To help them keep their family together?" he begs.

He isn't wrong. How can I champion love for others and not myself?

After all, we have so much history. We *worked* for our life together. Maybe James isn't entirely to blame. I haven't been the most present partner lately. Maybe we can get back what we lost and start fresh.

I feel I owe it to James to try, but the pit in my stomach never goes away, no matter how much I want to fix our marriage. Finally, after sleeping in the guest room for a week and a half, I'm about to agree to forgiveness on a trial basis, on the condition that we get a new bed and go to couples counseling of course. Maybe making the decision to move forward will help matters.

I am hopeful, until I walk into the house a week later to find him sitting on the couch in the dark. The light flooding from our entryway allows me to see that his eyes are red and puffy with dark circles underneath, like he's been crying. At this moment I realize he probably hasn't been sleeping much either.

"James? What's wrong? What are you doing in the dark?" I walk in, toss my stuff on the armchair, and begin turning on the lights. "I was thinking maybe I could ask Dr. Steiner for a recommendation," I begin, speaking quickly.

"Brittany is pregnant," he says numbly. When I don't speak, he continues, "You know...my TA."

I stare blankly at him. There goes my forgiveness. I take a deep breath. "Uh-huh. Yeah, I got that." My voice wavers, barely above a whisper. I cough and attempt to regain my composure, but my words come out wobbly anyway. "So, this wasn't just a one-time thing with her, I guess."

He begins weeping. I don't stick around to hear more.

We spent the past seven years struggling with infertility. I struggle to get pregnant, and when I finally do, I can't stay pregnant. The realization that someone else could sweep right in, steal my life, my husband, and his sperm hits me like a stinging slap in the face. Any ounce of forgiveness I had thought I'd be giving him when I walked in the door flies out the window. I retreat up to our room and throw everything that I can fit into a bag. I can't stay here with him another second.

He's still crying in the living room when my hand grasps the door handle. I pause and suck in a sharp breath. I can't believe what I'm about to say. I swallow hard and turn back toward him, slinging my duffel bag over my shoulder. He meets my eyes for the first time since I've walked in the door, shame and sadness clouding his expression.

"I want a divorce," I say, my voice stoney.

I let the door slam behind me, and I don't look back.

Chapter One

Sophie

Six Weeks Later

Cape May, New Jersey, is a picturesque Victorian beach town that I frequented as a child with my parents. The air is salty, and just a huff of the sea breeze can lower your heart rate to a blissful level. Each summer of my childhood was spent on these beaches, looking for seashells and Cape May Diamonds, walking the mall, and eating ice cream. My life and family have changed so much since those days, but I remember one thing clearly, almost as if it was yesterday. I remember that at the end of each of those summers, I felt whole. I felt peaceful.

Here I am now, trying to manifest the same peaceful feeling I had back then. I came here in search of that feeling, of a solace I realize I have been missing for a long time.

Today, I signed my divorce papers, a day that will be forever cemented in my mind as one where my dreams died. I had big plans. I wanted a family of my own, much like the one I grew up in, but my partner betrayed me in a way I still cannot fully wrap my brain around. The only place I could think to go to begin picking up the pieces is Cape May.

I'm realizing *now* that driving here straight from Scranton, Pennsylvania was maybe not my wisest decision. It's the first weekend in April, and while it's not officially the high season yet, I have no reservations and no plans. I called my assistant on my way down here and asked her to clear my schedule Luckily, my caseload isn't too heavy and my best friend Claire, who is also a therapist at the same center, agreed to take any emergencies. So, I have nowhere to be for two weeks. And, nowhere to stay.

I plop down on the cool sand, let out a breath, and reach for my phone. *I'm here now. This is going to be okay.*

I open the vacation rental app and search Cape May. The first listing catches my eye because the house reminds me so much of my grandparents' house with its large wraparound porch and big bay windows. It even has a turret tower, giving it the castle-like appearance that I loved about their home. I used to sneak into their bedroom and look out the window as far as the eye could see. Lucky for me, this old Victorian features an adjacent guest cottage with exactly the availability I need.

I quickly scroll through the description and then request a reservation from a woman named Eleanor. She doesn't reply immediately, giving me the chance to suck in a cleansing breath of ocean air. I'm letting the cool sand sift through my fingers and contemplating the meaning of life when my phone dings. Eleanor's picture is hard to see but she looks to be in her sixties and she has a kind smile. I click on the message:

> *The guest cottage is available for your requested timeframe.*
> *Would you mind calling or texting me? I hate the internet.*
> *609-555-3142 :)*

I chuckle and type her number into a text message. She tells me I can come over and check the place out if I am already in town. I stand up and brush the sand off my legs. I take in the smell of the salt air as I trek back up the beach, and I instantly feel at ease. I made the right decision coming to Cape May to heal. It has never steered me wrong before and I know it won't now.

This is the place where I will recover and pick up the pieces of my life.

When I pull up to the Victorian house on Perry Street

I am overcome with nostalgia. The home is even more like my grandparents' house than the pictures portrayed. My chest is tight as I swallow the memory of my last time staring up at their Victorian, a *for sale* sign firmly planted in the yard.

Before I march up the steps, I glance up and down the short block. Perry Street is shaded with mature trees, and each house is more beautiful than the next. A sense of serenity washes over me as I walk up the steps and prepare to knock. Just as I am about to grab the crab-shaped door knocker, the large burgundy front door swings open. I am greeted by a woman in a long sage green boho dress with long wavy hair that is a mix of gray and blonde. She is wearing red lipstick and dangly earrings at noon, but she has kind eyes, and I have a sense that they can see straight through to my broken spirit.

"You must be Eleanor. I'm Sophie." I hold out my hand to shake hers, self-conscious of my chipped nail polish and chewed cuticles.

She smiles warmly at me. "Call me Ellie, please." She holds the door open further. "Please come in." She starts walking toward the back of the house while speaking quickly. "This is the house I grew up in. I inherited it from my parents and now I live here all alone. I just love having company. You're also welcome to stay in the main house but I'm sure you'd prefer the privacy of the guest house. Is it just you who will be staying?" She turns around as she asks the last question. A baby cries in the next room. "Coming, Lulu!" she sings, dashing to the other room and coming back with a sweet baby girl on her hip. She has pink chubby cheeks and a mess of wispy blonde curls around her ears. "I'm babysitting." She smiles down at the baby. "This is Lucy."

I grin and reach for the baby's chubby little hand. "Hi Lucy, you're so cute."

Lucy is bashful as she nuzzles her face into Ellie's neck, tugging on the neckline of her dress.

Ellie adjusts Lucy's hand and leads me through a sliding glass door and down the steps of the deck to a small cottage. It has the same sage green siding and burgundy front door that the main house has, with a large bay window on the front and a smaller one on the right side. We walk by planters on the small patio with pink and purple petunias basking in the sunlight. If it's possible, the little house looks happy, and I feel like it's beckoning me.

"It's not much but I think you'll find yourself comfortable. It'll be perfect for just you." She unlocks the front door, and we step into a tiny living area with a teal crushed velvet couch, a small end table, and a small flat-screen TV. Behind that, there is a queen-sized bed with a night table. To my left is a small kitchenette, there is a cooktop and a fridge but no oven. I think, for now, I can work with this.

"Go on, have a look around. If you like it, you're welcome to stay. You'll have to complete the payment on that godforsaken website, because that's how I get paid, but I really don't follow the booking rules. Or any rules at all for that matter!" She laughs at herself. I really like her already.

I make a show of checking out the rest of the space, but I already know this will be where I find myself again. I walk into the small bathroom, thrilled to find a deep claw-foot bathtub. I envision myself soaking away my sadness in bubbles and wine. I haven't cared for myself properly in far too long. Between fertility treatments, the stress of getting pregnant, being in my strained marriage, and helping others at work, I am long overdue for some self-care.

I walk back out to the front patio, where there is a bench and a small café table. I think about the cups of coffee I will drink out here listening to the birds chirp good morning. I remember what Cape May did for me as a child, and I am manifesting that it can do the same for me now.

"I'll take it." I smile. "I think this place is just what I need." *Plus it sure beats staying at my dad's house.*

Ellie reaches for me and gives my shoulder a familiar maternal squeeze that strikes me as oddly forward, though not entirely unwelcome. "Wonderful! And you'll be with us for two weeks?" she asks, clarifying the availability I asked for in our initial message.

"Or is indefinitely okay?" I joke, then quickly add, "Yes. Two weeks should do it."

We are interrupted by the rumble of an engine, then the sound of a pickup truck door closing. Outside a man—tall, muscular, and bearded, with brooding blue eyes under a baseball cap—approaches the cottage. And he doesn't look happy to see any of us. "I didn't expect you to be out back," he says gruffly.

"I was just showing Sophie here the guest house. She's my new tenant," Ellie says, handing him the baby. "Sophie, this is my neighbor and longtime friend, Liam." She gestures at the man who is still wearing a salty expression.

I hold out my hand for him to shake but he doesn't move to shake mine. Feeling my cheeks flush, I stick my hand in my back pocket. "Hi, I'm Sophie." I offer him a smile. "Your daughter is beautiful."

He doesn't return it, and he doesn't meet my eye. "She isn't my daughter," he snaps. "She's my niece." He shifts her to his other hip and lets out an exasperated puff of air. "Is her diaper bag all packed?" he asks Ellie. "I'm sorry but it's been a long day."

"It's all inside, but she may need a snack." Ellie remains stoic, as if she is used to his cantankerous mood.

"Great. Well, I'll show myself out and see you tomorrow." He stalks toward the back steps and disappears inside.

Once he is gone, Ellie turns to me apologetically. "I'm sorry about him," she says, knitting her brow. "He isn't the happiest guy on the block. He recently got custody of Lucy, and I think it's been an adjustment for him." She shrugs as if to say, what can I do?

"Oh, you don't need to worry about that," I assure her. "I am preoccupied with my own shi–stuff, anyway." I pull out my phone and complete the reservation booking on Ellie's listing. "I just paid for the two weeks. I appreciate you accommodating me so last minute."

"No trouble at all, dear. It's still the off-season. I haven't been booked here all winter. This place is a ghost town until May." She starts to walk toward her house but stops abruptly. "I almost forgot!" She hands me a key on a ring with a keychain charm.

I take it from her and run my fingers over the smooth clear stone. "Thank you. Is this a Cape May Diamond?"

"That it is." Her eyes crinkle when she grins at me.

"I used to collect these all the time as a girl," I say wistfully, the memory sending a rush of nostalgia up the back of my neck.

Ellie nods solemnly, as if my nostalgia is palpable. Then she turns to go inside. "Just text me if you need anything!" she calls behind her.

I don't plan on needing anything.

ൣ

I wake up the next morning to the sound of chatter and giggling in the garden. I glance at my phone and see that it's only 7:15 a.m. When I sit up fumbling for my phone I remember the empty bottle of wine that I helped myself to from the liquor cabinet last night, sans dinner.

"Ugh..." I groan. I cannot believe I drank the whole bottle. And I never took my bubble bath. I frown at the realization. It's funny, even though helping to heal people is what I do for a living, I don't know the first thing about how to heal myself. I'm going to have to work on that.

I've had my phone on Do Not Disturb since I left yesterday. I specifically told my dad and Claire where I was headed and took off. So why do I feel a pang of disappointment when I see that I have no missed calls or texts from James? I know in ninety days, we'll be divorced; I know he's with someone else now.

I don't know what I expected, but suddenly I'm aware of just how alone I really am. It's disconcerting. I groan again, this time more audibly, and I worry Ellie has heard me when there's a soft knock at the door.

"Sophie, are you okay in there? I, uh, it sounds like you

might be sick?" Ellie sounds unsure, like she knows she might be overstepping.

"I'm okay!" I shout back, embarrassed. I throw the pillow over my face and whisper-scream expletives into it. "I am just waking up."

"Oh goodness, I hope Lucy and I didn't wake you!" Ellie replies apologetically. "We'll head inside."

I don't even have the courage to reply. My head is pounding, so I let myself drift back to sleep.

I wake up a while later, and my head still feels as if it's going to implode. I want to cry when I remember that I don't have any Advil or really any food in my new residence. It's 10 a.m., and I haven't eaten since lunch yesterday. No wonder that wine went straight to my head. I throw on one of my comfy lounge outfits, walk to Ellie's back door, and knock softly. She comes quickly, wiping her hands on a dish towel as she opens the door.

"Hello, dear! I'm so sorry if we disturbed you earlier." She pauses, giving me the once over. I hear a children's show playing in the background. "What can I do for you?" Her expression is warm and welcoming.

"I, uh, was wondering if you might have something for a headache?" I wince as I say it, partially out of embarrassment and partially because I don't even know how my head is still attached.

Ellie smirks. "Get into the wine, did you? The Cape May Winery makes a mean red." I must look embarrassed because then she smiles. "Sure, come on in. I was just fixing myself a little brunch. Would you care for some bacon and eggs? I'm intermittent fasting this week!"

I want to laugh at her usage of "this week" because if she is anything like me, she's tried everything to shed those few stubborn pounds. Fertility treatments have not been kind to my once trim physique. Where I once had abs, there's now a softer midsection. Up until now, I haven't found it in me to care. James loved me for me...or so I thought. My stomach grumbles audibly as I smell the bacon that she has in the oven.

"I'll take that as a yes, then!" Ellie laughs, reacting to its angry growl. "Come sit. Do you like coffee?" She ushers me into an old wicker kitchen chair with a homemade seat cushion tied on that reminds me of the chairs my grandmother used to have in her dining room. I take note of the empty highchair next to me and peer into the open living room where baby Lucy is in the playpen, holding herself up to a stand and bopping along to a toddler tune.

"Y-yes, please," I say. It's all I can manage. I'm overstimulated by the sunlight and the noise of the baby's music.

Ellie places a steaming cup of coffee and two Advil in front of me with a small pitcher of half-and-half and some sugar cubes. I fix my coffee, breathe in the heavenly aroma, and take my first sip.

"So, what brings you to Cape May, dear?" Ellie wonders aloud as she cracks some eggs into a bowl.

I take another sip of my coffee and a deep breath, feeling instantly better and more able to engage in conversation. "I just filed for divorce from my husband of thirteen years," I say, catching the melancholy in my voice but at the same time feeling relief having said it out loud. "I just needed to get away for a while."

Ellie drops the spatula on the floor and turns to me as she picks it up, eyebrows raised. "I'm so sorry. I can't say I was expecting that, but I thought I saw a sadness in your eyes," she notes. "I obviously didn't want to pry. If you'd like an outsider's perspective, though, I am a bored old bitty with a lifetime of experience."

I appreciate the sentiment, even though she doesn't look a day over sixty, and give her a grim smile. "The long and short of it is, I am broken, and he found someone else who isn't." I sigh, staring down into my coffee mug.

Ellie moves the spatula around the pan with her back to me but turns when what I said registers. "Sweetheart, I am sure you aren't broken," she soothes, speaking to me with a maternal kindness I can appreciate.

"Cape May has always been my safe place." I suck in a breath and then word vomit just pours out of me. I'm sure I am giving

Ellie way more than she bargained for with my life story. She is quiet but listens as she pours the bacon grease into a can to harden. From the other room, Lucy starts to cry, interrupting us. "Coming, Lulu!" Ellie calls.

I clear my throat. "How old is she?" I ask meekly.

"She just had her first birthday." Ellie smiles. Lucy whines again. "I'm coming, baby."

I swallow a lump in my throat. The intrusive fear that I may never get to be a mother floods my mind. I have always wanted to be a mother. I never in a million years thought I would find myself divorced and infertile at thirty-eight. More importantly, I never thought my husband would become a parent with anyone other than me. The realization slams into me with hurricane force. *I may never get to pick up my own crying baby.*

The words are out of my mouth before I can stop myself. "Please, let me get her."

I am out of my seat before Ellie can put the pan down.

Ɒ

It's 5 p.m. before I wander back to my little guest house, trying to think of a plan for dinner. I unexpectedly spent the day with Ellie and Lucy, and I had the best time. It filled me up in a way I wasn't expecting. I got to feed her lunch, then Ellie and I walked Lucy to the market, and I picked up some food for the cottage. Ellie and I got to know each other over afternoon tea while Lucy napped. It all feels so right, like I've been here all along.

I'm smiling as I unlock the door and hear the rumble of Liam's pickup pulling into the driveway. I must admit that I am curious about him, but I'm far too awkward and fragile right now to even attempt a friendly conversation, so I go inside and peek at him from my little front window.

Today, he seems jovial as he chats with Ellie at the side of the house, his eyes crinkling as he laughs at something Ellie tells him. Lucy grasps at the sides of his face, pulling it to hers. He laughs and kisses the side of the baby's head before waving Ellie goodbye. This display of tenderness is a world of difference from the man I met when I arrived yesterday, making me even more interested in who he is besides Ellie's single next-door neighbor.

I close the curtain and reach for my phone. I haven't looked at it since this morning. I have several text messages from Claire, my assistant Ashley, and surprisingly four of them are from James. I didn't expect to hear from him after signing the papers yesterday. I'm not sure if I have the mental capacity to deal with him right now so I decide to open Claire's messages first.

> **Claire:** Hi... Just checking in. I haven't heard from you much since you arrived in Cape May. I hope you're okay. Call me, please.

> **Claire:** It's been a couple of hours. Can you at least let me know you're okay????

> **Claire:** If you're okay, I am going to kick your ass. You're giving new meaning to the word solace!

I laugh to myself and quickly type out a text back saying I will FaceTime her soon. Then I open my assistant's message confirming that two weeks is enough time. I feel a smidgen of guilt over this. I know people depend on me for their weekly therapy sessions and here I am moseying around the beach, drinking away my feelings and my own need for therapy.

I text Ashley back and I make sure I let her know that I appreciate her. She is probably taking some heat from my crankier patients for the inconvenience. I told her to tell them I had a family emergency and I needed some time off. It's not a lie. Your husband having an affair, knocking the girl up, and then consequently having to file for divorce, is definitely a family emergency.

Before I bring myself to read James' text messages, I reach for another bottle of red wine. I pour myself a hefty glass, grab a fleece blanket, and settle on the teal sofa. Wine is about all I can think of for dinner now, despite purchasing several microwave meals earlier today. *Who needs food anyway?* With an exhausted sigh, I pick up my phone again.

> James: Sophie, I don't know what to say besides I'm sorry. I hate the way this turned out for us.

> James: I didn't want to become a dad this way. It was always supposed to be me and you.

> James: I know you probably don't want to talk to me and that's okay, but I wanted to tell you that I talked to a realtor about listing the house.

> James: When you're ready, we should probably chat about it. Take care, Sophie. I'm sorry for everything.

That last text was just sent within the hour. I have a hard time believing that he cares this much. He just wants to get on with his life with Brittany. They can ride off into the sunset and make a whole basketball team of beautiful babies. I don't know what to say back to him. It all feels too fresh. My eyes are just beginning to well up with tears when there's a soft knock at my door.

I bolt off the couch and over to the door, swinging it open just in time to see my new neighbor, Liam sneaking away. There's a bag of what smells like Chinese take-out at my feet.

"Liam?" I tilt my head, my brow furrowed in confusion.

Liam stops in his tracks and slowly spins around to face me. He runs his fingers through his tousled mess of almost jet-black hair and looks at his feet before meeting my eyes. "Sorry. I didn't mean to startle you."

"What are you doing here?" I eye him curiously but make sure to keep my voice light. "Did you bring me food?" I squat down and pick up the bag.

Liam rocks back on his heels and clears his throat. "Yeah. Yeah, I did. I think we got off on the wrong foot yesterday, and I thought maybe you didn't have dinner yet. I ordered too much food." An awkward chuckle bubbles out of him. "My eyes are bigger than my stomach I guess."

"Liam...that's," I suck in a breath, "that's really nice." I offer him a tight smile.

Liam shakes his head. "It's nothing, honest. I hope you like lo mein." He turns to go.

"Thank you," I call after him.

Liam looks over his shoulder and gives me a wave. "Good night, Sophie."

Maybe he isn't so bad after all.

Chapter Two

Liam

"So, what'll it be, boys?" Melanie's sultry voice purrs as she saunters up to the counter to place bar napkins in front of each of us. She shoots me a flirty gaze and leans her elbows on the bar.

Danny and Jack, both long-time married guys, are immune to her low-cut tops and seductive confidence. Melanie is only trying to attract my attention anyway. She and I have been doing this dance for over twenty years, and for some reason, I can never take it any further than the occasional banter that spirals her into false hope.

"Just whatever you have on tap, Mel," Danny says, gesticulating to the row of draft beers along The Ugly Mug bar with a wave of his hand.

Melanie rolls her eyes and mimics his gesture by dramatically opening her arm in the direction of the beers on tap. "There are like fifteen beers here, Daniel."

"Surprise me." He winks.

"Me too," Jack agrees.

Melanie drops her arms in defeat. "Ugh, fine." Then she walks a few steps over to me, an inviting gleam in her eyes. She traces her finger along my bunched-up fist. "What about you, Liam?"

She's asking what I want to drink but there is another implication here. Melanie wants to know where I've been and why I have been blowing her off lately. We're just friends—at least that's all we've been for the last couple of years—but Melanie always gives me the impression that if I went for it, she'd want more. Guilt nags at the back of my neck when I think about what a terrible friend I am to her. I often ignore her calls and texts for weeks on end, even though she's done nothing to deserve it.

Melanie has seen me through my darkest days, and for that, I'll always care for her, but my feelings for her ebb and flow with the tide. She probably knows me better than anyone. She's part of our group of buddies, and she's friends with their wives. We have history. I shouldn't be blowing her off. I should at least respect her enough to be honest about where this friendship isn't going.

A memory flashes in my mind of Melanie and I on side-by-side gurneys, twenty-two years ago, while the Jaws of Life cut Cara from my mangled vehicle. The shattered glass in the road reflecting the lights of the emergency vehicles, and all I can hear is Melanie's wailing. At the sound of her voice, I shake my head to clear the memory.

"Hello—earth to Liam?" She is waving her hand in my face. "Cat got your tongue?" She winks.

"Sorry," I sputter. "Just a Corona is fine."

Melanie clicks the gum in her mouth and makes some kind of "oookay" sound before sauntering away to get our drinks.

Danny nudges me. "What's with you, man? You're out there today."

"I'm just tired," is all I can offer him. It's true, and I don't have a lot of energy to take the conversation any further. I've had my niece Lucy for the past five months, but she's only been legally mine for three. It's been an adjustment, to say the least. My sister, Leah, died while serving in the Army Reserves, and she didn't have a will. She had just been called up to active duty when her helicopter went down in a training accident in Texas. She never even made it overseas.

"I remember those days," Jack commiserates. "Up at night with a cranky baby. Can't say I miss it." He grins. "What about your mom and dad? Have you talked to them recently? Maybe they can come up to help out a little."

I groan. "You know they're no help."

My relationship with my parents is rocky, to say the least. They left New Jersey twenty years ago for a retirement community in Boca Raton, after gifting me and Leah the house I live in. They have zero plans to return to New Jersey, but I thought maybe they would for Lucy. Turns out, coming back here was too hard for them. They can't even look at me, and with Leah gone, they can't look at Lucy either. I guess it's the two of us against the world.

"You'll figure it out, man," Danny reassures me with a pat on the back as Melanie brings our drinks to us.

"Figure out what?" She nib-noses, with a sideways glance in my direction.

"How to *dad*," Jack answers for me. "Liam here is *tired*."

I am not sure I like the mocking tone of his voice, but before I can say anything Melanie interjects.

"Well, if Liam would let *me* help him, he might feel a little better." She is being snarky because I have told her I don't plan to introduce any woman to Lucy unless I am prepared to be serious with her. She took great offense to that. I do feel bad, but it's not fair to Lucy to lose a mother figure twice. I don't want to confuse the kid by bringing around different women. It's better if I just don't date at all.

I groan. "We've had this conversation, Melanie. And if you don't mind, I'm really not up for it again today." I run my hands down my face in exasperation.

Melanie holds her hands up in defense. "Okay, okay." She feigns a smirk as she backs away, but I see the hurt behind her eyes.

I strung her along for years which wasn't fair to her. Now, we're both forty. Melanie could have found literally *anyone* else. She's gorgeous with a great body and strawberry-blonde hair that cascades down her back. When we were younger, she and I had an off-and-on thing, and Melanie is constantly trying to turn it back on. In the past, I was happy with the occasional tryst. I wouldn't let anyone closer than that anyway because if they really knew me, they'd probably run for the hills. I just can't give her what she's after, especially not now that I'm learning how to parent. Lucy has to be the only girl in my life.

When Melanie's gone, Jack changes the subject. "So what else is new besides you avoiding commitment?" He laughs at himself and Danny joins in.

I ignore it. I've known these guys for thirty years, and like Melanie, they have seen me through my darkest days. I know they're disguising a serious conversation with the cover of messing around, but I avoid it anyway. "Ellie has a new tenant in the guest house. I met her yesterday." Everyone knows Ellie; she has been the neighborhood auntie on Perry Street since we were kids.

Danny and Jack look at each other with raised eyebrows. "A woman?" Danny asks with a grin. "Is she hot?"

Jack holds up his hand. "Hold on. The more important question is, is she single?"

I roll my eyes. "Guys, I don't know. I met her for like a second. She was alone though." I take a long swig of my beer. When I put it down and glance sideways, they're both staring at me, waiting for more. "What? You asked what else is new. That's about it these days."

"Don't tell Miles. He will sniff her out like he does every other newcomer." Jack laughs.

Our buddy Miles is recently divorced and always looking for the next pretty lady to add to his bedpost.

"I don't plan to tell Miles." I roll my eyes. This town is small enough, especially during the offseason. Miles is a popular real estate agent in town—it won't take him long to find her if she decides to stick around.

"Is she at least hot?" Danny asks again.

I shrug in mock resignation. "I mean, sure. Yes, she's cute." I give them a smirk. "I was trying not to gawk at her."

I did look at her though, and she is cute, even if she looks a little sad. However, if I am not dating Melanie, I certainly shouldn't be trying to date the new girl in town either. I'll admit, I want to know her story but it's mostly out of curiosity. I only brought her food last night to be *nice* because I was a jerk the other day. At least that's what I'm telling myself.

"Well, do better," Jack scolds. "We want the scoop."

I drain the last of my beer. "I'm sure your wives will be happy to hear that, ya filthy animals." I stand up and push my stool in. "I gotta pick up Lucy before I take any more advantage of Ellie's kindness." I throw a ten-dollar bill on the bar for Melanie.

"Later," Danny says into his beer.

"Bye!" Jack calls after me as I'm walking away.

As an afterthought, and so I don't look like I am the jerk, I call back, "Tell Melanie I said bye."

❧

It isn't until later that night, when I'm outside with my golden retriever, Maggie, that I allow myself to wonder about the pretty brunette staying next door. She has big woeful green eyes and long wavy hair. I bet she has a beautiful smile even though I wasn't privy to it. Something about her face is so familiar and it's bothering me. I am less curious when Ellie rents the cottage to young couples during summer weekends over pretty, single girls. It's more than that though. I bet there is a lot more to her than a pretty face and sad green eyes.

Why do you care? I scold myself. This is ridiculous. I told myself that I'm going to focus on Lucy and my new role as her dad, *not* dating. Not Melanie, and not anyone else either. No matter how cute she is.

Maggie breaks my stare when she nudges me with her wet nose and her ball. I pat her head before throwing her ball.

Sometimes, I think it would be nice to share my life with someone though. Someone to wake up to, drink morning coffee with, and take a walk with the baby and the dog. But for that to happen, I'd have to really let someone in, and I'm not sure I'm capable of that. Even if I was, who would want me? I have a past that I'm not proud of and walls built up too high for anyone to want to climb.

Maggie comes galloping back to me with her soggy ball. She is two years old and thinks she's a lapdog, even though she weighs sixty-five pounds. Most nights, she is the only girl keeping me company. *I'm fine alone*, is a regular pep talk I give myself.

These are the nights I wish I could sit out here with my sister. Leah and I would often sit together after Lucy went to sleep and throw the ball for Maggie, just talking about our days.

"Did you build anything good today?" she'd ask me, a twinkle in her eyes.

"Nah." I would shrug. "Did you take anyone to jail?" I'd tease, nudging her with my elbow. Leah was a police officer when she wasn't serving in the Army Reserves.

"Why do you always think I'm arresting people?" she'd ask, laughing. "It's pretty uneventful around these parts."

Then we would sit in comfortable silence or talk about something cute that Lucy did. I can practically hear her voice in my head still. Leah was my best friend. I miss her like words can't describe. She was the person who never gave up on me. She never stopped believing that I would be okay, that I would find my footing again. I'm sure that's why she left Lucy with me when she got called up. She knew I would rise to the occasion. Now, what I wouldn't give to pick up the phone and call her. Sometimes I feel the same urge to call my parents, but the conversation is forced and often leaves me feeling lonelier than before.

Maggie nudges me again with a snort and forces her ball into my hand. "Okay, okay, girl. I bet you miss her too, don't you?" I wrestle the ball from the strong grip of her jaw. With a windup, I throw the ball as far as I can. Maggie takes off excitedly and I shake the doggy drool from my palm. Days like today, I'm especially grateful for this dog. I might otherwise give in to my loneliness and make a bad decision, like call Melanie for some physical comfort. Maggie quells that urge for me with her earnest company.

The thought of Lucy having lost her mom makes my chest

ache though. Maybe I need to try harder to find a wife or maybe even just a girlfriend. The problem is, I have too much baggage for anyone to ever accept me for who I am. I don't like the person that I used to be, but I work every day to make sure I am never that person again. I can't change what happened in the past, but I also know not everyone will accept it. I don't let my walls down because I am so terrified of ever feeling that level of pain again.

I have pretty much given up on the idea of that real world-series kind of love. I must focus on learning how to be a parent. I can't be a good dad if I am focused on dating and finding a mate who will accept everything about me.

I am just about to call Maggie inside when I hear the distinct sound of someone crying from beyond the fence. From my deck, I can see into Ellie's yard. That girl Sophie is sitting at the café table. She aggressively wipes her eyes as she reads her phone, then takes a big swig of her wine before typing quickly. Her body language makes me grateful I'm not on the receiving end of whatever that is. Then, she picks up her belongings and marches inside the cottage. Now I'm not only wondering about the cute girl next door, but I'm also wondering who hurt the cute girl next door. *Just what I need.*

I feel guilty thinking about how rude I was to her the other day. She is probably dealing with something that I wouldn't understand. Hopefully I made her day a little better by dropping off some food. I feel a rush of heat crawling up my neck. Now I also feel as if I invaded her privacy, listening to her cry and watching her send text messages.

"Come on, Maggie." I whistle. "Let's go, girl." Once inside, I pick up my phone. There's a message from Danny asking if I want to work for his construction company tomorrow. I text back that yes, I'd love the work. Diapers, after all.

I work for Danny as often as possible but custom woodworking is really where my passion is. I plop down in the wooden Adirondack chair on my deck—it was the first thing I ever built on my own and it's so special to me. It's old but every few summers I sand and polish it up to keep it alive and to remind myself that even when things look bleak, they will always get better.

Ellie's husband Eddie is the one who taught me how to do woodworking. For him it was just a hobby, but I found solace in it. He showed me how to use the tools needed to create the works of art we spent hours creating—cabinets, furniture, and even wall art. Eddie gave me a sense of purpose again. When I was in the woodshop, I didn't have time to think about anything except what I was doing so I wouldn't lose a finger. I may have blown my chance at school, but Eddie made me realize I had a talent, and I could have a future doing something entirely unexpected. He worked on projects for people around town and often let me assist him, until one day, he thought I was ready to take on projects myself. He told everyone I was his apprentice and that they could ask me to do jobs for them too. By the time Eddie passed away, I was as good as he was. I was in my mid-twenties, living mortgage free in my parents' house, and I realized I could make this my job. So, I did.

My phone buzzes. It's Melanie telling me I left my hat at the bar today and offering to bring it by.

Melanie is a good woman. That's the issue here. She is so nice, I can't bring myself to officially let her down. Maybe I should ignore my doubts and give the relationship a chance.

I wouldn't have to explain any of my past to Melanie, since she was there. She knows who I am, and she likes me anyway.

I rub my hand down my face. Is it better to be lonely, or to be with a woman I have lukewarm feelings for? I could see if Ellie can watch Lucy one day this weekend so I can take Melanie out and get a feel for where her head is at. I'm tired of thinking about it.

I pick my phone up and shoot Melanie a text back.

> **Me: Thanks. If you don't mind, I'm pretty tired. Want to bring it by in the morning?**

Melanie: Sure, I can do that. I'll see you then.

I turn my phone off and head upstairs, peeking at Lucy on the way to my room. She's sound asleep with her little butt up in the air. I flick on the lights and strip down to my boxers. Maggie hops right up in her spot on my bed. I always swore I'd never let a dog in the bed. She sure showed me who's boss. I turn off the lights and climb in. It doesn't take long before I'm dead asleep to the soft sounds of Maggie's snores.

CR

Morning comes quickly and I don't want to get out of bed when my alarm starts buzzing angrily. I groan and roll over, checking my phone. There's a text from Melanie confirming that she'll drop my hat off before I leave for work. I roll my eyes to myself. She could just as easily bring it by later in the morning instead of seven o'clock, but I have a feeling she's trying to make sure we see each other.

Construction starts early, and Danny will be expecting me so I get Lucy up and ready as quickly as possible. I am trying to avoid Melanie seeing Lucy at all. I know as soon as that girl catches sight of the baby or even more so, me with the baby, we're both doomed. Balancing Lucy on my hip with her diaper bag slung over my shoulder, I walk to Ellie's.

Ellie meets me at her front door and immediately takes Lucy from me. "You're a little early this morning," she raises her eyebrows and nods as Melanie's black Honda Accord pulls up to the curb. "Got company?"

I roll my eyes. I knew she would catch onto that. "What do you do, sit here and just look out the window all day?" I scoff. Ellie doesn't miss a trick.

Ellie scowls at me. "Hey buddy, neighborhood watch." She

jabs me in the chest with her index finger.

"Melanie is just dropping off my hat that I left at the bar last night." I hold up my hands defensively.

Ellie's lips press together. "If you say so," she says.

I scratch my jaw, hesitating. "There is one thing though that I was thinking about."

Ellie raises her eyebrows. "Well, go on," she shakes her head at me with a smirk.

"I wanted to ask you if you'd watch Lucy one night this weekend so I could take Melanie out." I am holding my breath.

"Take her out?" Ellie mimics. "You better stop playing with that girl," she warns, narrowing her eyes. "Melanie may not be your soulmate, but she is a nice girl. I know she thinks she can change you, but she probably can't, so please stop playing with her heart."

Ellie is serious now, giving me a stern look. She has known all of us since we were kids. She's always been my parents' next-door neighbor. When we were teenagers, Leah and I would putz around the yard and the streets with our buddies, and Ellie got to know and love them all.

"I know, Ellie," I say through gritted teeth. I glance behind me and notice Melanie watching us from her car. "Look, I'm not making the girl any promises. I just want to see where her head is at."

"You don't owe me anything, Liam; it's none of my business." Ellie folds her hands over her heart in an inward gesture. "But I am actually not around this weekend. I am going on a little book club retreat to the mountains."

"Oh. Okay. Well, I didn't even ask her yet so it's no big deal." I exhale and I realize I might be relieved.

Ellie taps her chin thoughtfully. "You know, you could ask Sophie. I don't think she has a lot of plans while she's here. Maybe offer to pay her though," Ellie suggests, winking.

I look at her dubiously, my jaw slack with surprise. "Haven't you known her for like two days? She could be crazy." But even as

I am saying it, I know it's not true.

"Liam! You surprise me that your judge of character is so poor," Ellie chides. "Sophie spent the day with us yesterday, and she is lovely. Besides, I think she could use the distraction. Give it some thought."

"Okay, whatever. I got to go." I turn and jog down the steps where Melanie is patiently waiting for me on the sidewalk.

"Hi." She hands me my hat, a tattered old Phillies cap that I honestly don't care that much about anymore.

"Thanks," I say giving her a tight smile and a nod.

"No problem." Melanie seems chipper this morning. "Can I see the baby?" she asks earnestly.

There it is.

"No. Absolutely not." I am firm on this. As I have said many times before, I will not introduce Lucy to just anyone. Not that Melanie is just anyone. "Mel, you know where I stand on this. I am not letting any woman get close to Lucy right now. Poor kid is confused enough without Leah. Maybe someday but not yet." I watch her face fall and immediately feel the need to acquiesce. I suck in a breath before adding, "But what are you doing on Friday?"

"Why?" Melanie eyes me warily and folds her arms into herself, as if to guard her feelings.

"I was thinking we could get something to eat. Maybe talk about some things," I suggest, trying my best to sound noncommittal.

Melanie softens, chewing on her lower lip. "Okay," she nods. "Yeah, I'd like that."

I force a smile. "Good. I'll touch base later this week," I promise.

We say our goodbyes and I hop in my truck to go to work, all the while wondering why I'm forcing myself to see something that really isn't there.

Chapter Three

Sophie

It's already Wednesday and I still have no idea what I am doing here or what I am doing with my life. I do know that I can't spend another day wallowing and avoiding the inevitable. I decided to wake up early and go for a run, which is really a walk/run since the last time I ran any sort of distance was about ten years ago. I let my memory guide me, and I can already tell, the exercise is so good for me.

I run up a block to a park I visited often as a girl and I take a lap around it, watching families play together and reminiscing about my own childhood. After that, I run up a few blocks to the beach and walk barefoot along the water's edge. As soon as the waves hit my toes, they trigger a dormant memory of childhood summers with sticky sand clinging to my feet, the salty tang of the ocean air, and bittersweet farewells to the summer days spent on a windswept beach. *How did I ever leave this?* I wonder. Then I put my shoes back on and run back to Ellie's house.

I am kicking myself now, though, as I approach her front stoop. One should never put sneakers and socks back on a sandy foot. I can feel a blister popping up on my heel, making damn sure this is the only time I will run this week.

I plop down on Ellie's front step and take off my shoe. I'm inspecting my wounds when I catch sight of Liam on the sidewalk, saying goodbye to a woman I have never seen before. She looks exactly like the type of woman a guy like him would go for. *Tiny waist, big boobs, low-cut top. Check, check, and check.*

I notice her but if she notices me, she doesn't make it obvious. She clicks the key remote for the black car directly in front of me and gets in at the same time he gets into his truck. I smirk to myself. *Well, clearly, he is unavailable.* I scold myself for the envious feeling that catches me by surprise. In the six weeks that I've been single again, it has seemed to me that literally *everyone* else is attached. I'm going to have to get used to the feeling of loneliness, I think.

Shaking Liam out of my head, I dust off my sandy feet and head for Ellie's front door, because naturally, I don't have any Band-Aids in the cottage. I find her sitting at the kitchen table with a gentleman who also appears to be in his sixties. He has glasses, a balding head, and is sipping coffee while Ellie chats away.

"Oh, Sophie! I'm glad you're here." Ellie smiles and holds up an empty mug. "Would you like some coffee?"

I hesitate. "I, uh—I'm sorry, I didn't mean to interrupt. I need a Band-Aid and of course, I didn't bring any." I duck my head, feeling embarrassed.

Ellie waves her hand in dismissal. "Don't be silly, dear. They are in the medicine cabinet in my powder room. Go help yourself and then come back and join us!"

"I'll just be right back then." I give them a shy smile. I know there is no getting out of this coffee date with Ellie. As soon as she heard about James, the woman convinced me to hang out with her all day yesterday, saying that I shouldn't be alone at a time like this. Ellie means well, and I will certainly enjoy her company when it's offered to me.

When I return to the table, Ellie has poured me a steaming cup of coffee and put a cinnamon roll on my plate. "These rolls are from Sticky Ricky's," Ellie shares excitedly. "Robert brought them over. They're famous here."

"Oh, I know that place," I say nodding. "We got them all the time when I was a little girl. My grandparents lived just a couple of blocks up on Jackson Street." I sit down and inhale the scent of the sticky bun, immediately awakening a dormant memory.

"Sophie, this is my dear, dear friend, Dr. Robert Stevens. He's the only psychiatrist in town and we've been friends for years." She's beaming. "I wanted you to meet him. He helped me so much when my Edward passed away," Ellie gushes, eying Robert carefully. "Sophie is a marriage and family therapist. I think you two might have stuff in common!" Ellie looks very pleased with herself.

I blush, wondering about the reason for this visit. Is Ellie implying that I should talk to someone about my failed marriage? On the one hand, I probably should, but I'm confident I can handle it myself. I am bothered by the insinuation, but then I shrug it off. I'm sure she's just trying to help. It doesn't seem like Ellie has a mean bone in her body.

"Hi, Dr. Stevens. It's so nice to meet you." I pick up my coffee and take a big sip. Ellie is an expert with the French press, and the caffeine instantly picks me up.

"Please, call me Robert." He smiles. "Ellie was just telling me you're here visiting Cape May because you're recently divorced, is that right?" His face is amiable and curious, but I feel embarrassed anyway.

I sigh. "I am. I know I should probably talk to someone to help me navigate this. I take for granted that this is what I help other people do."

"Oh, Sophie, I don't want you to feel like this is an ambush! Robert was over for our weekly breakfast anyway," she says, glancing his way.

Is she mooning over him? Maybe Robert isn't just a friend, I wonder silently.

"I just wanted to introduce you because Robert is a great friend to me," Ellie says apologetically. "Please don't feel like I'm butting my nose in your business!"

I don't know why, but I feel my heart expand. Ellie seems to care about me in a nurturing way, the way my mom would have. My dad means well, but since my mom's death, there are some things he just doesn't know how to help with. Maybe an outsider's perspective will help.

I do need to determine where to go from here. If I am being honest with myself, going back to Scranton is not appealing at all. Scranton isn't a small town where I would constantly run into James, but I just feel as though there is nothing left for me there. For the first time, I'm starting to envision myself here in the long term.

☙

I spend the morning drinking coffee with new friends and playing with baby Lucy. Lucy is a joy on an otherwise mundane day in my post-divorce life. She seems to be enjoying herself as we play on the floor and when I push her on the swing at the park. Her giggles are melodic and contagious.

Ellie is more than happy to let me play a role, so after we feed her lunch, I rock her for her nap. She falls asleep in my arms, clinging to the collar of my T-shirt with her chubby baby fingers. I can't bring myself to put her down, instead enjoying snuggling her for the duration of her nap.

Spending time with Lucy is becoming therapeutic for me, and I find myself smiling much of the day.

Back at home, I'm saying goodbye to Lucy when Liam enters the front door. "Hey everyone," he says from the kitchen entryway. He eyes me holding Lucy but doesn't move from the doorway. His greeting hangs in the air, and I don't know what to say after hellos are exchanged. I move to hand him the baby, and he takes her from me, nuzzling her a hello with a peck on the head.

"I should be going..." I say awkwardly. "Thanks, Ellie, for a great day." I give her a warm smile as I move toward the back door.

"Wait, Sophie," Liam stops me by touching my arm. He moves it quickly but the place he touched is tingling. "Ellie says you've been hanging out with her and Lucy the past couple of days. It seems like Lucy is really comfortable with you."

"Well, she's an angel," I say, gazing affectionately at Lucy.

Then I meet his eyes and nod. "She's really brought joy to me the last few days."

He gives me a look I can't read. "I was wondering," he says, pausing in hesitation, "Ellie isn't around this weekend. Is there any off chance you'd be able to watch Lucy on Friday night?" I can feel the heat rising up my neck from the way he is looking at me. I immediately think of the food he left on my doorstep, followed by the memory of the woman I saw him with this morning.

"Oh...sure. I mean, I don't have much going on." I force myself to look him in the eyes again. *Poor lonely Sophie. He probably thinks you have no life.*

My inner mean girl needs to shut up.

Liam smiles broadly. "Great! That's great. Thank you. It'll just be dinner and then I'll come home. I won't be long."

I force a laugh. "Take your time. Everyone deserves a break once in a while." As I turn to leave, my phone starts buzzing. Claire is calling me. "I need to get going but I will touch base with you tomorrow or Friday morning to firm up our plans." Then I duck out the sliding glass door.

"Hi," I say quietly, picking up the FaceTime on the deck.

"Where have you been? My goodness. And who is that fine-ass man behind you? It looks like he is staring at you," Claire asks, laughing. I'm confused for a moment, thinking Liam followed me outside. Then I realize she can see through the sliding glass door, and he is standing right at the door with Lucy, watching me. The back of my neck tingles just knowing he is looking at me.

"Oh, that's Liam, the neighbor. No, he's not available. And no, I hadn't even noticed," I lie, indignantly. I have definitely noticed. "What's going on?"

"*Well,*" Claire drags out her words dramatically. "You've been a little MIA since you got there. I just wanted to make sure you're okay." Since Claire and I work together, she's not only used to talking to me every day, she's used to seeing me daily too. We give new meaning to co-dependent friendships.

"I know, I'm sorry. I've been spending a lot of time with Ellie, my landlord, and the sweet baby Lucy she watches each day." I sigh, walking down the deck steps. "It's been sort of healing for me to take a step back and stop analyzing my next move constantly. Just sort of *be*, you know?"

"I get it," Claire says nodding. "I miss you though. I guess I'll just have to hang out with Derek," she grumbles. Derek is Claire's very loving and supportive husband of five years. They're madly in love. And while I know she's being playful about my return, Claire is much more impulsive than I am. She'd prefer I figure out my life there as opposed to here and the sooner the better.

I plop on the patio chair outside the cottage and let out an exasperated breath. "I just think I need this time to figure out what I want now. I don't know what my life looks like without James. I really thought we were a success story, you know? Like we may not have been able to have kids the traditional way, but I thought we had made it through some pretty hard stuff. I didn't see this coming at all. Thirteen years is a long time to be married. It just goes to show you can think you know someone and be *oh so* wrong."

My voice catches, and I force myself to swallow my grief. Even six weeks later, the weight of it all catches me by surprise sometimes. Maybe if I keep up a tough exterior, my heart won't completely crumble.

Claire relents with a grim smile. "Okay, I understand. I'll just have to man up and carry on without my bestie. In the meantime, you have some soul-searching to do, girlfriend. How many more days are you there?"

Claire can be a little pushy. I know it's because she cares so much about me, but it's only been four days. I haven't even let myself start thinking about what's next. She follows it up with a heartfelt, "I just want what's best for you," and I let it slide.

"I'm honestly not sure, maybe forever." For the first time, I admit to the possibility out loud. I don't hate the way it sounds but Claire probably does. "Want to come for a visit?"

CR

By Thursday, I haven't seen Liam at all, and since I am babysitting for him tomorrow night, it's time to touch base with him. I don't have his number, so I decide after some dinner to saunter over to his place and knock on his door. *Relax.* I tell myself. *This is a favor you're doing for him. For Ellie really, nothing more. Who cares if he's tall and muscular and probably wearing one of those too-tight T-shirts that shows all his muscles in a completely agonizing way.*

It has been a long time since I've been curious about a man other than James. I think that's why I am so nervous. For all I know, he asked me to babysit because he wants to go out on a date, which is none of my business. I glance down at my phone to check the time, 7:45 p.m. Another text from James catches my eye at the same time but I ignore the unread message and stick my phone back in my pocket.

Okay, here goes nothing. I walk up Liam's front steps and immediately notice the video doorbell. Nothing like being on camera to make me feel self-conscious in my monotone loungewear. I press it anyway.

The front door swings open, and Liam appears momentarily surprised to see me. He recovers quickly, offering me a smile that immediately puts me at ease, though I can't pretend I don't notice him looking delicious in low-slung gray joggers and a fitted black T-shirt. *I knew he'd be wearing one.* I force myself to look only at his face. Meanwhile, I am fully aware he is taking in my entire ensemble while I stand there hoping my underwear doesn't show through my beige pants under his porch light. For what feels like an eternity, even though it's only a few seconds, we're both standing there sizing each other up. *I didn't think this through.*

"Sophie, hi." Liam rubs his palm down the length of his face. *Is he flustered?* "I wasn't expecting you...anyone," he corrects himself quickly.

"I just realized I never touched base with you about tomorrow night, and I don't have your number so..." I force myself to swallow any minor embarrassment I'm feeling. We're both adults. Presumably, he has seen pajamas before. *This is not a big deal.* Yet, seeing Liam up close again, looking this effortlessly good in the glow of the golden hour of all times, is really doing something to me that should be unwelcome, but strangely isn't.

"It's cool. Now we're both guilty of sneaking up on the other's porch." Liam grins at me again and runs his hands through his messy hair. He is gorgeous when he smiles like that. He is so fit that I wonder when he has time to go to the gym. His dark hair is cropped on the sides and longer on top, and he has just a shadow of a beard. His clear blue eyes have a weight behind them, like he's carrying something on his shoulders too.

"So..." I look at him expectantly.

He leans against the doorframe and licks his lips. My stomach flutters, which once again catches me off guard. I need to stop imagining the feel of those lips, especially considering the fact that I haven't dealt with any of my own shit. Think about literally anything else, Sophie.

"Right. Sorry, Sophie." My name rolls off his tongue as if he's speaking a romantic language. "Why don't you come in for a minute, and I can show you some things for Lucy?" He steps back and gestures for me to enter. I want nothing more than to shrink into myself.

First of all, I internally reprimand myself, *you left your house with nothing presentable to wear, like twelve pairs of underwear, and some chargers.* I feel like I need to go shopping before I can realistically babysit for the guy. If I show up like this, he is going to... *Why do you care?* I scold myself again. *Because some male attention wouldn't be the worst thing for my fractured ego.* I can admit that at least.

"Okay, sure," I say, following him inside and glancing around. Liam's house looks like a once loved and cared for home that has been taken over by a bachelor. To the right is a formal sitting room, but boxes of things take up most of the space. To the left is an oak staircase with various collage photo frames from the '90s hung up in the stairwell. Shoes are stacked on each step, presumably waiting to be carried upstairs. A jacket is draped over the handrail. I follow him down the short hallway, passing a powder room before we enter the kitchen. A table and highchair sit amid various clutter—dishes in the sink, mail on the countertops, leftover dinner, and a bottle of milk resting on the highchair tray.

"I, uh, didn't get a chance to clean up dinner yet. Lucy was a handful tonight." His lips twitch into a sheepish smirk. Just then a lazy golden retriever comes up and sticks its nose right in my crotch. I laugh and skirt away. Liam winces. "Oh...are you okay with dogs? I'm sorry. This is Maggie. She's pretty calm and will probably leave you alone once she sniffs you. She may or may not jump on your lap as soon as you sit down." He pats the dog on the head affectionately, and my heart swells a little. Maybe Liam is a little softer than I thought.

I nod. "I'm fine with dogs. Hi Maggie." I ruffle her ears.

Liam's entire upper body relaxes with relief. "Good." He clears his throat. "So, you can see, this is the kitchen, and the family room down here is usually where I hang out with Lucy. This is where most of her toys are." He walks one step down to a living room off the kitchen where there is a couch, recliner, a pack-and-play with some toys in it, and a bouncer that Lucy is probably too big for now. I follow him, looking around at the pieces of his life.

The TV on the mantle has the evening's baseball highlights on. We both turn our attention to it as the newscaster is showing a replay from today's Phillies game. On the screen, Trea Turner scores the game-winning run for a final score of 5-3. "Yes!" Liam whispers as he watches.

I am surprised to find myself smiling. "Do you like baseball?" I ask him, even though it's obvious he does. Small talk is not my strong suit.

"I do. I played my whole life until I graduated high school. I love the Phils," he says with a wistful smile. The conversation hangs in the air for a minute, and I wait for his lead. "Anyway, I'm just planning on going to dinner. It shouldn't be real long. If you don't mind feeding Lucy and putting her to bed, you can come over at about 5:45?"

His relaxed demeanor is putting me at ease. I find myself wanting to spend more time with him but also knowing what a terrible idea that is. I'm nowhere near ready to start something new.

I nod. "Sure, I can do that." My phone buzzes in my hand. *James.* A picture of us from our wedding day flashes on my screen as it rings. I catch Liam noticing it.

"Do you need to get that?" he asks, taking a step back toward the kitchen. Maybe he wants to give me privacy.

I hit decline. "Definitely not," I mutter quietly. I take a deep breath. Liam looks so good, and my emotions are all over the place. I am lonely and attracted to him. I have to get out of his house. It's too tempting.

The need for male attention to heal my bruised ego is clouding my judgment. I am a therapist. If I were a patient, I would tell myself to run and not look back—at least not until I've had the chance to digest these major life changes of the past few weeks.

I have to figure out my life. I will. I will figure out my life. Tomorrow.

Liam moves back into the kitchen and walks over to his fridge. "Can I get you something to drink?"

He's being so nice. I sigh. "That sounds good, but I really ought to be going." I follow him back into the kitchen with intentions of heading toward the front door.

"Are you a wine girl?" He cocks his head at me, a smirk playing on his full lips. "I think I have some red wine in the cabinet. You know, if you don't want to be alone." He almost convinces me.

Not only is he hot, he's thoughtful, too. I saw evidence of that when he door-dropped me food the other night but now, he's further proving it. He's enticing me. *Be strong, Sophie. A rebound is not what you need right now. Run. Away.* "I can't. But I will see you tomorrow at 5:45."

"Okay." He catches me by surprise when he walks over and lifts my phone out of my hand, holding it up to me so my face can unlock it. Then he starts typing. "Here's my number though. I am going to call myself, so I have yours." He watches my face while it rings. Our eyes stay locked until we hear his voicemail pick up, sending a shiver up my spine. He hands it back to me and our hands graze.

Is it my imagination or did his touch linger a second too long? My breath catches. I've got to go.

"Great. Thanks. See you," I say abruptly. I am out the door before I can hear him say goodbye.

Chapter Four

Liam

I keep telling myself I shouldn't need a beer every night, but tonight was one of those nights where it was definitely needed. Lucy was a handful, and the dog followed me to every room I went into. As soon as I get back downstairs, I head for the fridge and pop the cap on a beer before making my way to my favorite recliner.

These past few months have been an adjustment that I wasn't prepared for. I feel like I have no personal space. I couldn't put Lucy down tonight and had to rock her to get her to sleep. She felt a little warm, but it's probably from crying all night. Times like this I really wish she had her mom. Or I wish I knew *literally* anything about raising a baby. Anything at all besides that they're expensive as fuck.

As exhausting as my new role is, though, I do relish the quiet moments with Lucy. I found myself looking down at her red, chubby cheeks, matted to my T-shirt from tears and snot, her eyelashes so wet they were stuck together. And yet, even in her sleep, she clung to me for comfort, fisting my T-shirt as if she couldn't get close enough to me. It makes my heart swell seeing how much she needs me, because if I have discovered anything these past few months, it's that I really need her too.

֍

Hours later, I'm lying awake in bed thinking about Sophie. She seemed so shy when she stopped over, and I can't help but find it endearing. When she showed up on my porch looking embarrassed in her pajamas, all I could think about was how she doesn't seem to realize how pretty she is. It's not just that though. I see a woman trying desperately to put on a brave face for the world before her when clearly, she has a burden she is carrying.

Her green eyes are beautiful with little flecks of gold in them, but they also carry a sadness. I feel a kinship with Sophie from that alone. I want to know more about her and how she got here, but she couldn't get away from me fast enough tonight. I'm trying to think of ways to befriend her when Lucy's cries wake me from the other room.

I groan and get out of bed, preparing myself to have to rock her back to sleep. I find Lucy sitting in her crib, looking toward the door, wailing. I immediately pick her up and she snuggles into me, hiccupping into my shoulder. "Shhh. I'm here," I whisper, walking over to the rocker.

I need to clean my house before I can let Sophie back in here to babysit. I gathered from the phone call she got when she was here that she has been married so she probably knows how most guys live, but I was embarrassed that my house was in disarray nonetheless.

Once again, I start the gentle back-and-forth motion with my bare feet, resting my head back on the rocker. Lucy settles almost immediately in my arms, so we rock. I'm hoping she falls asleep but every few minutes, I startle because *I'm* the one dozing off. When I look down at Lucy, she's still gazing up at me, sucking her thumb. Every time I make a move to put her back down, she cries again. Thank god I told Danny I can't work tomorrow.

"Okay, little lady, let's try to get back in your crib so Dad–Uncle Liam–can get some sleep too." I catch myself almost saying Daddy. I don't know who I am to her at this point. I rise to put her down and before I even get near the crib she is screaming again.

What. The. Fuck. I am trying to remember what Leah used to do when she was teething. I think we have some baby Tylenol in the bathroom, so I carry Lucy in and get her some, reading the dosing on the bottle super carefully. I have never given her medicine before. In fact, she probably is due for some kind of pediatrician appointment. I feel anxiety creep up. I remember Leah taking her to the pediatrician often. I make a mental note to ask Ellie when Lucy is supposed to go. I'm sure she'll know.

Lucy is whimpering and grasping at my T-shirt while I fill the syringe with the sticky red liquid. I carefully feed her the medicine, silently praying it helps her sleep. She sips it but dribbles some out, so I wipe it off her face. When we go back to her room, she still won't let me put her down and every time I so much as get near her crib, her eyes widen with panic and she starts wailing again. I let out a frustrated groan. It's not her fault; clearly she doesn't feel well, but I am bone tired.

I sigh. "I know this is against all the rules, baby girl, but we have to get some rest." I walk down the hallway to my room and arrange extra king-sized pillows on the bed. Then I place Lucy in the middle of the bed and lay down next to her. *Just until she's out*, I tell myself, but before I know it, we both drift off into a deep restorative sleep.

❧

When we get up the next morning, Lucy seems okay. She wakes me by climbing on top of my chest and patting my face with her drool-covered hand. This is a relief because I cannot imagine canceling on Melanie. The girl has already confirmed with me three times.

I woke up this morning with a pit in my stomach though, because after seeing Sophie last night, my gut is telling me that this thing with Melanie has run its course. I am going to have to make it clear to Melanie—once and for all—that we will only ever be friends. We need to have a real honest conversation about our situation, and I have to let her go. It's just not there for me anymore with her and I can't pretend it is. I have never talked to Melanie about anything that I carry around in my heart and mind, even though she was witness to it all. I leaned on her initially all those years ago, but when that turned sexual, I shut down the emotional. It all felt too heavy back then and now, I have to figure out how to be someone's dad. I can't keep running circles around an old relationship that I feel lukewarm about.

There is nothing like the pressure that becoming an instant parent puts on you. Usually, you get married, and you have time. You build your lives together, talk about the future, get a home. You have nine months to prepare for a baby with your partner. Leah didn't get that when her baby daddy took off, and I didn't get that because I made up my mind a long time ago that marriage and a family isn't something I deserve anymore. I've had my walls up now for longer than they were ever down. I've never let a woman get close enough to hurt me and my reasons were always related to Cara. Now, my reason is Lucy. I must do right by her.

I decide since I can't hit the gym today, I will take Lucy in the jogging stroller and go for a run. The late April air is warm with a cool sea breeze, the sun is shining, and it's amazing what a little vitamin D can do. Before I know it, I have jogged three miles. I slow my pace, take a right on Lafayette Street, and plop down on a bench at the park near our house. Lucy has fallen asleep in the stroller, so I guess I won't disturb her for any playtime at the park.

I lean back and look around. The street is quiet for being the center of town. I notice some local businesses are opening up, and I can see Dr. Stevens' office right from my spot on the bench. I have been going to Dr. Stevens since I was eighteen. He helped me through more trauma than any eighteen-year-old kid should have to endure, so there's that. He is probably one of the few reasons I couldn't leave this place behind. Someone in my situation, fresh out of high school with an uncertain future might've wanted to get the heck out of dodge. But I knew if I did, Doc would come after me.

I'm just contemplating stopping for a coffee and making my walk back leisurely when Lucy stirs in the stroller and starts crying.

"Uh-oh, Luce. What's the matter?" I lean down, resting my elbows on my knees and look at her. Her cheeks are flushed and her eyes are glassy.

Her cries slow to a slight fuss when she sees me though, and she does that thing where she is half laughing and half crying.

"Did you wonder where I was?" I ask her, rubbing the side of my finger up her chubby little arm. She grabs it with her other hand. "I would never leave you," I promise her.

Lucy gives me a gummy smile, and it looks to me like that promise made her feel better, even though she probably doesn't understand. I reach under the stroller and pull out an apple sauce pouch. I unscrew the top and hand it to her. She immediately perks up, sending relief up my spine. I physically feel my shoulders relax. *See, we're getting this. We're learning together.*

"We're gonna be okay, Lucy," I reassure her, standing up from the bench. "Let's go home."

Chapter Five

Sophie

I wake up this morning with a tightness in my chest that gives me the sensation of suffocating. I feel like I'm paralyzed in bed. I wiggle my fingers; they're tingling. My heart is thumping so hard I'm sure Ellie can hear it all the way in her house. I'm scared, like I'm trapped and can't get out.

Thoughts of James and my future swirl in my mind. *What will I do now that I'm all alone? Where will I go? I can't keep staying at my dad's house.* I sit up and put a hand over my pounding heart that is threatening to shatter my ribs, but I am immediately dizzy and have to lay back down. *What would people think if they knew what James did to me? I can't get pregnant, and my husband found someone else who could.*

I am drowning, gasping for air. I've never had one before, but I recognize these symptoms to be the result of a panic attack. It was only a matter of time. My chest aches, like there is an elephant sitting on it. I was awake through the night, tossing and turning, all the while my anxiety increasing. Dreaming about James and then dreaming about Liam—*WTF?*— and sweating profusely. I sit up and try again to get a good breath. My heart is still racing. I pick up my phone and call Claire. She answers on the second ring.

"Hey, stranger!" She sounds chipper.

"I'm having a panic attack and I'm alone," I blurt out, huffing and puffing in her ear. My eyes well with tears. I have never felt this out of control of my mind and body.

Claire's voice instantly softens. "Okay, honey, take a deep breath. In through your nose, out through your mouth. Do it with me. We're going to do this three times."

"Okay, okay." I try to breathe but my breaths are shallow. I know what to do but I cannot make my own brain do it.

"Are you breathing? We're going to count to five and breathe in, and then we're going to let it out for another count of five. In... one, two, three, four, five...and out...one, two, three, four, five. Good girl. I hear you breathing." Claire is my best friend in the world, and she has the benefit of *knowing* me and knowing the *cause* of this panic attack—fucking James—and how to help me through it the way she would a patient. "Remember, this feeling will pass."

My pulse hammers in my ears and the lump in my throat feels as if it grew three sizes. There is nothing for me to do except listen to Claire's directions and wait for my breathing to even out.

"Tell me five things you see," Claire says soothingly.

"I see the teal sofa across the room," I murmur. Sucking in a breath, I continue. "The window looking into the backyard, the bottle of wine I drank last night, my suitcase, and the TV."

"Good. Now what about four things you can touch?" Claire urges.

My fingers tremble as I try to sit upright, the weight in my chest still pinning me down. Hot streaks of tears carve a path down my cheeks. A flood of emotions—fear, sadness, and rage—that I've been harboring for the past six weeks crushes me all at once.

"The blanket on the bed, my pajamas, my hair, and the glass of water next to me," I breathe.

"What do you hear?" Claire asks patiently.

"The birds outside, you, my erratic breathing," I grumble, closing my eyes.

"Is there anything you can smell?"

"Wine and my deodorant." I start to feel myself relax when Claire giggles.

"At least you smell good," she murmurs. "What do you taste?"

"Morning breath," I scoff, disgusted with myself.

Claire continues, "Take a few more soothing breaths for me, Sophie. In and out."

Finally, after a few moments of deep breathing, my heart rate begins to slow and my lungs remember how to pull air. I still feel hollow, but I wiggle my toes, stretch my arms overhead, and breathe deeply. "Okay. It's slowing down. Thank you. I wasn't going to be able to talk myself through that one."

"Happy to help you, babe. What was your trigger?" Claire, always cutting to the chase and bringing me back down to earth.

"I don't know where to start. I think my trigger was my mixed-up dreams. It happened right as I was waking up. I was having terrible dreams about Liam—"

"Liam!" she gasps. "The cute neighbor? Sophie Lynn, why are you dreaming about *Liam*?"

"Relax. You cut me off. I was dreaming about James and Liam. I went to Liam's last night—in my only clean loungewear, mind you—because I am babysitting for him tonight. I am pretty sure it was see-through. While I was there, James called me. I didn't answer but he has been texting me about calling a realtor to sell the house. I know Liam saw his name come up on my phone because he asked if I needed to take the call. That's what triggered the dreams, I'm sure of it."

"Not the fact that he's an attractive guy with a cute baby on his hip?" Claire laughs at her own joke, then her voice turns serious. "Girl, put on your shoes, go for a walk. Go shopping. And make yourself a plan."

I know she's right. I don't have a plan, and I am just floating around waiting for answers to come to me. I know that I am done with my marriage. I've signed the divorce papers for goodness' sake. But as soon as we sell the house we made a home, then it's *really* over. I'm not ready to admit that this part of my life is over—that I'm really all alone.

"Ellie introduced me to her psychiatrist friend recently. I

think I am going to give him a call today," I tell Claire, knowing it will reassure her.

"I think that's a good idea," she deadpans. I can always count on Claire not to sugarcoat anything. She tells it like it is. I appreciate that most of the time, but right now I am feeling delicate. She must sense it because her voice softens. "Hey, I'm always here for you, you know," she says gently.

I let out a deep breath. "I know. I'll call you later."

◌◌

I called Dr. Stevens, who still insists that I call him Robert and that any friend of Ellie's is a friend of his, and he told me his morning was slow. I guess he could hear the trembling in my voice because he asked if I wanted to come down and chat with him. The idea of being the one on the couch feels foreign to me, but I know it's something I have to do. I walk slowly up Perry Street, my feet still sore, until I hit Lafayette Street where Dr. Stevens's office is.

As I walk, I take in the sights, sounds, and smells of downtown. There is minimal traffic for 8:30 a.m. Shops are getting ready to open, little cafés are bustling, and a few people are getting their early morning jogs in. The salt air is everything I need to calm my nervous system.

Dr. Stevens's office is in a strip of stores, the second from the corner. The building is white stucco with a black awning and bold black lettering on a large window that says *The Psychiatry Office of Dr. Robert M. Stevens*. I open the door and a little bell chimes. The office is bright, airy, and welcoming. Instead of the standard doctors' office chairs, several plush gray armchairs line the walls and the open space. Raw-edge teakwood tables bookend the row of chairs and a bigger teakwood coffee table sits in the middle. They are gorgeous and exactly what my style would be if I were decorating a beach house.

While I wait for someone to appear at the front desk, I walk around and check out his various diplomas and accolades hanging on the wall. He was voted best psychiatrist of Cape May County for several years in a row. I let out a breath through my mouth. *At least he knows what he's doing.*

I mosey over to one of the plush armchairs and sit down. I nervously pick up a copy of *Psychology Today*, and I am thumbing through it when Dr. Stevens comes out. I have only been waiting about five minutes, but the anxiety in my chest has me feeling like it's been five hours.

"Sophie, how wonderful to see you." He smiles warmly, walking across the room to embrace me.

"Hi, Dr. Stevens," I squeeze him back and then pull away. "Your office is lovely. I was looking at all your accolades. And I just love these end tables." The nervous energy is real.

He chuckles. "Thank you. I'm not sure if you know him, but they were made by Ellie's neighbor, Liam. You know, the one with the baby she watches." He starts walking and gestures for me to follow. "Please, this way."

I feel my cheeks warm and my neck tingle at the mention of Liam. I'm surprised at the level of craftsmanship he is capable of. "Oh, yes, I know Liam. I am actually watching Lucy for him tonight. I didn't know he could build such beautiful things." I always did love a man who works with his hands. The realization makes me even more curious about this beautiful, broody man.

"He's one of the more popular artisans in town. You can find his work down in some of the stores at the mall." Dr. Stevens says. He leads me into his office, gestures toward a very comfortable looking tufted couch, and takes a seat in the chair opposite me. "So, Sophie, how are you feeling today?"

I take a moment to appreciate that he isn't behind some big desk and making this feel all clinical. He's simply sitting in an armchair opposite me, like I'm talking to a friend. I take a deep breath before I unload on him.

"I had a panic attack this morning, and I can't help but feel that I am avoiding all of the important things in my life by being here in Cape May. I haven't answered any of my ex-husband's calls or texts. He has reached out multiple times about selling our house and I have done nothing but avoid the situation. It's easier to just put on a front and immerse myself in the present moment so I don't have to think about it. I'm not ready to think about it."

I plop backward on the couch. Dr. Stevens makes it feel very casual here. I feel like I am complaining to Claire over margs and that makes me feel like I can speak freely.

"I see," he says. "Why do you suppose you feel like you're avoiding important things? You came here seeking solace, right?" He jots something down in his notebook.

I shrug. I feel the tears well up, threatening to fall. I haven't spent a lot of time talking about my own feelings. Generally, I am talking with *others* about *their* feelings. This part feels unfamiliar and scary.

I let out an unsteady breath. "This morning while I was having the panic attack, I called my best friend Claire. Usually, I know what to do to bring other people out of their own panic attacks, but I have never had one of my own before. I couldn't find a rational thought. She helped me breathe through it. Then she encouraged me to get outside for a walk and to make a plan. But I'm paralyzed. It's been six days that I've been here, and I haven't put one thought into what happens next."

"Can you tell me a bit about how you got to this place?" Dr. Stevens' voice is gentle, making me want to open up to him.

I give him the recap of the past six weeks and it all tumbles out of me like word vomit. I tell him how James not only carried on an affair, but that his mistress is pregnant. I tell him how this is a particularly hard pill to swallow because James and I struggled with infertility for seven years, eventually finding out that the reason we couldn't have a family had nothing to do with him and everything to do with my inhospitable uterus. I tell him that I drove to Cape May the day I signed my divorce papers. In the state of Pennsylvania, there is no separation period if it's a mutual divorce. James didn't even try to convince me to work it out. We both knew it was over as soon as he told me she was pregnant.

"Now I'm in a ninety-day waiting period until the divorce is final in court. Coming here for the first few weeks seemed like a good way to heal and figure out what comes next." I sniffle and shudder a deep breath. When I'm finished, I wipe my mascara-streaked cheeks, blotting under my eyes for any excess with a tissue Dr. Stevens held out for me while I cried.

Dr. Stevens appears thoughtful and then he speaks. "Sophie, you shouldn't be so hard on yourself. Not many people would know what to do with this turn of events," he says gently. "I know you feel you should be doing more right now, but there is nothing wrong with taking your time. This is your life and your well-being." He is so sincere when he says this that I instantly feel relief.

"You're right. But I haven't even thought about where to go from here. We were married for *thirteen* years. I never thought he would do this to me." I sniffle as my eyes fill with fresh tears. "I never imagined I wouldn't be the person he became a parent with. It's gut-wrenching."

Dr. Stevens listens intently. Periodically, he makes a note in his notebook, but mostly, he just lets me talk and cry—and I didn't realize how much I needed this.

I swallow and reach for another tissue from the box Dr. Stevens is holding out to me before continuing. "I think maybe if she wasn't pregnant, I would have wanted to try to work it out. I believe in love. I help other families and couples work through these issues. We said for better or for worse." I pause, hiccupping, and use the tissue to wipe under my eyes. "Unfortunately, I don't think the worse part included infidelity."

Dr. Stevens makes a note in his book and then looks up at me with a reassuring smile. "It's natural to feel a sense of loss and grief after a divorce. Mourning this change is an important step in healing."

I nod, letting out a post-cry shudder. "My therapist brain knows this. I just never thought I would be the person in this position," I admit, looking down at my hands.

"It's important to give yourself time to adjust. Coming here for a change of scenery is good but it's also okay if it's overwhelming." He pauses. "If you don't mind my asking, why did you pick Cape May?"

"I came here all the time as a child. My grandparents were locals, and my parents brought us down on the weekends every summer until I was sixteen and my mom died..." I trail off. "I have wonderful memories here and it just felt like the right place to come to clear my mind for a fresh start."

Dr. Stevens nods and jots down something else I can't read. "Have you thought about journaling? Writing down your big emotions as they come can help you process them."

I bite my lip and stifle a self-deprecating laugh. "I am really bad at journaling," I admit with a weak smile.

Dr. Stevens chuckles, putting me at ease. "It was just a suggestion. I'd like you to try to set yourself a routine. You're in a new physical place and you're in a new emotional place, too. It may help you to feel as though you're in control of something. But a new place can also be a fresh start—a chance to build something new and meaningful for yourself."

"I agree," I say emphatically. "A routine for the next couple of weeks feels manageable."

Dr. Stevens startles when the sound of the front door jingles, indicating someone else arriving. He looks at his watch and then back at me. "Sophie, this is great, great stuff. You have kept all of this bottled up inside you for a few weeks too long. I'm so glad you talked to me."

"It was pretty cathartic," I admit, attempting a small smile. I stand up and collect my things, sensing my time for today is up.

"I think you should come back next week, for a real appointment. In the meantime, I'd like you to make time for activities you enjoy or that help you feel calm, like exercise, reading, or spending time in nature. You're at the beach! Go get yourself a nice coffee from Coffee Tyme, put your feet in the sand, and decompress. The salt air cures everything." He touches my shoulder as he guides me out of his office. Gesturing to the receptionist who is getting settled behind the desk, he says, "If you talk to Angie here, she'll get you set up for next week."

"I will come back, thank you. I needed this." I blow my nose into the crumbled tissue I'm still holding.

After making my appointment, I decide to do exactly what he suggested. I walk up to Beach Road, get myself a piping hot vanilla latte, and plop my butt in the sand. There really isn't much that the beach can't cure.

Chapter Six

Liam

I am pacing around my living room after running all over the house, trying to tidy it up. *Why am I nervous?* I glance in the front room at all the boxes of Leah's belongings that I have yet to go through. I am going to have to do that eventually, but I can't bring myself to do it yet. I think it will trigger the mourning process all over again. I am scared to go back to that level of pain. I need to focus on now, on tonight. Lucy has been a little fussy all day. I hope Sophie isn't overwhelmed. I will give her the heads up and leave the Tylenol for her. She seems like she doesn't have a frustrated bone in her body, and Lucy really seems to like her.

My palms are sweating. *What the fuck, Harper, calm down.* I check my phone, 5:38. Sophie and Melanie will be here any minute. I am wearing faded J. Crew jeans and a black thermal. I still managed to get Lucy in her highchair and feed her some dinner. She's sitting there now watching a show on the TV and giggling every few minutes. *This is fine, everything is fine.*

I have reassured myself that this evening is a good idea at least fifteen times today. I'm worried about Lucy and agitated from not getting enough sleep. I'm nervous about setting things straight with Melanie and for some reason, I can't get Sophie out of my head. All of these sound like great reasons to bail but it's too late now because the doorbell buzzes right as I see Melanie's black car pull up in front of my house.

I pick up Lucy and open the front door to greet Sophie. I

immediately realize she isn't the reason I am nervous. Just the sight of her smile and relaxed demeanor eases my nerves. Then Sophie grins and reaches for Lucy who wriggles out of my arms to get to her.

Sophie giggles. "Hi, Luce." She plants a kiss on the top of the baby's head. "I'm happy to see you too!" Lucy nuzzles into Sophie's shoulder as if it's the most natural thing in the world for her. A sharp, unexpected twinge of longing twists in my chest, taking me by surprise.

Sophie seems to be feeling a lot better than she was last night, wearing a tight pair of black leggings and a fitted pink long-sleeve pullover. Her chestnut hair is down and falling wildly around her shoulders. She's completely at ease with Lucy and I find it undeniably attractive.

"Hi," I rasp, biting back a smile. There is a nagging feeling in my gut. I want to know *Sophie*. It's a feeling that is so foreign to me that I can't dismiss it.

"Hi," she chirps back. She grins and shifts Lucy to her other hip.

We don't get to say anything else before Melanie walks through the still-open front door. "Hey," She smiles tightly at me. "You ready?" She doesn't look in Sophie's direction at all.

I clear my throat. "Almost." I decide a formal introduction is the best course of action here since they don't know each other. Before I can say anything, a look of irritation crosses Melanie's face. I gesture to Sophie, holding Lucy. "Melanie this is Sophie. Sophie, this is Melanie."

A look of recognition passes over Sophie's face and her brows furrow for just a second before she says, "Hi, Melanie. It's nice to meet you." She offers her a warm smile.

In return, Melanie is the epitome of unfriendly. "Hello," she says curtly.

I stifle a cough. "Sophie is renting from Ellie for a bit, and she's been helping out with Lucy." I feel the need to explain even though I don't have to.

"Ah," Melanie says, as if it's clicking for her now.

Now here they stand, sizing each other up in a way that shouldn't matter but for some reason does. Melanie is wearing tight skinny jeans and a black bodysuit that accentuates her curves. She has big silver hoop earrings, and her sleeve tattoo of Hawaiian flowers is on display. She's taller than Sophie by about three and a half inches because of the black knee-high boots she is wearing.

Seeming uncomfortable, Sophie shifts Lucy from one hip to the other and looks back and forth between us. I find myself wondering what she is thinking about me and Melanie. An awkward silence has fallen upon the three of us and I know I need to break it, but Sophie beats me to it.

"Oh, yeah. I think I saw you leaving here after my morning run the other day."

I realize the second the words are out of her mouth and her cheeks turn a faint shade of pink that she thinks she shouldn't have said it. It seems she's a nervous rambler, but at least she tries to be kind. It also occurs to me that Sophie probably thinks Melanie slept over, and I want desperately to clarify but of course, I can't. Not now anyway. I can't help thinking though, *why is it so important for me to make sure that Sophie knows I'm not with Melanie?* The feeling nags at me, awakening a foreign longing I don't fully understand.

"Mm-hmm," Melanie nods, clearly uninterested. Then turning to me, "Ready? It's 5:50."

I nod. "Sophie, you have my number. Lucy is fed. If you want to give her a bath you can. I treat baths like an activity to occupy her," I laugh. "Anyway...she was a little fussy today. I think she's getting another tooth. There's Tylenol in the upstairs bathroom if you think she might need it."

Sophie smiles. "We'll be fine. Won't we, Lucy girl?" She brushes some hair from Lucy's forehead and grins back at me. Then she steps toward the door as if to usher us out. "Go, go. You kids have fun." She pats my back as we walk out. "Bye, Melanie. It was nice to officially meet you!"

Melanie ignores her, and as we climb in my pickup, I can't help but wish I was staying home...with Sophie.

⚯

We arrive at Taco Cocina, and the bar area is crowded. I recognize some familiar faces from around town but thankfully no one in our inner circle is there. The hostess says it'll be a few minutes despite our six o'clock reservation, so we head to the bar. I order us both a margarita on the rocks and close the tab. There's only one open seat so I pull it out for Melanie and stand behind her.

There is a familiarity between us that feels safe and reassuring. I can't get hurt with Melanie. I know she's more invested in us than I am, and there's a sense of safety in that. She wants me despite how well she knows me, despite how much I have been through, how emotionally unavailable I am. She *still* wants me. And I am probably holding her back from meeting someone who will be emotionally available for her. She is forty, I am forty. We're not kids anymore, and I have to set her free. We're just making small talk as we wait for the text message that our table is ready.

"I'm surprised you let someone you've known all of five days watch Lucy. But I'm not even allowed around her." Melanie goes right in for the kill.

Oh, here we go again. I roll my eyes. "Melanie, we have been over this. I am a new dad. And not the kind that has nine months to prepare. I am trying to protect Lucy at all costs. I'm not going to let her get close to someone I care about and then lose them if it doesn't work out." I'm surprised at how tightly my jaw is clenched as I have this conversation for the zillionth time.

She spins in the bar chair and tickles my chest up and down. "Well, who says it won't work out, babe? We've been doing this thing between us on and off for years."

"Yeah but, it's been off for quite a while now," I mutter, glancing anywhere around the bar except at Melanie.

"Sophie just looks like a train wreck, that's all," Melanie says snootily, taking a long sip of her margarita. "How can she take care of Lucy when she looks like she barely takes care of herself?"

I can see that Melanie is just jealous, and it doesn't look good on her.

"What? What's that supposed to mean? She's *nice*," I counter, feeling a little defensive of my new friend. I give an exasperated sigh just as my phone buzzes. "Our table is ready," I tell her and turn toward the host stand, leaving her to follow.

☙

For some reason, getting through this dinner feels like an eternity. Not only am I feeling all sorts of pressure from Melanie, spoken and unspoken, but I just have a sinking feeling about the whole evening. Melanie is coming off as jealous and bratty. She wants a future with me because of everything we've been through together. I'm still trying to work up the courage to tell her that this isn't what I want.

"So, what do you say to *dessert?*" Melanie looks hopeful, her voice flirtatious. "Like you said, I'm sure Sophie is very capable with Lucy. We could go back to my place," she purrs, stroking my hand.

I need to get out of here.

"Honestly, I told Sophie I would only be gone for a couple of hours. I don't want to take advantage of her kindness." I pull my hand away from Melanie's, hoping that sends a message.

"How about your house then? I'm sure she'll be asleep when we get back." Melanie picks up her drink and takes a long sip.

I'm not sure if it's because she's had years of me pulling away from her, then getting close again, then pulling away again, but all she does is push. And when she pushes, I pull away. It's this vicious little circle we've got going. My stomach drops. Melanie isn't the person I want to be with. Ellie is right. I need to let Melanie go.

I feel myself growing irritated. "What exactly are you trying to make happen here?" I ask, even though I know the answer.

Melanie isn't deterred. "Come on, Liam. You know how good we are together," She murmurs. "Don't you remember?"

"I do remember," I growl impatiently. I suck in a breath to steady my voice. "But that was the past. I'm really sorry, Mel, but I think I've been clear with you that we're not going back there."

For a moment Melanie looks taken aback but then she smirks. "That's what you say until you want someone to warm your bed at night."

I narrow my eyes at her. "Melanie, that hasn't happened in a long time. And never for more than a month at a time. You have to admit, it was mostly because we both missed Cara." I wince as I say it. In high school, Melanie was my girlfriend Cara's best friend. Cara was my high school sweetheart until she died in a fatal car accident that I'm not convinced wasn't my fault.

"That might be how it started, Liam, but I always thought there was more to it."

Melanie's voice wavers and I must actively swallow the acquiescence building in my throat out of guilt.

"I'm sorry, Mel." I soften my voice. "But I have been honest with you from the start about the level of commitment I am capable of. You can't fault me for that. I didn't ask you to keep hanging on or to hold out hope that you could fix me." I keep my voice calm so I can stand my ground.

"Then why did you ask me here tonight?" Melanie scoffs, pushing her plate away and folding her arms.

"I asked you here so I could be really honest with you and tell you it's not going to happen. I've been avoiding the conversation, but I can't anymore. I have Lucy now, and I have my own demons I am battling. I have too much work to do on myself." As soon as I say it, I relax, relief flooding my muscles.

"I see," Melanie mutters, refusing to meet my eyes.

"I'm sorry, Melanie. I am. It's just—"

A text from Sophie interrupts me, then quickly, another.

> **Sophie: Liam, I think Lucy is sick. She's really warm. I was going to give her a bath but then I realized she definitely has a fever and she has a red rash all over her belly.**

> **Sophie: What do you want me to do? I can give her some Tylenol to lower her fever but I'm not sure about the rash. Does she have a pediatrician I can call?**

I tip my head back in frustration and look at the ceiling, pinching the bridge of my nose. Of course she has a pediatrician. Do I know who it is? Nope. Have I taken her at all in the almost six months Leah has been gone? Nope. I'm barely surviving. It's a damn good thing I'm not starting a relationship. I quickly type back.

> **Me: Uh...I'm sure she does have a pediatrician but I don't know who it is.**

> **Sophie: What? Okay. What about urgent care?**

> **Me: I'm coming home, I'll be right there.**

"We've got to get the check," I say hurriedly.

Melanie takes a bite of her food and frowns. "I'm not done eating," she says, even though not five minutes ago she pushed her plate away.

"Lucy is sick." I raise my arm to get the server's attention to ask for the bill and some boxes. "I'm sorry."

"Right. Sure." Melanie pushes her plate away. "Okay, let's go then."

Chapter Seven

Sophie

I'm pacing around the upstairs hallway, attempting to soothe Lucy and waiting for Liam to get back. I'm trying to remember, but I think my brother's wife, Laura, told me once before the twins got rashes with viruses. Maybe that's what this is. It must be so overwhelming for him to be in this new role. But he has to figure it out. I will help him if he'll let me.

I hear the front door open and close, and I shout to him that we're upstairs. He bounds up the stairs and grabs Lucy from me, holding her up so he can look her over. "She's fine," he says abruptly, taking me aback.

I look at him as if he has three heads. "Uh, no, Liam, she is not fine. She is sick. It's probably just a cold or a virus, but she has to go to the doctor," I say firmly.

I watch Liam carefully as he walks into his room with Lucy in his arms. I wait a moment before following. I'm not sure what to say to him so I don't set him off. He seems a little edgy, perhaps because his date got cut short. When I walk in, I find him sitting on the edge of the bed, holding Lucy close and stroking the back of her head.

I lean in the doorway and wait for him to notice me.

"I don't know what to do," he admits, his voice raspy. "She's never been sick before."

I sigh, my empathy for him growing. I walk over and sit down next to him, so close our thighs are touching. "I can help you," I tell him.

He shakes his head vigorously and scoots over so I can no longer feel the heat coming off his body. "No. You've done enough." It doesn't sound outright mean, but it sounds like he really doesn't want my help.

"Maybe we should call her doctor. I'm sure we could look in your sister's boxes..." I trail off when he stands up and walks out of the room.

I follow him and find him rooting one-handed through Lucy's pajama drawer while he holds her with the other. "I told you. I don't know who her doctor is," he growls. "I will figure it out."

"Liam, why don't you let me help you? It's Cape May, it's small. How many pediatrician's offices could there be?" I try to take her back from him, but he turns away, surprising me with his unwillingness to accept my help.

"With all due respect, Sophie, this is my problem. Not yours. It's 8 p.m. on a Friday night. No pediatrician would be open anyway." He walks away from me, back into his bedroom, and lays Lucy on the bed to dress her.

"They have doctors on call. Or we can try an urgent care. This qualifies as urgent." I push harder and right away I realize that's a mistake.

Liam is visibly frustrated, but I don't think it's with me. Not directly anyway. Maybe he's frustrated with the situation. I'm trying not to take it personally.

"No, Sophie. Just stop. I've got this," he says curtly, holding up his hand. Then he walks back into Lucy's room and sits down in the rocking chair. She is tense and starts to whimper, probably because she can sense the tension between us. He pats her back and whispers "shhh" in her ear. He clearly loves her, and maybe he is mad at himself right now. I just wish he would let me help.

"Liam, please. I want to help you both," I try again, forcing myself to steady my voice.

"Sophie, I appreciate all you've done tonight, but I'm here

now so please, I don't need your help. Please just let me handle it."
He holds his hand up at me as if telling me to back off.

My lips are trembling. I am speechless at this point, and I don't know what else there is to say. Obviously, Liam and I are not becoming friends like I thought we were. *He doesn't want my help.* It stings. I suck in a breath, willing myself not to cry. I look at Liam, but he won't meet my eyes. He wears a mix of emotions on his face—fear, frustration, sadness, shame, maybe. I can't quite pinpoint it, but there is nothing more I can do if he doesn't want my help. Without another word, and with one last long look at Lucy, I leave.

࿇

"What a *douchebag*!" Claire shrieks when I am FaceTiming her fifteen minutes later. "You know, the nerve of that guy. I cannot even believe he acted like that to you when you are *helping him*! I am infuriated." Claire props her phone up on her dresser and paces around her bedroom.

"I mean, I was pretty pushy about him letting me help," I reconcile, feeling so silly now that I laugh at myself.

"So what? You were helping him. You were giving him advice as a woman who knows a hell of a lot more about babies than he does!" She is yelling at me now.

"I mean, I'm not a mom so I don't know how much I really know," I mutter, feeling my typical self-pity creep up once again. Here I am, on a Friday night, miles and miles away from my best friend, my ex-husband, and my *life*, feeling sorry for myself instead of doing whatever else I should be doing. I don't know what that is yet, but it is *something*. Who even cares about Liam?

"And he told you to *let him handle it*!" Claire shouts ignoring my remark about motherhood.

Claire and Derek are DINKs. Double Income No Kids. They are choosing not to have kids and instead to embrace life together, travel, make a shit ton of money, and roll around naked in it, probably. So, while I know she empathizes with me and my journey toward motherhood—that has now abruptly come to a halt—I would say she doesn't totally get it.

"You know what? I'm coming there. Tomorrow. *Derek*!" She shouts to another room, "I am going to see Sophie in Cape May tomorrow!" She is such a firecracker.

I love Claire; she is my best friend. My ride or die. She's mad for me, but I also secretly think she misses me. "I think you're more upset about this argument with Liam than I am. I hardly know the guy. I thought maybe we could be friends but now it's just clear that I need to stay out of his way." I kick off my shoes and lay back on the couch. "I mean, you can come if you want to but it's a long drive."

"I'm coming. You need some moral support. I should have been there already! You need me to kick your ass in gear and help you figure out what you're going to do next." She begins throwing things in a duffel bag erratically. "What's the weather like there right now?" I laugh because she *would* ask about the weather.

For the last weekend in April, it's actually quite nice. I wished that I had shorts earlier in the week because it's been in the 70s but cooler at night. I love it when there is a sea breeze. I can crack open the window in the cottage and smell the ocean all the way over here while I sleep. "It's warm-ish during the day and cooler at night," I tell her.

"Great. I'm leaving first thing in the morning. Book us a spa appointment for tomorrow afternoon or something. I mean it. Let's get massages, pedicures, nails, really relax. Wait. Do you have space for me to sleep?" Claire is talking so fast I'm having trouble keeping up, but she already helped me forget how riled up I was when I called her so that's a plus.

"I have a queen-size bed we can share, otherwise this super cool teal sofa." I laugh, holding my phone up so she can see where I am sitting.

"Okay, great. We can snuggle." She laughs. "I will see you tomorrow!"

"Bring wine," I chirp.

"You know it! I'll see you tomorrow." Claire grins and with that, she's gone.

I immediately go in search of a spa that will let me book online at 9 p.m. on a Friday night.

Chapter Eight

Liam

I berated myself as soon as Sophie closed my front door. The entire time I was refusing her help, I knew I was being a dick. The logical part of my brain was setting off alarm bells, but I couldn't stop being irrational. The other reason is because I know Sophie is right. I do need help. I just don't know how to ask for it and for some reason when she offered, it made me feel weak. I was just starting to think I am getting this parenting thing and today it seems like I'm back at square one. Lucy is dozing in my arms now, but I know I won't sleep at all tonight if she's as sick as Sophie seems to think. I stand up and place her in her crib; she stays asleep.

I head downstairs but find myself just standing in the kitchen, unsure what to do next. I glance over at Maggie who is camped out under my kitchen table. "Come on girl, let's go outside," I tell her, gesturing to my sliding glass door. She doesn't move. "Maggie, don't you have to go pee? Let's go." In typical stubborn golden retriever fashion, she continues to stare at me. I'm sure she heard the argument and is pissed at me too.

I reach down and slide her out by her collar and walk over to open the door. Only then does she walk out. I follow her out and look over the fence at Ellie's house. It's dark of course. The cottage is lit up and I can see Sophie on the couch in the window laughing at something. She's absolutely beautiful when she laughs. She must reserve those smiles for people who aren't unnecessarily rude to her.

For a minute, I think about going over and apologizing, but I can't let go of my pride. I mean, I am the parent. I don't need her unsolicited advice. Anyone who knows me knows what I've dealt with and that I'm trying my damnedest to do right by Lucy. *Forget it. I don't have anything to apologize for.*

I watch Maggie sniffing around the trees that line the fence, and I am about to call her in before she picks up a dead bird or something when my phone buzzes in my pocket. It's Melanie. I brace myself for a fight but the message only says:

> **Melanie: Even though it hurts, I appreciate you being honest with me, Liam.**

I swallow hard and put my phone back in my pocket. I want to say the right thing and I know I'm not in the right mindset to do that. I flash back in my mind to the first time Melanie and I connected as more than friends, about a year after Cara passed away.

We are at a house party in Lower Township. The houses here are on large lots of land. I don't know whose house it is, honestly, but the party is a rager. Since I can't cope with anything happening in my life, I am drinking heavily. There are about fifty people here and multiple kegs in the backyard with a huge bonfire. I remember doing a keg stand and not much else after that. I am stumbling around the woods when I trip on a raised tree root and fall. I lay there on the ground for I don't know how long. I am starting to pass out when I hear leaves crunching nearby, and then Melanie is lying next to me.

"What are we doing?" she asks, looking up at the stars.

"Just...laying," I say. I look over at her and feel her grab my hand and intertwine her fingers with mine.

"Okay. I will just lay with you," she says, leaning her head on my shoulder.

Melanie strokes my hand with her thumb and forefinger.

We are so quiet that I can hear her breathing. Before I know it, I am crying. Full-on beer tears. Melanie knows it too, and she does nothing but continue to stroke my hand.

"Shhh," she says. "You're okay. You're safe. You're not alone," she whispers to me.

"It is my fault," I croak. I squeeze my eyes shut, remembering the worst day of my life. I was driving with Cara in the front seat, and Melanie in the back. Then we were T-boned by a large pickup truck at a four-way stop. The driver had been drinking. I saw him coming but it was my turn to go and it was his turn to stop. I saw he wasn't slowing down. I thought I could make it or maybe I was showing off by putting the pedal to the metal, but either way, I was wrong. He ran the stop sign. A loud sob escapes me at the memory.

She wipes away one of my tears and puts my fingers to her lips, kissing them. "It's not your fault, Liam," she whispers.

I can't say anything back but before I know it, we're kissing

Kissing was as far as it went that night, but through the years, our relationship got to be very intense. Both of us missed Cara in our own ways, and Melanie was the only one who understood the guilt that I experienced from that night. I have blamed myself ever since.

I think if you asked me back then, I would have told you that I loved Melanie. She took so much of my guilt and hurt and carried it for me. All she asked for in return was that I give her my heart, and I never could. If Cara had never died, I would never have gotten swept up with Melanie. I might have even married Cara. We were headed in that direction. I was going to play baseball at Duke University. Cara applied to their nursing program. We were in love. Our futures were bright...until they weren't.

I let out a big, defeated sigh and call Maggie inside. I wander into the front room and look at Leah's boxes piled high and not labeled well. My parents put everything together after Leah's funeral. I couldn't bear to help. It was too painful, so I have no idea where everything is. After three boxes of childhood photo albums, I find one that says *Important Papers*. I open it and find several file folders with Leah's birth certificate and sadly, her death certificate. I feel something in my heart shift at the sight of it.

I find her military papers and IDs but nothing pertaining to Lucy. Finally in the third folder, I find Lucy's birth certificate. I take it out and study it. Lucy Elizabeth Harper. Under mother it says Leah Grace Harper. The father line is blank. I knew the jerk took off when he found out Leah was pregnant, but she must've had no contact with him whatsoever to leave his name off the birth certificate.

The rest of the stuff in the folder is just Lucy's baby footprints from the hospital, the "It's a Girl" card that they put on her hospital bed, and finally the discharge paperwork. I scan the papers and find a pediatrician's name who checked her out in the hospital. Dr. Andrew Philips at Rainbow Pediatrics. There's a phone number, so I call and leave a message on the recording. There is nothing more I can do tonight. I pack up the boxes once again and just as I'm about to bring Maggie up for the night, I hear Lucy crying upstairs. It sounds like she's saying "Dada."

Chapter Nine

Sophie

Promptly at 10 a.m., I am greeted by a car horn beeping excessively with the Spice Girls blaring in the background. I know immediately that Claire is here, and she made excellent time. I run out of the cottage and toward her car. She sticks her head out the window.

"I made it!" she shouts excitedly. She turns off the ignition and gets out of the car at the same time I get there. She throws her arms around me, and we squeal. "I missed you, Soph!" she says into my hair.

"I missed you too, Claire Bear!" I sniff. "Thank you for coming to see me." We separate and I grab one of the duffel bags out of her trunk.

Claire hesitates before we head toward the cottage. "I drove by your house before I left," she begins cautiously. "I wanted to see if it looked like James was still living there."

I nervously chew on my lower lip. "And? What did you see?"

Claire takes a breath and reaches for my hand. "There were two cars in the driveway. James' car and I guess the girl's car? And a FOR SALE sign in the yard." Claire squeezes the hand she's holding. "I'm sorry, Soph."

I exhale and nod. "I expected that, honestly. I've been avoiding his calls, but he's been telling me he was going to list the house. I guess he didn't need my blessing to do it." I shrug, because what else can I do? "It's really over."

Claire nods sympathetically, her mouth turning downward

in sadness. "It is. But you'll be okay. I'm here."

"Thank you," I whisper and start walking toward the cottage. Right then I decide we need mimosas with brunch.

❧

Several hours later, I am laughing harder than I have laughed in a very long time. I didn't realize how much I needed my best friend. We had brunch, walked around the Washington Street Mall, popped in and out of boutiques, and bought pretty things that we don't really need. We walked on the beach, charged into the icy waves, and got ourselves soaking wet. Now, we're sitting in the quiet room at Stillwater Spa, waiting for our massages, and we're not being very quiet.

"Shh!" An older lady glares at us and points at the sign next to the door that reads *Relaxation Room. Quiet Please. No Cell Phones.*

Claire and I look at each other and giggle. I look at the lady and pretend to zip my lips and throw away the key. She turns back to her book, ignoring me. I lay back and close my eyes.

"Let's go out tonight," Claire whispers, forcing me to peek at her. "I think you need it."

"I think I do too," I agree.

❧

It's been ages since I got myself dressed and ready for a night on the town. I'm wearing my favorite boyfriend jeans and plunging red bodysuit that I haven't worn in forever because James and I rarely went out. I got my hair done at the spa and then came home and put on makeup for the first time in way too long. My skin is soft and glowy from my massage, and I am feeling pretty good as I slip into my dressy black sandals.

"Girl, you are a knockout!" Claire gasps when I come out of the bathroom and do a little spin. "James who?" Then she squeals and throws her arms around me. "This is going to be okay.

Everything is. And tonight, we party! When was the last time we went out together without *husbands*?" She scrunches up her nose in mock distaste.

I laugh and shake my head. "You're right. We need this. I need this. It's Saturday night. Tomorrow I will figure out what I am doing with my life. I keep saying tomorrow but I really mean it. Tomorrow."

"You got it, sis. I'm calling an Uber. We're not taking any chances tonight." She requests the Uber while I spritz on some of her perfume and a little guava lip gloss. By the time I finish our ride is here. We slide into the backseat of a white Toyota Prius. The driver is a young guy in his twenties.

"Va va voom, ladies! Where we going?" He looks at his driverapp. "The Rusty Nail. Groovy. There's live music there tonight!" He pulls away from the curb and for the first time in a long time, I feel free.

☙

I feel like my younger self as we take seats at the bar closest to the live music. A cover band is playing all kinds of beachy tunes, like Jimmy Buffet and Kenny Chesney. I can tell the crowd in the bar is mostly locals, but everyone seems to be enjoying the mid-spring vibes on a Saturday night.

Claire waves her hand up to the cute bartender and he saunters over.

"Hiiii, can we have two shots of tequila please?" She gives her best flirtatious smile even though her two-carat diamond engagement ring is casting a glare in all directions.

"Sure thing, girls. What are we celebrating?" he asks. When Claire and I look at each other with raised eyebrows, he adds, "You always have to be celebrating something on a Saturday night, even if it's just because it's the weekend." His smile is infectious, and I can tell this is his MO with all the women who come in here.

Claire looks at me and shrugs.

"Divorce!" I say, holding up my nearly empty margarita left over from dinner with a big smile. "And moving on."

"Here, here!" A guy next to me holds his drink up in agreement. "Marriage sucks!" He has a lean build, tousled brown hair, and kind hazel eyes. And he's very cute. We take our shots, and he takes a sip of his drink before turning to us. "I'm guessing you girls aren't from around here," he drawls in a very Jersey accent. He grins and the dimple in his left cheek catches my attention.

"You would be correct," I say with a smile.

"I'm Claire, this is Sophie. We're from Scranton," Claire offers. "I'm here just for the weekend but my girl, Sophie is here..." She pauses to glance at me, cocking her head. "How long are you here for?"

"You know," I mimic her head tilt. "I'm thinking about staying a while longer."

"Staying, eh? In that case, I'm Miles." He offers his hand to Claire first. "This is Danny and Jack. We've lived here our whole lives."

The other two guys give "married guy" waves in our direction, and they aren't nearly as interested in engaging with us as Miles is. Before I know it, Miles has conned us all into more tequila shots.

Miles and I share several dances up front near the stage as Claire watches from our bar seats. Miles is cute, and the tequila is making me forget all about the fact that my life is crumbling. Then I'm back at the bar, laughing and taking shots and singing along to Jimmy Buffet's *Margaritaville* when Danny turns to me. "Did you say your name is Sophie?" he asks, raising an eyebrow.

I nod, taking another big sip. "That's me. Cute little lonely recently divorced Sophie." I bop my shoulders up and down to the music. I'm going to cringe thinking about this tomorrow, I just know it.

"Are you staying with Ellie?" he asks, clearly more interested now.

"I *am*," I slur. "For the foreseeable future, I think." I am getting a little sloppy now. "Why? Want to come over?" I give him my best flirtatious wink. Claire puts a water glass in front of me.

"Drink," she says firmly. "I think you're flagged."

"I am not flagged!" I huff and turn back to Danny. "Am I flagged?" I pout.

Danny smiles and nods his head. "I think so. No, I'm not coming over." He points at his wedding ring. "But I do know Ellie well, and Liam."

"Oh, Liam! That asshole," I shout. Miles barks out a laugh, as if it is the funniest thing he's ever heard. Danny shoots him a look I am too drunk to interpret.

"Liam is an asshole," Miles agrees, nodding vigorously.

Danny holds up his hands in defense. "Okay, okay. Liam can be...difficult, but he's my best friend. Knock off the Liam bashing." He puts his beer down and turns back to the band.

"You started it," I challenge, a hand on my hips.

Claire takes my drink out of my hands. "Well, boys, it was super great to meet you, but our Uber is here so we're going to go." Claire signs the check for the tab that I didn't know she asked for, drapes my jacket over my shoulders, and leads me out of The Rusty Nail before I can even say my goodbyes.

❧

"But I don't want to leave!" I whine as Claire puts me in the back of a car.

"It's time, babe. You've had a lot to drink, and you won't like either of us tomorrow." Then to the Uber driver, "Hey, can you stop at a CVS or a grocery store?"

"Sure thing," he says, which is the only thing this driver says the entire drive. He's probably not interested in engaging two drunk girls.

"Oooh...What are we getting?" I ask Claire, excitedly.

"You are waiting in the car. I am getting Liquid IV and ramen." Claire chuckles, grabbing her bag as the driver pulls up to the CVS on the next block. "Be right back. Don't move." Back in college we ate ramen after every night out, and to this day we still swear it's the magic hangover preventer. Something about the salt balancing out all the alcohol.

I sigh and lean back on the seat. I pull out my phone and see a text from James.

> **James: I listed the house but you need to sign some things. We really need to talk, Sophie.**

Maybe it's all the tequila but for the first time, I want to text him back. I hesitate, my thumbs moving over the touch screen. I'm not sure what to say.

> **Me: I'm drunk. And I danced with another man tonight. And I think I am moving to Cape May.**

> **James: Come home and talk to me.**

Decisions made while drinking are never the best ones but after spending the day in Cape May with Claire, meeting locals this past week, and seeing the town with new adult eyes, I really can envision myself here. *I don't want to leave next week.* I know my judgment may be clouded by tequila, but maybe I can take a leave of absence from work or see clients virtually. Maybe I can stay here a little longer.

> **Me: I will. If I am staying here, I will have to get all of my things from my dad's house.**

> **James: I have some things of yours still.**

> **Me: Well, you can bring them over there.**

> **James: Okay. I'll do that. I'm sorry.**

That's it? That's freaking it? I realize that I have started to cry right as Claire slides her butt back in the car. Her brow creases and her face falls. "What's wrong?" she asks with great concern.

I sniffle but I can't talk or the dam will break and it will no longer be just a few tears. Instead, I hold up my phone screen so she can read the exchange. She skims the text chain and then puts my phone in her purse. "Fuck him. I'm making us ramen."

Chapter Ten

Liam

Lucy is definitely sick and it's a damn good thing I called the on-call line last night. They called me back an hour later and scheduled me to come in first thing this morning. My first priority when I wake up today is to get Lucy feeling better.

I make myself coffee, let the dog out, and shower all before Lucy even wakes up. The poor thing must have needed the rest. When I finally go in to wake her, the sight of her makes my heart ache. Her eyes are red and glassy, her cheeks rosy, and she is super congested.

I dress her in warm clothes and head for the pediatrician's office. We check in at the desk and then we're taken to a small blue room with a couple of chairs and a long exam table with paper covering it. Fish decals adorn the walls in bright colors. Lucy is fussy and not interested in anything except being held and her sippy cup of water, even when I try to point out the pretty fish to her.

Dr. Philips comes in and greets me with a smile and a handshake. He's probably ten years older than I am with a lean build and salt-and-pepper hair. Behind his silver-rimmed glasses, his eyes are kind. "Hi, Mr. Harper. I am Dr. Philips." He smiles at Lucy. "Hi, Lucy. Are you not feeling so well?"

"You can call me Liam. Thanks for seeing us so quickly, Doc. I don't know what I was thinking. My sister passed away and I was thrust into full-time parenthood. I didn't know babies got shots and well visits so frequently. This is so new to me." I am nervous and rambling.

Dr. Philips holds up his hands to reassure me. "It's okay, Liam. I am so sorry to hear about your sister. This is a small practice, and I know most of my patients well. I had wondered what happened to her. How are you guys holding up?" he asks, genuinely concerned.

I clear my throat. Any time I have to talk about Leah is hard. I don't always know how much information to give, but I also don't want people thinking she did drugs or died in vain. "We're doing okay. As well as can be expected. It's been a tough few months. Leah got called up to active duty, but her helicopter went down in a training exercise before she even made it overseas."

Dr. Philips shakes his head. "Gosh, that is just awful, Liam. I'm so sorry for you both. Thank you for her service, truly." Perhaps sensing that it's getting too emotional, he asks if he can take Lucy from me, then places her on the table. "Let's check out this rash, Lucy." He lays her back. He does a thorough examination, listens to her heart, checks her ears, eyes, and throat, and inspects the rash. Then he picks her up and turns to me. "A lot of times, these rashes are viral. Babies often get viruses and once the immune system responds, they develop a rash. There are several childhood illnesses that present like this. But unfortunately, there isn't always a clear answer. It could be any number of childhood viruses. There's no need to test for these because Lucy is presenting like a baby with her first cold. If she worsens, or if her fever doesn't break in a couple of days, you'll need to bring her back." He hands Lucy back to me.

I nod, taking her back from the doctor. "Okay. So, we just do nothing but wait and keep her comfortable?"

"We'll swab her throat to make sure it's not more serious, but in the meantime, treat this like any illness you might get. Rest, fluids, Tylenol when needed. She'll be feeling better in a few days," Dr. Philips smiles. "And once she's feeling better, let's get her back in here for those shots she is behind on."

Dr. Philips wraps up the appointment by swabbing Lucy's

throat and says he will send out the test to the lab. I won't hear anything for a few days. We get in the car, and Lucy falls right to sleep. I decide to cruise around a bit so she can rest. I drive past our house without pulling in, and I can't help but notice that Sophie's car is gone. I feel awful about how I spoke to her last night. I would love to talk to her, but she seems to be preoccupied with company now. I have to wait until I can catch her alone. In the meantime, I will do the best I can to help Lucy feel better.

I get home, put Lucy in the playpen with Elmo, and fix myself some coffee. I haven't had any caffeine yet and I feel the headache starting. I sit down in the recliner with my phone. I have several texts that I have ignored all morning.

> **Melanie: How is Lucy this morning?**

> **Ellie: Liam, Sophie said Lucy is sick. How is she? Are you alright?**

> **Perry Street Boys (Group Text): Anyone want to go out tonight?**

All of a sudden though, I don't have the energy to answer anyone. I put my phone on the end table with my untouched cup of coffee and drift in and out of sleep.

℞

I wake up with a startle. *It was just a dream.* I exhale deeply and rub the sleep out of my eyes. I was dreaming of Cara, the night she died. She was trying to get in my car but non-dream Liam knew what was going to happen so dream-Liam tried to stop her.

I shake my head and look around the room, breathing a sigh of relief. I'm still in the recliner, Maggie's wet nose is nudging my hand, and Lucy is sleeping in the pack-and-play. I am relieved that she's resting. Maggie whines and nudges me again. "Okay, you have to go outside, girl?" I ask her. I get up from the recliner and walk over to Lucy. I look down at her sleeping, feel her sweaty forehead and then her back to make sure she is breathing. She is. I think I googled that sweating could mean her fever is breaking.

"Okay, let's go." I motion Maggie toward the door.

I look down at my watch. 3 p.m. We must have been asleep for quite a while. I know I have to get back to everyone who texted me, but I am haunted by the dream I just had. I can't stop remembering the night like it was yesterday, not twenty-two years ago. But my dream was different because this time, I know the ending. Everything leading up to the accident was the same, but in my dream, I didn't want to get in the car.

"Come on, Liam! Let's go!" Cara skips down my front steps and out to my beat-up old Ford Mustang. I feel so cool driving this car. I had it repainted to be a metallic navy blue that glistened in the sun. I put bright neon green rims on the tires and tinted the windows. I can only fit two additional people because I put a large bass in half of the backseat so people can hear me coming. "Unlock my door!" She squints at me, shading her eyes.

I am paralyzed on the steps. "No. I don't want to go anymore," I say carefully.

"Liam! Melanie is waiting for us. Come on." Cara stamps her foot. "This is the first football game of the year! Don't you want to get a good spot?" She puts her hands on her hips. "Besides, I'll make it worth your while," she teases.

There isn't much that Cara can't convince me to do. She smiles mischievously and makes a come-hither motion with her index finger. I huff and stomp down the steps.

Although it's a night game in September, it's not completely dark yet. We stop to pick up Melanie, who squeezes in the backseat. We are blasting Blink 182 as I approach a four-way stop off the Garden State Parkway. There is no one stopped on the other side, but I do see a large pickup making its way pretty quickly. Feeling cocky, and a little amped up for the evening, I gun it through my side of the four-way, but the pickup never stops.

Cara was killed instantly, and I will never forget the painful scream that I heard last.

The sound of the crash in my dream is what startled me awake. For years, I have had dreams like this. I could generally work through them with Doc during my weekly sessions, and we discovered that high levels of stress brought them back. Shocker. I have been abnormally stressed the last few months. No wonder the dreams are coming back. The last few days, I have been short-tempered and irritable. And lonely, oh so lonely.

Chapter Eleven

Sophie

"Oh my god." I cover my face with a pillow. "I am going to die," I groan. "Why did you let me drink so much?"

Claire snorts. "Girl, you did that all by yourself." She is sitting up on the velvet sofa with a piping hot mug of coffee. "Would you like me to fix you a coffee?"

My stomach rumbles, and I can't answer her because I'm running for the bathroom. I'm going to be sick. I emerge a few minutes later with nothing left in my stomach and plop down on the couch next to Claire. She hands me a cup of coffee and a beer. "Hair of the dog? Or coffee?"

I pick up the beer first and take a swig, swishing it around in my mouth. Then I pick up the coffee deciding the beer is *definitely* not what I need. I smell it first and then take a sip. "Did you put Kahlua in this?" Ellie has an old liquor cabinet in the cottage with a note on it that says *Help Yourself* in case her guests don't bring any alcohol.

Claire grins mischievously.

I laugh at her. "You're impossible."

Claire laughs too, throwing her head back. "Hey, you know the hair of the dog is a proven method to feeling better after a night of drinking too much. There's more regular coffee in the pot." She gestures with a shrug. Then, more seriously, she looks at me and says, "You told James you're moving to Cape May last night. Is that true?"

I moan loudly. "Ugh. I don't know." Then I walk over to the sink and dump the horrific Kahlua coffee and the beer. I'm quiet as I turn back to the pot, pour myself a fresh cup with some half and half, and make myself busy rummaging in the fridge for something to eat. Surprise! There's nothing because I have literally bought nothing of substance since my second day here.

Claire clears her throat and looks pointedly at me. "Is that what you really want?"

Claire is always demanding when it comes to important conversations. She doesn't beat around the bush, and she forces me to think about things I'd rather not. Sometimes I avoid her so I can avoid my own feelings about hard topics, but today, despite the wicked hangover, I am grateful for her straight-shooting. I need a kick in the ass to really figure out how to move forward.

It's been seven weeks since my birthday and a week since I signed the divorce papers. I've only been here for a week, but it feels like much longer. The only thing in my life that feels right at the moment is being in Cape May. I haven't worked much in the six weeks since my life imploded, but I think I could figure out virtual appointments or even a sabbatical. I don't think I can go back to life in Scranton knowing my heart and my marriage were annihilated there.

I turn to Claire and take a deep breath. "I think so," I say sadly. "I just don't know how I can go back to living there, without James, knowing someone else got everything I have ever wanted with him." My voice cracks and my eyes fill with tears for the thousandth time since all of this started. I shudder and let out a big breath.

Claire puts her mug down and stands up. "Okay, then let's go move you the hell out of your dad's house and down here!" She walks definitively over to me and puts her hands on my shoulders. She gives them a squeeze, looking me in the eyes with a grim smile. "You've got this. This is going to be okay. You are going to be okay." And then she gives me a hug.

Everyone needs a Claire.

CR

I decide to pack everything, even though I hope Ellie will let me stay longer. I can't take any chances. I get dressed quickly, take a couple Motrin, grab some bottles of water, and I'm out the door. I'm driving right to my dad's house, and I shoot him a text to give him the heads up that I want to talk to him and the family.

"Can we stop at McDonald's first?" Claire asks before opening her car door.

"We better," I call back before plopping in my driver's seat. "Give me a minute before you pull out," I yell.

I pick up my phone and quickly type out two texts—first to Ellie. I haven't talked to her since she's been away except for a few texts yesterday morning to let her know about Lucy. I also not-so-subtly let her know that Liam rudely told me he didn't want my help.

> **Me: Ellie, I am going home to Scranton for a couple of days. I need to figure out what's next for me. I'd love to talk to you about the potential of a longer lease. I'll be in touch.**

And then I send a text to James.

> **Me: I'm going to be at my dad's house this evening if you want to talk.**

I don't wait for a reply from either of them. I put on a '90s bangers playlist and back out of the driveway.

When I was a kid, the drive to and from Cape May was agonizing. I could only play so many car games or read so many books before getting car sick or bored. The drive today feels cathartic. I am singing my heart out to songs of my youth and reflecting on the choices I have made that led me to this moment.

This week has been very nostalgic. I found myself reflecting on moments from childhood that are burnt in my memory but not often at the forefront. I thought about how my parents would take Simon and I with our beach friends to Sunset Beach to look for Cape May diamonds. They are little pieces of naturally occurring quartz that wash up to shore where the river meets the bay. The changing tide transforms them and makes them new. Today as I drive back to my hometown, I think about how a person can be like a Cape May diamond. A dull piece of quartz but when the tide changes, as it always does, they can become new again too. *Maybe once I get through this, that will happen to me.*

I had so many Cape May diamonds when I was a kid that I needed a box to keep them in. No matter how many I collected, I always wanted to find more. There was just something so magical about combing through all the pebbles and finding that one diamond in the rough.

After we searched our little hearts out, we would go into the gift shop at Cape May Point and show the lady behind the counter all the diamonds we had found. She would always be very impressed and make us "offers" to buy them to sell in her store, but we would never take the bait. These diamonds were our treasures. I have an overwhelming urge to go in my dad's attic and pull out all of the boxes from our times in Cape May. I know there were pictures of all of us kids on the beach holding up our treasures dripping wet from the surf with bright, red-lipped smiles. I can practically see it now, as if it was yesterday. I also know that pulling out those boxes would be very painful for my dad so I won't do it. At least not now.

I think about the first time I brought James to Cape May. By then, my grandparents' house was long sold but we stayed a weekend at the beautiful and infamous yellow hotel, Congress Hall, for one of our wedding anniversaries. I took him around and showed him all the things I loved about this little beach town, my grandparents' house, the lighthouse, the old railroad, and Sunset Beach.

James was polite. He smiled in all the right places, and I would say he enjoyed our weekend together. But he didn't get it. He didn't see the reason to go back to Cape May repeatedly, year after year, summer after summer. So, we didn't. Looking back, I realize how much of our adult love and attachment for places is reflective of our childhood memories. James couldn't love Cape May like I do because he didn't grow up there and he didn't have the same memories. My only hope was that we could grow our family, and I could make new memories with him and our children there. Now *that's* out the window.

I have been so lost in my thoughts, I didn't realize the four-hour drive was coming to an end. For the first time in the three and a half hours I had been in the car, I tap the CarPlay button on my car's touchscreen. I see multiple text messages but I tap James' first.

> **James: I am looking forward to talking. Let me know a good time to stop by.**

Here goes nothing.

Chapter Twelve

Liam

Now that Lucy is down for a midmorning nap, I allow myself to think about my tense conversation with Sophie on Friday. I really do need to make things right with her, if only to keep the neighborhood peace. I'm sure she wants to know how Lucy is, too. She only told Ellie two weeks, but it sure doesn't look like she is going anywhere any time soon. I probably need to reach out to her. I pick up my phone and send her a quick text. It's the first time I've texted her casually and it feels strange.

> **Me: Sophie, it's Liam. Are you around today so we can talk?**

I realize after I send it that she'll know it's me and I am an idiot, but too late now. Then I text Ellie to see what time she'll be home. She texts back right away.

> **Ellie: I'll be home within the hour and you have some explaining to do, sir!**

I can almost hear her voice admonishing me with that text message. I groan. I might as well own up to it. Ellie is the closest thing I have to a parental figure. She has helped me in more ways than I can count. I can't imagine how disappointed she'll be when she hears how I treated Sophie. Nonetheless, she has seen me do much worse, so I know once we talk, she won't be mad at me anymore.

I let Maggie outside and peer over the fence line at the cottage. There are no lights on, there is no movement, and Sophie's little white Mazda SUV is gone. I glance down at my phone. She still hasn't texted me back. I am going to have to find a way to distract myself until she does.

I leave Maggie in the yard and go back inside to get my sketchbook. Before I build anything custom, I usually draw it. I have been thinking about redoing the nursery for Lucy. Her crib is probably as old as I am. So first on the agenda is a new crib for Lucy. I want it to be fit for a princess because that's what she is. Drawing out my designs and building them in my workshop gives me a sense of peace and purpose. It helps me feel like I am contributing to the world and not just taking up space. I don't get very far though because my phone starts buzzing again. It's the Perry Street Boys group text.

Danny: Yoooo Liam, we met your girl Sophie last night. We hung out with her and her friend. She's a cutie.

Jack: Not very fond of you though. ROFL

Miles: She doesn't need to be fond of Liam, she's fond of me. You don't mind, do you, buddy?

Danny: Maybe he's drowning in baby puke.

Jack: Maybe he's drowning in Melanie.

Miles: That would work out great for me.

Me: What are you assholes talking about?

Danny: He lives!

I feel the hair on the back of my neck stand up imagining my friends chatting up Sophie without me there. Even more so because of the way we left things on Friday. *What did they talk about? Did she tell them she knows me? She must have.* I decide I can't show them I care.

Me: Where did you meet Sophie?

Jack: Oh so he does care!!!!

Danny: Rusty Nail last night. She was with her red-haired friend. Totally wasted. Miles was trying to tap that until her friend flagged her and took her home.

Miles: Yo I am a nice guy. I wasn't gonna take her home.

Me: Stay away from her, Miles. She's got baggage.

Jack: Sounds like someone is jealous to me!!

Me: Not jealous. I just know Miles.

I throw my phone back on the table and try to focus on my sketch, but I can't get Sophie flirting with Miles out of my head. If they hook up, I will lose my mind. It dawns on me like a freight train. I like her, but I also feel protective of her. Just thinking about her with Miles makes my blood pressure rise. I glance back at my phone—still nothing from Sophie. *Nothing ever goes the way I want it to.*

I stop sketching and put my head in my hands. I feel myself regressing again and I know I'm on a dangerous path. Even when Leah was still alive, I was still coasting along. Part of me wondered why she didn't ask my parents to take Lucy while she was gone. But if I knew Leah, she wanted to give me the opportunity to rise to the occasion. Until now, I hadn't surpassed anyone's expectations for me, but caring for Lucy the past six months has kind of made me want to.

I don't know if I'll ever be ready to forgive myself or fall in love, but I could try. I do think Cara would want that for me, and I know Leah would love for Lucy to have a mother. But more than that, I could be applying myself more to the important things in life. I am going to fix up this old house. I am going to work on getting more jobs doing what I love, and in time, just maybe I can fall in love.

✦

I wait until the afternoon before I sheepishly drag myself over to Ellie's and knock on her front door. I am holding a very happy Lucy as a peace offering. Lucy has improved so much in just twenty-four hours. She hasn't had a fever all day and the rash that covered her tiny body is starting to fade. To say I am relieved is an understatement. I should have known better and seen the signs to take her to the doctor much sooner. I do feel more confident after talking to Dr. Philips though. He eased my concerns by letting me know that the first time a baby gets sick is hard for everyone. I know I'll do better going forward.

Ellie swings open her front door, giving me an exaggerated scowl and then the biggest smile to Lucy. Lucy smiles back and reaches her arms out to Ellie who gladly takes her from me.

"Hi, Lulu!" Ellie coos. "Ohhh, my poor baby!" She cradles Lucy's head to her shoulder and bounces. Then smacks my shoulder. "Why didn't you call or text me? I would've taken one look at her and known you needed to take her to the doctor."

I shrug. "I'm a stubborn ass, I guess." I don't have another excuse. I know I rely on Ellie for so much. I didn't want to bother her on her book club retreat. She's probably sick of bailing me out all the time.

"I left you for two days and you have made multiple women angry at you, so I don't know about the stubborn part, but I am pretty sure you are an ass." She turns to bring Lucy inside and I follow. She puts Lucy in her highchair and moves to fill the teapot. I plop down in one of her cushioned kitchen chairs and sigh.

"So, where should I start?" I ask her expectantly.

"Hold on, hold on," she waves her hand. "I need to make my tea if you're going to spill the tea." She laughs at her own joke, and I instantly know she isn't really mad at me. She reaches into the cabinet and grabs some crackers for Lucy and two mugs for us. She sets them down before going back to the fridge for the cream and sugar. Finally, she's sitting in front of me with her legs crossed and hands folded in her lap, looking at me eagerly. "Let's talk about Melanie first."

I roll my eyes. "Well, okay, Ms. Neighborhood Watch. What have you heard? I guess you heard that I'm a dick." I lean back in my chair and rest my hands behind my head.

Ellie sighs. "You're not a *dick*, Liam." Her face contorts like she swallowed vinegar, as if saying the word *dick* is repulsive. She recovers quickly. "In fact, I have wanted you to set this girl free for a while now. I am proud of you for that." The tea kettle whistles, interrupting her. She gets up to retrieve it and two Earl Grey tea bags for us. Before she says anything else, she quietly makes our tea. I have a feeling she is dragging out whatever it is she wants to say next. I raise my eyebrows at her waiting for her to speak. "To answer your question, I saw Danny and Kristen at the grocery store this morning. Kristen was all fired up."

I groan. "It's none of their business, Ellie." This town may be packed in the summertime, but during the off-season, it feels mighty small.

Ellie rolls her eyes. "Whatever. She seems to think it's their business. She said Melanie is heartbroken that you don't want a relationship with her," Ellie retorts. Sometimes I can't tell whose side she is on. "If you ask me, she has no self-confidence to have put up with you for as long as she did." *It sounds like mine.*

I laugh. "Thanks a lot. Look, Ellie, I am a good guy. I was always upfront with Melanie about what I wanted out of our friendship, and it was never going to be me falling in love with her. What am I supposed to do if she is hopeful? She is responsible for her own feelings. She could have stopped seeing me instead of trying to change me." I cross my arms, indignantly.

Ellie nods her head with a lazy smirk playing on her lips. I know she knows more than she is letting on. "Okay, so, you just let her down gently? Just called her up and told her how you felt?"

A hot wave of embarrassment washes over me from being under the Ellie microscope. "Well, not exactly." I swallow. "I took her out while Sophie babysat and broke it to her over tacos. I was gentle though! But then Sophie texted to say Lucy was sick and I cut the conversation short."

Ellie nods, putting her teacup down and folding her arms across her chest, taking me in. She must see a haggard mess of a man. My beard is long and scraggly. I know I look exhausted, and I didn't bother to put anything nicer than gym clothes on today.

I'm having trouble remembering if I brushed my teeth or when I last showered. I look back at her warm, motherly countenance and instead of disappointment, all I see is pity. Ellie feels sorry for me. I hate it, but I appreciate that she won't stay mad at me for too long. Ellie and Eddie could never have children of their own, and I know she thinks of me as the son she never had. She may be the neighborhood mama, but I am her favorite. "And Sophie? What happened with her?"

I look down and once again feel my cheeks heating up with embarrassment. "Well...I sort of told her I didn't need her help. And to just let me handle it."

Ellie gasps. "Liam! After she helped you on her own time!" She makes a tsk-tsk sound that makes me feel worse.

I might as well be entirely truthful. "She was just pushing so much for me to accept her help. And Melanie was pushing me all night. I got home and the baby was screaming and I just couldn't take anymore *pushing*." I grimace thinking about the hurtful words I threw at her. "I told her to just go."

"Oh, Liam. And now she's *gone*," Ellie moans. "Who knows if she'll be back now."

I feel the color drain from my face. "What do you mean, who knows if she'll be back? She left because of me?"

Ellie shrugs, and I can't tell if she's playing coy with me to punish me or if she knows something I don't. Either way, I hate it.

Chapter Thirteen

Sophie

I call James as soon as I drive through the Lehigh Tunnel. He answers right away. As it turns out, the house isn't officially listed because we both need to sign the paperwork. He has it there and asks if I'd come by instead of him meeting me at my dad's house. Truthfully, he probably can't face my dad and my brother, and I can't blame him for that. I must be getting soft because I agree.

It's a quiet Sunday afternoon on a warm spring day and my old neighborhood is abuzz. I wave at a neighbor who is walking her yellow labrador retriever around the main road loop of the neighborhood. Kids are playing basketball and tag and riding their bikes. A rush of sadness that I won't be living here anymore hits me like a punch in the gut. I had such big dreams when we moved here. It was one of the first houses we looked at. I had just started working at the center, James had gotten tenure with the university, and the future was bright. We saw this beautiful white colonial with a two-car garage and black shutters and both fell in love with the *what if*. Nine years ago when we closed on the house, we made love on the kitchen island. I never would have imagined this would be our fate.

I park in the driveway, next to James' white Tesla. I am grateful that there doesn't appear to be anyone else here, but I need to sit in the car and collect myself for a minute before I go inside. I note the For Sale sign with a magnetic banner that reads *Coming Soon!* A queasy sensation twists in my gut and I practice taking in a few slow, deep breaths. Then I march up our beautiful brick paver pathway to the front porch that we used last year's tax return to pay for.

James meets me at the front door. "Hi," he says, his voice hoarse. "Do you want to come in?" I glance down at his feet and see a single box of some of my personal items and I realize, he probably doesn't want me to come inside. The inside is probably crawling with evidence of another woman living there.

I shake my head. "No, that's okay. We can talk out here."

James lets out a sigh that I realize is probably the result of relief. He picks up the box and steps out onto the front porch. I sit down on the top step, and he puts the box down next to me, following suit. I realize now this is the first opportunity we've had to have an honest conversation since the day I left. I filed for divorce pretty much immediately, and James didn't contest it. There are so many questions I haven't gotten answers to but suddenly, I'm not sure if I even want them anymore.

"James, I—" I begin to speak but he cuts me off.

"Please. Can I go first?" he asks earnestly.

I shrug. "Sure."

"Sophie, I feel horrible. I never meant for this to happen. I feel like the past few months I have been so depressed. I was going through the motions of life. Everything felt black and white and lifeless."

I want to laugh at him because his description feels like a farce, but I do my best to keep eye contact.

"I think things between us had become so strained. We were both so tired of the fertility treatments, the miscarriages, the hormones. I know you were so sick of it and ready to give up many times, but you hung on for me. You know how much I wanted to be a dad. I know you wanted to be a mom, too, but it has taken such a toll on us. Don't you agree?"

"Of *course* I agree, James." Our problems seem so obvious to me now. We never actually *talked* about anything. "I wanted to explore other avenues. I wanted to foster or adopt. That never seemed like something you wanted to do. And look, now you're going to be a dad, and I am *still* not going to be a mom." I am exasperated, like he is placing the blame for his affair on me. "I would never have had an affair," I mutter under my breath.

"I know, Sophie. I really do know that. We hadn't had spontaneous sex in so long. It was like through all the years of disappointment, something died between us. And then when we had the miscarriage in January, I felt like something died in you, too. You weren't the Sophie I fell in love with anymore. You were sad all the time. I know that doesn't make it right. I'm sorry if I am making excuses." He pauses and sighs. "I just want you to know, I tried to stop seeing her. But I would get home from work and find you in a funk again, and I'd lose my nerve to break things off with her. I tried so hard every day to make you happy. I know you don't think I was trying but I was. And then eventually, I got tired of trying. I didn't know what to do anymore. If you had said you wanted to do another cycle, I would have. But once you decided to give up, I couldn't pull you out of the black hole you were living in. Being with someone else relieved me of that. I never meant for it to go this far. I just needed a break." He puts his head in his hands. "It was always supposed to be me and you."

I look sideways at him, and he slowly turns to meet my gaze. I exhale deeply. "It was. But now it's not. What's done is done."

Therapist Sophie understands where James is coming from. One of the things that no one talks about is the effect that infertility has on a marriage. Our marriage had a hole in it, and it would have taken both of us to save it. But I couldn't see my way out. I needed him to throw me a life preserver and instead, he drove the boat away.

We're silent for a few moments before James says, "Are you really going to move to Cape May?"

"I'm going to move to Cape May, yes," I tell him. "It's the only place I have felt peace for the last seven weeks." Not wanting to prolong this conversation anymore I say, "Do I have to sign something?"

James pulls some paperwork from a realty office out of the box between us. He's already signed all the highlighted areas required of him, but there are several places for me to sign and initial. He hands me a pen. We're silent while I flip through the documents other than him pointing to a few places I missed. When I finish, I stand up and move to take the box, but he beats me to it. We both peer inside. Right on top, there is a small selection of loose wedding photos. Beneath that is a purple embossed keepsake box that if he dug into, he'd find my infertility keepsakes, which are mostly ultrasound pictures and used pregnancy tests—gross, I know.

He reaches in and picks up a wedding photo of us holding hands as we're walking away but looking back at the camera. Our happiness is palpable. We study the picture together for a moment and then catch each other's gaze. We're both tearful as we stare into each other's eyes. James speaks first. "I guess this is it. I never meant to hurt you, Soph." He wipes a stray tear away from his rosy cheek with his thumb. For the first time, I can see that this has been hard on him too. We've been through the wringer together. I hoped we'd come out together, too, but somehow, we got separated along the way.

"I guess so," I sniffle and shrug. I am sure my tears are a combination of anger and sadness but for some reason, I can't let him see me ugly cry. He's held me many times through many dark days, but this is different. He was on my side then. Now he has someone else's side to be on. He's never been the cause of the big fat raindrop-size tears threatening to fall. "The end of an era." I try a small smile. Rubbing my arms to self-soothe, I walk over to the passenger door. I open it and James sets the box on the seat. I walk around to the driver's side and he follows, watching as I climb in and buckle my seatbelt.

"I will call or email you and let you know what the realtor says." He ducks his head in the car and kisses my forehead.

All I can do is nod my head before my eyes again fill with tears. I pull the door shut and start the engine. James gives the roof of the car a farewell tap, and I back out of the driveway.

It's only when I'm on my way to my dad's house that I let the tears fall.

Chapter Fourteen

Liam

Ellie wants to keep Lucy for the rest of the day. I assume it's because I look as bad as I feel. As soon as I get back, I head right upstairs and fall into bed. I decide a nap is exactly what I need but my sleep is restless.

And then I'm dreaming again. *"Liam, come on. We've got to go," Cara is telling me. She's stomping her foot outside my car again. "I don't understand you. You said you wanted to go to the game." She indignantly puts her hands on her hips and purses her lips. She's pouting. Next, she'll try to persuade me with a flirtatious curl of her lips and a come-hither motion with her index finger. I shake my head vigorously, fighting the internal conflict. Do I follow Cara? My heart races at the thought of letting her down but I'm determined to stop her from getting in that car.*

"I don't want to go anymore," I tell her again. "It's going to rain anyway. Let's stay here and watch a movie," I try.

"No, Liam. Melanie is waiting for us. We have to pick her up." Cara crosses her arms and then her eyes light up. "I'll make it worth your while," she coos, waving me over. Dream Liam always caves to this. If only Cara could see what our life would be like if we skipped this football game.

❧

We're at our college graduation at Duke University. I am waiting to hear my name. *Cara Cote has been called already and is sitting back in her seat, diploma in hand. "Liam Harper," the president of the university calls me up to receive my diploma. My hand is sweaty as I try to conceal the handmade sign I have rolled up in my left hand, camouflaged by the sleeve of my gown. As soon as I shake the president's hand, I drop down to one knee and hold up my sign. "Cara Cote, will you marry me?" And the crowd goes wild. Cara hops out of her seat and runs to me to say yes. When we kiss, the audience hoots and hollers, applauding enthusiastically. We're on top of the world.*

Then it's our wedding day. "I now pronounce you husband and wife! Liam, you may kiss your bride," the preacher yells.

I dip Cara backward and kiss her passionately as all our friends and family clap. Everyone's face is a blur as we walk up the aisle holding hands, our love and excitement evident. The world is at our feet.

We're in a dimly lit hospital room. "Come on, Cara! One more push. You got this." And then a baby cries. The baby is placed on Cara's chest, and we look at each other lovingly. I kiss her softly and then kiss the baby's head. I've never been so in love.

We are leaving the hospital in my navy blue mustang with the green rims. There is no room for the baby's car seat because Melanie is there too, so we put the car seat on top of the bass. And then we're back in Lower Township heading for that four-way stop. We're blasting Blink-182 again and singing at the top of our lungs. A baby is crying in the distance as I awaken with the sound of the crash.

I jerk awake, disoriented. I run my fingers through my hair and down my face. My eyes are wet. I must've been crying this time. It's been a long time since my dreams have gotten this bad or have felt so real. It's the first time I've ever clearly seen what might've been. I am gutted by the visions of what our life could have looked like if I hadn't been so overconfident behind the wheel that night.

I prop myself up in bed and lean my head against the headboard. I'm not sure what to do about the recent and unwelcome return of these dreams-turned-nightmares. I thought I had a good handle on things. I am finding my groove with Lucy, hitting the gym, working regularly. The only thing that has really changed is the stress of the last few days—and my drinking habits are starting back up again. Not enough to really cause a problem, but enough that I should probably cool it a little with the after-bedtime beers.

I throw the blanket off me and walk into my master bathroom. It is one of the only rooms I have remodeled in this house and something of an oasis. Black-and-white penny tiles cover the floor, leading into a six-foot-long, black-framed glass shower with a rain head and six wall sprayers. The walls are white subway tile with white grout, and the shower floor is pebbled tile. My vanity is natural wood with black fixtures, a marble top, and a black faucet. I am truly proud of it because I did all of this after my day job, before Leah left. My plan was to do Leah's bathroom next. I look in the black-framed mirror at my ashen expression. I turn the cold water on and splash it on my face. Then I trim my beard back to a regular five o'clock shadow and brush my teeth.

I pick up my phone to check my messages, but there are none—not even the group thread with my guy friends talking smack to each other. I click on Sophie's name. Nothing back from her, either. I must've really made her angry on Friday. I contemplate sending her another one, but ultimately decide against it. I don't know much about Sophie. Maybe she needs more time to cool off after an argument. Maybe she holds grudges. I have too much going on in my life to grovel.

I text Ellie to make sure she doesn't mind if I head to the gym for an hour before grabbing Lucy, and she's fine with it. When I get back, I'll call Doc. Maybe it's time I get back to seeing him regularly. I decide to run there to help me blow off some steam. Gradually, as I run, the post-dream sadness begins to ease.

∞

"Hello! You're looking better!" Ellie says as she swings open the front door to greet me. The smell of dinner is wafting down the hall and straight to my nostrils. I don't realize how hungry I am until my stomach audibly growls. "I hope you're staying for pot roast. Otherwise, I will be eating it for the next seven days." I hear Lucy's adorable sounds coming from the other room and I smile. This is as close to a Sunday family dinner as I'll get. Ellie makes me feel cared for. And I know she cares about Lucy. I can't imagine where I'd be without her in my life. A hell of a lot worse off, I bet.

I walk into the kitchen and pick up my little girl, snuggling her close. "Hi, Lucy girl. Thanks for letting me take a break," I say to Ellie sincerely. "I didn't realize how much I needed it until I woke up from a horrible nightmare about Cara."

Ellie makes a clicking sound with her tongue as she reaches in the cabinet for some dinner plates. "You'd better call Dr. Stevens, Liam. These dreams coming back are not a good sign for you. You know how they have haunted you in the past." She walks over to me, puts the plate in front of me, and then touches my shoulder. "You make me worry." Her expression is grim. "I know what an adjustment the past six months have been. I haven't exactly given you a lot of grace. But I am here for you, and I love you like a son. You know that, right?" Her clear green eyes meet mine, like she can see right through to my damaged soul.

"Yeah, yeah. I do. I love you and appreciate you too, Ellie. I don't know where I'd be without you." I clear my throat and wrap her in a sideways squeeze. This display of emotion is not comfortable for me, and Ellie knows it, but I guess she felt she needed to let me know.

She shifts her tone to lighten the mood. "Which is why," she pauses and looks at me with an I-told-you-so expression, "I can tell you that you need to apologize to Sophie." She walks over to the oven and pulls out the pot roast. Its aroma is heavenly, and my stomach growls again which makes me realize I really haven't eaten much today.

I groan. "I mean, do I really have to talk to her? How much longer is she even going to be here? She's already gone," I huff, putting Lucy back in her highchair. I pull out my chair and sit down as Ellie places the pot roast in front of us. I pick up the toddler plate that Ellie took out for Lucy and start cutting up some pieces of beef, carrots, and potatoes for the little one to try. She is delighted when I place it in front of her.

"She'll be back," Ellie says, serving herself. "And when she comes back, you will apologize for treating her poorly. Sophie has been through a lot too. Things you wouldn't possibly understand." She takes a bite of her pot roast, and I know Ellie means business.

"Yes, ma'am," I agree with a groan. We spend the rest of the meal eating in the comfort of familial silence and I count my blessings with each bite.

Chapter Fifteen

Sophie

Sunday dinner at my dad and Carol's house is a regular thing most weekends. Usually, James and I would go, along with Simon and Laura and their five-year-old twins, Sammy and Sarah. Sometimes Carol's sons Josh and Drew would come with their wives too, but rarely is it all of us at once. I am grateful tonight when it's just my dad, Carol, Simon, and Laura. I am in a very delicate headspace, and I can't take discussing the nitty gritty with everyone. In my mind, this is my last Sunday dinner for a while. I already cannot wait to get back to Cape May.

I pull up to the curb of my dad's white rancher and walk up the front steps. My dad must have seen me pull up because he meets me at the door. He doesn't even have to speak. He just opens his arms, and I fall into them. He rubs my back as I squeeze him tight.

"That bastard," he mutters in my ear, and I can't help but smirk. My dad is a man of few words. Although I have been staying here since I left James, he still hasn't figured out what to say to me to help me feel better.

As we walk through the foyer, he squeezes my hand and says quietly, "I told everyone you didn't want to talk about it. They won't bring it up unless you do it first." I smile at him sadly. While he may not know what to say, he is always thinking of his little girl's feelings. His empathy is immeasurable. I want to cry thinking about how I won't see him every week anymore. I hope he'll come visit me in Cape May, but if he won't, I will make an effort to see him.

"Thank you," I whisper back. It will be a hard conversation, but I think I need to tell my family what is going on and where I will go from here. I am filled with gratitude again when Carol greets me at the kitchen door with a glass of red wine. Simon comes up behind her, takes it from my hands and sets it on the counter, and immediately wraps me in a tight bear hug. His hugs are so good that they are now referred to by most people as "Simon Hugs." Happy or sad, they are a constant, and he has a knack for knowing just when I need one.

"I missed you, sis," he says into my hair. "I'm going to kill that bastard." Like father, like son.

At this remark, Dad smacks Simon on the back of the head. "You weren't supposed to bring it up first!"

"Ow!" Simon laughs. "Sorry, sis." He gives me a lopsided grin.

I smile and shrug. "I do have some things to talk to you all about so at least you broke the ice, Si."

With our wine in hand, we gather around the kitchen island and a magnificent charcuterie board, something that Carol is known for. Periodically, the twins come running in and swipe some olives off the board with their grubby fingers, but for the most part, everyone is making small talk and waiting for me to address the elephant in the room. So, I talk. I fill them in on the day we signed the divorce papers, the 90-day waiting period, and how I took off for Cape May before the ink dried.

"I never liked him," Simon growls. "How could he do this to you, Soph?" His eyes are sad, and he gives my arm a comforting squeeze.

"What will you do now?" Laura asks, who up until now has been quiet. "Well, that's the thing. I'm thinking about staying in Cape May for a while. I could use a fresh start and I really can't see myself staying here at Dad and Carol's for too long." I glance at both of them and force a smile. "No offense, you've both been lovely. I just feel too old to run home crying to my parents."

"You're never too old to come home, sweetheart." My dad pats my hand.

"I know, it's just...Cape May feels right. My landlord is so kind and I feel most at peace by the ocean." I take a sip of my wine and wait for someone to speak.

"You always did love that place," Dad offers, his voice hopeful.

I nod. "Yeah. I feel really close to Mom there." When I say this, Carol gets up to stir something on the stove as if she feels like she is eavesdropping on a private conversation. I continue, "But the real reason is, I know I need to go *somewhere* and the ocean is healing for me. I can't stay here and risk running into him and his new girlfriend and baby." I shrug half-heartedly. "I just need to get away for a while."

"We understand, Sophie. Do what you need to do." Carol comes around to my side and puts an arm around me.

"What about work?" Simon asks, always the responsible one.

"Well, I'm thinking of resigning completely. At first, I was going to ask for more time off, but I haven't had many patients the past six weeks anyway and then I took these two weeks' vacation. If I'm going to resign, now is the time to do it." I hadn't really thought this through until this very moment. On the way up here, I'd decided I'd ask for a leave of absence. But if I see myself in Cape May and that's where things feel peaceful for me, then what is the point of prolonging it? I have only seen three patients virtually over the past seven weeks. I think the center will be okay.

Simon nods as if he understands, and then Carol puts a big bowl of spaghetti and meatballs on the table. Laura calls the twins in to eat, and the conversation seems to shift.

"My plan is to stay here tonight," I whisper to my dad, "and then I'll leave in the morning."

He smiles and puts his arm around my shoulders, pulling me close. "You can stay as long as you want, Soph. There is no rush."

ℭℜ

After dinner I am sitting in Dad and Carol's guest room. Carol brought me a cup of tea, and I am snuggled up in bed with the duvet pulled up to my chin. I've done the hard part, which is talking to James and telling my family my plans. Next in order is to text Ellie and see if I can stay longer.

I know her busy season is coming up, so I want to be courteous. Without income, I'll have to be strategic and cautious with money, too. Then there's the whole needing to resign and not knowing what's next thing. Strangely enough, instead of feeling apprehensive about all of this, I feel exhilarated. For the first time in a long time, I feel free.

I look at my phone. There's a message from Claire wanting to know how I made out telling my family. I shoot her a quick text back letting her know all went well and that I'll call her tomorrow. There's a text from Liam asking if we can talk. I'm sure he wants to fill me in on Lucy, but I am so emotionally exhausted, and last time we spoke he was not very nice. Pass.

I scroll down to Ellie's contact and shoot her a text.

> **Me: Hi, Ellie. How was your book club retreat?**

> **Ellie: Hi, doll! It was great. How are you?**

Me: Well, this is kind of awkward for me to ask you, but do you think it would be okay if I stay at your place a little longer? I want to come back to Cape May and get as far away from here as possible. But I know your busy season is around the corner...

Ellie: Sophie! Of COURSE you can stay with me. On one condition.

Me: What's that?

Ellie: Stay in the main house with me.

Me: Right. So you can rent the cottage out weekly. That makes the most sense.

Ellie: No, silly. Because I love your company.

Me: Ellie, you're the sweetest. But you must charge me the full rate!

Ellie: We'll discuss. :) When are you coming back?

I'm smiling as I tell Ellie I will be back tomorrow morning and tuck my phone away before pulling out my laptop. I have a feeling that Ashley knows what is coming, and I will certainly give her the heads up, but I have to get the resignation letter off my chest. I open an email to my immediate supervisor and start typing. I thank her for the opportunity to work there and help the patients of Scranton Center for Guidance but due to a change in my personal circumstances, I will be relocating.

After it's written, I feel myself physically relax. That was the last step I needed to take to start my next chapter. I pick up my phone and text Ashley to fill her in and thank her for being the best assistant. I close my laptop and turn off my phone for the night. Right now, in my dad's house, in his guest bedroom, is right where I need to be.

I roll over and turn off the bedside lamp. Tomorrow I will embark on a new journey, a new path to finding my one true self. I can see the light at the end of the tunnel. I just hope I make it through.

ᘒ

I'm lost in thought, driving back toward Cape May the next morning when Claire calls me. I told her I would call her, but then I shut my phone off and never did.

"Who will I have wine nights with now?" she bellows when I answer, not bothering with a hello.

I laugh. "We can still have wine nights, just on FaceTime instead."

Claire turns serious. "Are you sure a move four hours away is what you want? You are welcome to stay with me and Derek. We'd love to have you." I can't tell if she is really trying to convince me or if she's saying what she thinks she should say.

"I'm sure. I think I need a clean slate. Being around too much familiarity is just too painful." I bite my lip to stop myself from crying on the highway.

Claire is silent for several seconds before she says, "Okay. Then I am happy for you, Sophie. I think you will find whatever it is you're looking for."

I exhale a breath I hadn't realized I'd been holding. Having my best friend's support means more to me than most people's. I need her to realize why I am doing what I'm doing in case it's a horrible, life-altering mistake. "I hope you're right."

Chapter Sixteen

Liam

Monday morning, I wake up early, haunted by another dream about Cara and the accident. My dreams have been progressively worsening and I have tried to avoid the inevitable, but I can't anymore. Before Lucy wakes up, I pour myself a cup of coffee and sit out on my back deck while Maggie does her business.

I haven't been taking care of myself. That much is apparent. Now that I have Lucy, I need to so I can be a solid presence for her. I want to do it differently than my own parents did. They weren't the most affectionate parents around, but they weren't bad parents either. I was the kid who would get in trouble and think, "Oh man, my parents are going to kill me." I could never talk openly with them. It was the '90s; everyone I knew had a similar relationship with their parents. Adults would tiptoe around uncomfortable topics, and we learned about the world through experience, often by doing things that were dangerous or just plain stupid.

Nevertheless, I feared their disappointment until my fear became apathy. I think it was the fifth time I showed up to school drunk that my dad reached his breaking point, and they realized they were in over their heads with me. They called Dr. Stevens, and even though I didn't say much to him for months at a time, I *did* hear him.

Doc became the only adult I could say things to who wouldn't run in the other direction, no matter how dark it was. He recognized the pain I was in, but he didn't crucify me for the things I did to numb it. He never patronized me, he empowered me. As years went on, I continued my therapy with him, and I learned to recognize the signs that I was falling back into my old ways. I learned my triggers. In a way, he saved my life. That's why calling him this morning and asking for his help again is a no-brainer.

"Liam! What can I do for you?" he says, answering the phone jovially. I was awarded his personal number the day it became apparent that I would need to be a lifetime patient.

"Hey, Doc," I say, hesitating before I remember that I can tell this guy pretty much anything and he won't turn away from me. "I think I need to come in and see you. The nightmares are back."

Doc is quiet for a moment and then he says, "Okay, Liam. I understand. You've had a lot happen in the past few months. How is tomorrow at nine?"

"Tomorrow at nine is great. Thanks," I say, breathing a sigh of relief. "How 'bout them Phils?"

※

I've spent much of this Monday in my own head. After waking up and handing Lucy over to Ellie, I run to the gym for a workout, reflecting on life the whole way there. Despite having every possible wrench thrown in my path, I still try to improve each day. I am a good person; I know who I am. Making a decent living, following my gut, and focusing on my family, even if they're found family, are the only ways to overcome my demons. I'm doing the best I can.

I'm halfway down our street when I see what I think is Sophie's white SUV pulling into Ellie's driveway. I pick up my pace to a sprint to make sure I catch her. She hasn't even gotten out of her car when I reach the driveway in record time. I put my hands on my knees to catch my breath, and I'm huffing and puffing when she gets out of the car. I look up in time to see her giving me a sidelong glance. "You ok?" she asks, giving me the side-eye.

I take a gasping breath and stand up, wiping the sweat from my brow. "I'm good. Just doing some sprints." I put my hands on my hips and pace back and forth, playing it cool while she opens her trunk.

Neither of us speaks for a few moments. Me, because I'm still trying to get my lungs to physically pump oxygen, and Sophie because she appears to be making herself busy rummaging around in her trunk for god knows what.

"That's a lot of boxes," I muse, attempting to break the ice. *Smooth. Real smooth.*

Sophie raises her eyebrows and nods at me as if to say *duh*. She probably doesn't know how to be rude though so she just says, "Yeah, I have them stuffed in every square inch of this car. I hope Ellie doesn't mind all of my crap."

I can't hide my surprise and Sophie notices because she has a small smirk playing on her lips. She seems like she's holding back, and I wonder if she is remembering Friday night. "Oh... Are you moving?" Now I'm fishing for information.

"Yeah. I am," she says and moves to grab one of the boxes from her trunk.

I attempt to take it from her, but she turns away too quickly. "I can help you," I say.

"That's okay," she says with a bite. "I loaded it all in by myself. I've got it." She starts toward Ellie's front step, but I catch her elbow.

"Sophie," my voice comes out hoarse. *Why is this so hard for me?* I clear my throat and try again. "Did you get my text? I wanted to see if we could find some time to talk."

Sophie opens and closes her mouth for a beat before she says, "I did. It's okay, Liam. We don't need to talk." She looks away but doesn't move.

I realize she isn't going to give me the opportunity to explain myself unless I do it right now. I swallow, working up the nerve. "Sophie, I'm sorry. I had a weird night on Friday, and I realize you don't even know me or care about me so maybe you don't want to hear it. But I took my shit out on you and I'm sorry. I shouldn't have said what I said." I'm still holding her elbow, and I'm trying not to focus on the fact that my fingertips are vibrating at the closeness of our skin.

Sophie sighs and puts the box down at her feet, breaking the contact. "It's okay, Liam. We all have our own problems. Consider it forgotten." She gives me a half-smile, but it's not warm.

I exhale. "Okay. I know. I was rude... It won't happen again." I bend down to pick up the box she set down. "So...inside?"

Now I see it, the slight upward pull of her lips that tells me she wants to relax with me, but she's still got her guard up. I can work with that.

Chapter Seventeen

Sophie

Liam is holding my heaviest box that's full of every shoe I own and looking at me expectantly. I bite my lip to keep from fully letting him read me. I know he probably is curious about why we're going inside and not back out to the guest house. I'm already distracted by the sizzle I felt when he touched my elbow, and I'm annoyed at myself for wishing he'd do it again, especially because the last time we spoke was so contentious. "Uh...yeah, inside. I'm going to be staying there for the next few weeks until I figure things out."

Could this be any more awkward?

Liam nods but doesn't ask me any more questions. "Inside. Got it." He brushes past me with the box, and I follow him without grabbing another one. "Ellie!" He bellows as I follow him in. "Sophie's back!"

Ellie rounds the corner from the kitchen and smiles so genuinely I think of a mother seeing her long-lost child. "Sophie! I'm so glad to have you back." She embraces me and I'm covered in maternal warmth. "And staying in the house with me! We're going to have so much fun together! Like *The Golden Girls!*"

Wait until you see all the crap I brought, I think to myself but instead I say, "I, uh, sort of have a lot of boxes. I didn't realize how much stuff I had in that house. Thirteen years of my life. I hope that's okay?" I search her face for annoyance but find none. Ellie is as accommodating as ever.

"Not to worry, dear! I gave you the largest guest room.

Everything will be just fine." She wraps an arm around my shoulder and guides us toward the stairs. "Liam, Lucy is napping in the living room. Be a good boy and bring in Sophie's boxes," she calls over her shoulder and winks mischievously at me.

"On it," he says, already jogging out the front door.

CR

The room Ellie has chosen for me is the first bedroom at the top of the stairs, and it may just be one of the most beautiful rooms I have ever stayed in. The hardwood floors are polished oak and it smells faintly of lemon which makes me think that Ellie has cleaned for me. A plush gray area rug covers most of the floor. The bed is a beautiful four-poster canopy with a plush white duvet and lilac-colored accent pillows that match the walls. A welcoming window seat in the rounded alcove of the turret tower of the Victorian-era home faces the front of the house. It's just like my grandparents' bedroom. The window seat looks cozy with a plush cushion, a soft throw, and various purple pillows.

Built-in bookshelves line one side of the cozy alcove, and I quickly scan the shelves to see Ellie likes her romance novels. I imagine myself sitting here reading with a warm cup of tea. I walk around the room and take note of the lovely Victorian wardrobe painted white, and a four-doored closet that should hold most of my clothes. An ensuite bathroom with a beautiful clawfoot tub and a corner stand-up shower completes my new oasis. The room itself is a bit dated but has exquisite Victorian charm. I know I will be very comfortable here.

As much as I want to, I can't leave Liam outside to carry in my boxes himself. Once Ellie shows me the room, I jog quickly down the steps. He has already piled most of the boxes on the porch and is just starting to bring them in. I can't help but notice my keepsake box is open and right on top. I blush at the thought of Liam seeing my wedding photos. If he picked up the box, he wouldn't be able to miss them.

Liam brushes past me. "The purple room?" He asks.

I can't seem to find my voice. "Yep," I manage to squeak. I pick up my keepsake box and follow him up the stairs.

Liam is carrying two boxes at once and even though I shouldn't notice, I am distracted by his back and shoulder muscles bulging in his tight sleeveless gym tee. My attention is then drawn to his waist and his ass. He has great looking calves too. *Woo, am I sweating? It's got to be that it's warm for the first week of May at the shore.*

James always took good care of himself, and he wasn't a big guy by any means, but he also wasn't this fit. I allow myself a moment to admire the sharp edges of Liam's back and his sinewy forearms as he hoists box after box up the steps. I may be broken-hearted, but you can't blame a girl for noticing an attractive man walking up the stairs ahead of her. Plus, the apology he gave me when I got here seemed difficult for him and I find myself softening toward him a bit for trying.

"All of Ellie's rooms have a color theme." Liam smiles genuinely at me when I follow him into my new room. I might feel a tiny flutter in my chest. Maybe.

"Oh...really? That's nice. And vaguely OCD." I laugh and he does too. *Yep. Definitely a flutter.* I clear my throat and will myself to calm down. *A rebound is fine, Sophie, but it should not be this guy.* Not *Liam!* Alarm bells are ringing in my head loud and clear.

"I used to stay in the green room when my parents had enough of me," he offers, awkwardly laughing. I get the sense there is a lot more to that story, but I decide now is not the time to inquire. He must sense my reluctance because he says, "Let me grab the rest of those boxes for you," and jogs out of the room before I can say another word. *Do not watch him go, Sophie,* I scold myself.

And then I watch him go.

CR

Liam is able to bring up all of my boxes pretty quickly. They're heavy, and it would have taken me way longer. I decide I will spend the rest of the afternoon and evening putting everything in its place so I can get settled quickly, but first, I need a snack. I find Ellie in the kitchen cooking up a storm. It smells heavenly and I realize I am famished when my stomach audibly growls.

"Oh my gosh, what are you making?" I peer over her shoulder as she is seasoning a pot of soup.

"Clam chowder," she says, offering me a taste from the spoon.

I lick the spoon, and my eyes roll back in my head. "It's divine," I moan. "Is this a late lunch by any chance?" I ask, feeling hopeful.

She turns me around and walks toward the table with her arm around me. "This, my darling, is part of our dinner. But I do have a cheese plate in the fridge for you if you're hungry." She ushers me to a chair and then opens the fridge. She hands me a plate of assorted meats and cheeses and a water bottle.

"I'm eternally grateful." I sigh, taking my first bite of prosciutto and gouda. "Moving is hard work."

"I know it is, sweetie. I am cooking us a feast tonight!" She claps her hands together and then points the wooden spoon at me. "But don't get used to it." And then she giggles as she walks back to the fridge to retrieve some vegetables.

"I like to cook too, so I can certainly cook for us some nights. Also, please don't feel like you have to feed me, Ellie. I don't want you to think of me as a guest...more like a roommate." I hesitate as I say this because I don't want to offend Ellie. She's so maternal that I feel like she will get her feelings hurt if I don't allow her to nurture me and my broken heart, but my intention is not to impose on her.

"Nonsense! A guest is what you are!" She waves her hand at me.

"That's another thing, we need to discuss payment. I can just send you a Venmo or write you a check each week or month, whatever you prefer." I feel awkward bringing this conversation up, but I have to.

This time, Ellie puts the spoon down and turns around to face me, wiping her hands on her apron. "Now, Sophie. You're going through a very difficult time. I don't want you to pay me the price of summer rent. You'll pay the off-season rate." Ellie has clearly put some thought into this, and I am treading lightly so as not to hurt her feelings.

"Ellie, you aren't used to having an extra person here, using up your electricity and water. Those things cost money. I have to pay you the full rent. I have savings and I can afford it." I cross my arms and try to look defiant.

Ellie puts her hands on her hips. "But you just picked up and moved away from your home. You're getting divorced. I presume you left your job. I cannot take money from you when it might be tight for you right now." She sighs and has her arms folded over her chest. We're at an impasse, but I think I can win.

I chuckle at this back-and-forth we're having. It's so much like a conversation I imagine I might've had with my own mom. Ellie is the kindest woman I have ever met. I can't take advantage of her, especially when it seems like Liam takes enough advantage for the both of us. I roll my eyes at that thought and Ellie gives me a curious look. "Look, you let me worry about that. I have money to live, Ellie. Just tell me an amount I should pay you, please."

Ellie huffs like a child and drops her arms. "Fine. The winter rate is five hundred dollars a month, she says with a reluctant sigh. "And that's my final offer."

I laugh until she laughs with me. Before we know it we're both cackling with tears in our eyes and I think, just maybe, this might be an arrangement I can live with. "Fine. Five hundred. Let me get my purse and I'll write you a check," I say, walking out of the room. Yes. I can live with this.

"Liam and Lucy are joining us for dinner," she calls after me.

I stop in my tracks. *That part...is the part I might not be able to live with.*

❧

I spend the next two hours up in my room with my boxes, and I make a pretty good dent in organizing. I am able to use the shelving over the toilet in the bathroom for my toiletries and makeup, and I hang up most of my dressier clothing items in the closet. I am excited to wear real clothes again since I've spent a good amount of time the past few weeks wallowing in my pajamas. I am organizing my underwear drawer when I hear the front door open.

"Ellie, we're here!" Liam hollers. Then I hear Lucy giggle.

I just want to finish what I'm doing but a few minutes later, I hear footsteps coming up the wooden staircase. Then Liam is in my doorway, and he takes up all the space.

He stands there for a moment, wordlessly watching me pull clothes out of my suitcase, and I can't stop sneaking glances at him, too. He changed out of his gym clothes and is wearing relaxed-fit jeans and a snug black T-shirt that hugs all of his muscles. *God. The muscles.* The scent of too much cologne permeates the air but he smells *really* good. Like evergreen and eucalyptus. It's so dangerous. He is leaning in the door frame in the same way he did the night I stopped over at his house, and how comfortable he looks there is doing something to me between the thighs. *This guy looks like he belongs here.*

There you go with those dangerous thoughts again, Sophie. I silently reprimand myself. *He is just a man. And from what you've seen, not a very nice one so stop letting him make you tingle.* Liam is looking at me with a mischievous twinkle in his eye, like he is reading my thoughts, and that would be very dangerous. I don't even realize I'm holding a pair of red lace panties in my hand until he clears his throat and smirks like he is absolutely loving every second of it. I force my mouth closed and hide the panties behind my back, shoving them in my pocket.

Liam scratches his beard with a coy smirk playing on his lips. "Ellie says to tell you that dinner is ready," he clears his throat again. Maybe he has a tickle in it. "It looks like you've gotten a lot of organizing done."

"I...yeah, I'm trying," I stutter, wiping my sweating palms on my pants.

"You'll get there." He offers me an encouraging nod.

"I haven't moved in nine years, so this feels like a lot," I admit with a frown.

"I could help you, if you want some company." Liam raises his eyebrows, stepping further into the room.

I open my mouth, then close it again, shaking my head. "Oh, that's okay. I've got it."

"I know it didn't seem like it the other night, but I promise I'm a nice guy." He looks down at his feet and then his eyes drag up the length of my body before meeting mine again.

"I know. I mean, I'm sure you are," I stammer. *Did he just check me out?*

"And, I really am sorry for the way I treated you on Friday." He rasps, taking a step closer to me.

I suck in a breath. This guy makes me too nervous. "I know you are," I murmur, walking back over to the wardrobe. I pull the thong out of my pocket and shove it quickly in the drawer. Biting my lip, I look back at Liam to see if he noticed. "I'll see you down there."

Liam winks and gives me a head nod. "See you down there," he says, biting back a grin.

I'm going to need a pitcher of ice water with my dinner.

Chapter Eighteen

Liam

I caught Sophie red-handed, clutching a pair of red lace underwear, sparking thoughts I definitely shouldn't entertain. *What is it with this woman?* I mean to be fair, I barged in on her and caught her off guard. She didn't want me to notice what she was holding judging by how quickly her hands went behind her back. I can't help it though; I love the fact that her cheeks got pink with embarrassment, and she couldn't formulate sentences.

I'm sitting at the dinner table next to Lucy in the highchair when Sophie comes in. I can't help but notice that she changed clothes. She has her wild wavy hair down around her shoulders again and she's wearing a pair of tight black leggings and a tight T-shirt that shows off her petite shape. I find her insanely attractive, even though I know that is the absolute last thing I should be thinking at this moment. I imagine Ellie would be lecturing me about being a gentleman and not flirting if she knew what was going on in my head.

It's more than that though, I am so curious about her and where she came from. Right now Sophie is nothing more than a neighbor, but maybe eventually she'll be a friend.

"Uh... hi. Sorry. I hope you weren't waiting for me," Sophie says sheepishly as she pulls out her chair next to Ellie and across from me.

Ellie gets up and takes Sophie's empty soup bowl over to the stove. She fills it to the brim with clam chowder and brings over a personal-sized bowl of oyster crackers for her to sprinkle on top. "Nonsense, darling," she says as she puts the bowl in front of Sophie. "There are no rules in this house. You come when you're ready." She squeezes Sophie's hand, and I can't help but notice how happy Ellie seems to be to have people around her table again. This used to be me and Leah, most nights, before she left. Ellie would call one of us and say she cooked way too much food and could we come over and help her eat it. She used to always act like she did it accidentally, but we knew better. Ellie needed company, and we were more than happy to give it to her.

"So, Liam, as you can see, Sophie is officially a Cape May resident. Aren't we just so happy to have her?" Ellie takes a big drink of water and then stands up hurriedly. "We need wine! We've got to toast to Sophie." She rushes over to her liquor cabinet.

"Oh no, that's really not necessary." Sophie looks down at her hands, she looks embarrassed. "I mean, I appreciate it, Ellie, but I'm not here under the happiest of circumstances..." She stops talking and glances at me. I know she doesn't want to elaborate.

Ellie walks back over with a bottle of red wine and three glasses and sets them down. She wipes her hands on her apron and smiles. "Okay then, we'll just toast to new beginnings." She pours the wine and hands us each a glass. Sophie and I meet each other's gazes and hold our glasses up, waiting for Ellie's cue. For some reason, my heart is racing with our eye contact.

"I am just so happy to have friends around my table. And whatever the circumstances that brought you here are, I just know you are in the right place. I feel it in my gut. This is where you are supposed to be right now. I know you don't want a fuss made over you, so I won't do that. To new beginnings." Ellie holds her glass up and we all clink and take a sip. Her smile is contagious. Even Sophie has a small one working the corners of her lips.

"Here, here," I say, taking another drink. I glance at Sophie again, but she won't meet my eye this time. Her focus is on Lucy shoveling banana in her mouth. "Sophie, what do you do for a living?" I ask her, genuinely curious.

Sophie's eyes widen and she looks surprised to be asked a direct question. She clears her throat. "I am a marriage and family therapist." She takes a sip of wine. "I mean, I was. I just resigned actually, to move here."

Ellie pats Sophie's hand. "You are. You will figure things out, dear." She gives her a reassuring smile.

"I guess so. I don't really know what to do now. Luckily, I have a little bit of savings until I figure things out. I've always wanted to start my own therapy practice but if I start over, it's really starting over. I don't know anyone here. I don't know how I'd even find patients." Sophie shrugs. She doesn't seem to be comfortable with the conversation, and I want to reach out and hold her hand. It's a foreign feeling for me and I can't say I hate it.

"Give yourself some grace, sweet pea. The right answer will come," Ellie soothes. She is always the most optimistic. She looks at Sophie as if she can sense her discomfort with the subject matter, patting her hand. "And in the meantime, you do whatever you need to do to feel better."

Sophie's sudden display of vulnerability sparks something in me. "You know... I've picked up daily work with Danny for the foreseeable future. And I think I've taken advantage of Ellie quite enough... Maybe you'd like to be Lucy's babysitter for the time being? I could pay you of course." I blurt this out without even thinking about how this might embarrass her more or make her hate me more but when I meet her gaze, she's smiling.

"I would love that." She grins, and I get the feeling she genuinely means it. When I saw her with Lucy the other day, both of them looked content. Sophie is a natural with Lucy and it tugged at my heartstrings seeing it.

"So, I guess I'm out of a job, then?" Ellie scoffs playfully. "And why haven't you ever paid me?" She kicks me under the table and laughs. I have a feeling she's happy to give up her job to help Sophie, and I am happy to give Sophie something to do.

Where is this coming from?

"Sorry, El. I think Lucy likes Sophie better," I tease.

"That is *not* true!" Sophie giggles—a bona fide giggle. "But I can't start until Wednesday. Tomorrow I have some things to do. And Ellie and I can share the job, if you want?" Sophie looks at Ellie.

"Darling, there is nothing I'd love more." Ellie picks up her soup bowl and slurps the rest of the soup and we all laugh.

℃

Tuesday morning, I wake feeling refreshed. I slept soundly, and so did Lucy. Her rash is completely gone now, and I'm seeing solid glimpses of my happy baby girl again. I still haven't heard from the doctor, but maybe it wasn't too serious after all.

I take my time getting ready. I put Lucy in the highchair, cook us both some scrambled eggs, and toast myself a bagel. I sip my coffee slowly and listen to the birds chirp through my screen door while I watch Maggie sniff around the yard. I know I need to see Doc, but this morning I feel good, and I almost want to cancel it.

That's the problem with battling demons though. I can have a good day, or a few good days, and think they're gone. Then out of nowhere, they knock me on my ass again, leaving me feeling desolate. I have been here many times. The highs are *really* high, but the lows are lower than I ever imagined. I'm thankful to have Doc as a guide through these emotions, and it makes me emotional thinking about everything I have overcome.

By 8:30 a.m., I am ready to drop Lucy over at Ellie's and head over to my appointment. I'm standing in the foyer attempting some small talk with Ellie, casually looking around when she cuts me off. "She's not here, Liam. She left already." She gives me a knowing smirk that embarrasses me.

I'm more than a little disappointed, I was hoping to catch a glimpse, but I can't let Ellie see that. "What are you talking about?" I play dumb.

"Sophie. She left early this morning. She didn't say where she was going, nor should you care." Her lips are pursed as if in disapproval, but the faint twitch at the corner of her mouth betrays her. "I know what you're thinking and it's a bad idea."

I hold up my hands. "Whoa there, Ellie. I'm not thinking anything," I say defensively. "I am just curious, that's all."

Ellie raises an eyebrow, the ghost of a grin softening her otherwise serious expression. "Yeah well, curiosity killed the cat." She takes Lucy from me and walks toward the kitchen. Calling over her shoulder she says, "I'll let Sophie tell you about herself but forgive me when I say, *you* are the last thing that lovely girl needs." Then I hear her chortle to herself because for some reason Ellie thinks she is hilarious.

I shake my head with a smirk, miming a silent "*Oh really?*" at her back. *Challenge accepted.* "Okay... I'll be back in a couple of hours," I call after her.

She turns her head just enough to cast a sidelong glance over her shoulder. "Stay out of trouble." She winks and then she's gone.

↊

I decide to jog to my appointment. Ellie disguises her warning with jest, but I think she assumes I am after some tail, instead of just genuinely curious about Sophie. I get it. She's trying to be protective, but honestly, it's not like Ellie has seen me bring home multiple women. Sophie is *nice*. Sure, she's also beautiful and if I am reading her correctly, a little broken, but she is warm and intriguing, and I can't help but be curious.

I get to Doc's office as he's unlocking the front door and I catch him by surprise.

"Hey, Doc." I grab the door behind him.

"Oh hi, Liam. Come on in. I don't have any other appointments until 10 a.m. so Angie isn't here yet." He shuffles in and turns on the lights. He walks behind the counter and switches off the answering service on the desk phone. Then he goes into the single bathroom and comes back a moment later with a filled watering can and mills about hydrating the house plants. It's like

I'm watching Ellie's counterpart. Finally, he puts the can back and turns to me. "Let's go in my office, shall we?" he offers, and then turns toward the small hallway.

I follow him as he turns on his office light, opens the blinds, and cracks the window before sitting down behind his desk. Doc is a creature of habit. I'm observing him do the things he very likely does every morning, with the same thoughtful care. I can't think of anything I do so methodically besides taking care of Lucy and going to the gym. I bet there's a sense of calm in the consistency of it all. I plop on the couch and lean back, waiting for him to speak.

"How are you, Liam?" he asks me, his brow furrowing with concern.

"Today, I am okay," I tell him. I wait for him to ask something else and when he doesn't, I continue. "I guess I've been stressed lately because I'm having a lot of dreams about Cara."

He nods and writes something down. "Mm-hmm...and what do the dreams entail?" He peers at me from behind his glasses.

"Usually, it's us right before we get in my car the night she died. I am trying to convince her to do something else instead of going to the game. I try to keep her from getting in the car, but she always wins." I rub my hands over my eyes and down my face.

"I see." Doc makes another note on his paper.

"But this last dream was erratic," I continue. "I was standing on my front steps, trying to convince her not to go to the game, and I saw what our life might have been like together if we skipped it. I saw us going to college, getting married, and then having a baby. I felt so happy in the dream that if I'd have woken up right then, I would have been thrilled. But then we were in my car leaving the hospital with our new baby. It was my old car so there was no passenger seat for the baby because Melanie was also there. We were back in the same spot the crash happened, the same music is playing, but a baby is crying in the background and I woke up to the sound of the crash. When I woke up, I was crying." I shift my body so I am laying down on the couch now. Just recounting the dream was exhausting for me.

"These dreams are definitely stress-induced, Liam. I know you don't want to be medicated but you need to reduce stress in your life. Tell me a bit about what you're doing leading up to bedtime." He looks at me expectantly. When I don't immediately answer, he continues, "Just tell me what your nightly routine is after work."

I cough to clear my throat. "Okay. I usually pick up Lucy, get home, and have a beer while I figure out some dinner. I feed us both. Lucy and I sometimes take Maggie for a walk when it's a nice night. If we don't get to do that, then I bathe Lucy and put her to bed. I have been having to rock her to sleep because she's been under the weather. By then I'm usually exhausted. I have another beer, throw the ball for Maggie, and then pass out." I rake my hands through my hair.

"Do you have a beer every night?" Doc asks, frowning as he scribbles on his clipboard.

I scratch my chin, awkwardly. "Usually," I admit.

"More than one?" Doc raises his eyebrows.

"Yes. But no more than three. It's just to unwind, Doc, not to get drunk. I can stop any time." I fold my arms across my chest and cross my ankles.

"Okay, Liam, then I want you to stop. Or drastically cut back." Doc cocks his head at me. "You'll need to create an evening routine for yourself that signals that it's time to calm down— without alcohol."

I sigh, nodding my head, "I know." The truth is, I'm just going through the motions some nights.

Doc scribbles something else on the paper before speaking again. "What else are you doing to manage your overall stress levels? I know you go to the gym regularly, but why don't you try a meditation or yoga class downtown?" Doc puts his pen down and looks at me directly. "You'll need to get a handle on this before it worsens."

I groan. I know he is right. "The thing is, it isn't every night that I'm having these dreams. It's usually after a stressful day."

"Okay, what was the trigger this time?" He leans back in his chair with his pen and clipboard expectantly.

I sit up and rest my elbows on my knees, covering my face with my hands before I talk. "This time... Well, it was a stressful weekend." I fill Doc in on my Friday night, the ensuing argument with Sophie, and Lucy's illness. Getting it off my chest helps a lot. I pinch the bridge of my nose and suck in a breath before I admit the next part. "And I cleared things up with Melanie. I let her know that we're just friends and that's all it will ever be." I lay back down as the words tumble out of me. I forgot how exhausting talking about emotions is.

When I'm finished, Doc exhales. "Phew. Yes, that is a stressful weekend," he agrees. He pushes his glasses back up on his nose. "How do you feel since you talked with Melanie?"

I hesitate. "Relieved...I think? She was just causing me so much extra stress. And I can't give her what she's after."

"Which is what?" Doc asks me, as if he doesn't already know. As if we haven't gone back and forth on this a thousand times before.

"A serious relationship... I can't do it. At least not with Melanie. Maybe with someone else someday but..." I shrug. *Someone else.* At this moment, a visual of Sophie with her bright smile and warm demeanor pops into my head. I shake my head to push it aside.

"After all this time and all of the things you have been through, why do you think you can't be serious with someone?" Doc has asked me this question periodically throughout the years, and my answer has always been the same.

"I still have lingering guilt that I'm responsible for Cara's death. Any time I think about being in a relationship, there's a little voice in my head telling me I'm unworthy of love. And I have never *loved* Melanie. Sometimes on good days, I think I could love someone else, but it's not Melanie for me." I close my eyes and take a deep breath, sitting up.

Doc's timer beeps on his desk. "Liam, there is a lot to unpack here. The bottom line is you do deserve love. You do. And you need to work backward to get to a place where maybe you can feel healthy enough to date someone, if that's what you want. In the meantime, I'm giving you some homework." He points his pen at me. "I want you to try a yoga class."

I smirk at his mention of this, and he rolls his eyes. "You'd be surprised how much yoga can do for your mental state, Liam. And it's gentle. It's not you pushing yourself into fight-or-flight in the gym."

I drop my hands in defeat. "Fine. I'll try a yoga class. Anything else?"

"Yes. We need to get to a point where you can come to terms with the past. Whenever you have a dream that leaves you upset, I want you to write it down. I want you to give yourself a period of time—five, ten, fifteen minutes, whatever you think you need—to sit with the feelings. Then I want you to tell yourself you're a good person, and I want you to move on with your day. Do you think that's something you can do?"

"I'll try," I promise, letting out a breath. I stand up and start moving toward the door when the front door jingles, signaling that someone else has entered the office.

"Good. And Liam, same time next week." He points and winks at me.

I groan as I walk out of his office. He yells after me, "Send my next patient in, will you? I don't think Angie's here yet."

I am shocked when I enter the waiting room and see none other than Sophie sitting and flipping through a copy of *Food & Wine* magazine. She hasn't spotted me yet, so I pause at the end of the hallway and allow myself to take her in. Her wild hair is tamed in a loose bun on the top of her head. Black sunglasses rest on the crown of her head. She's wearing a loose-fitting pair of jeans and sandals. I can smell her perfume from where I am standing and it's intoxicating. She looks beautiful as she flips the pages, biting her lip while she pauses to read something. A tingle rises in my chest at the sight of her. This woman is a mystery—a beautiful broken mystery—and I am determined to make her trust me.

I clear my throat. "Hi...uh, fancy meeting you here." I walk toward her.

"Liam... hi." She stands up and all but throws the magazine on the coffee table I built. "What are you doing here?" She clearly didn't expect to find me here.

I try to make light of the situation. "Oh, you know, a good old-fashioned therapy session to start my Tuesday." I force a laugh.

She awkwardly mimics my laugh and shifts her weight side to side. Neither of us know what to say next so I decide to put her out of her misery. "Doc is ready for you. He told me to tell you to go on back."

"Oh." She turns to pick up her purse. "Okay. It was nice seeing you." She sidesteps me so as not to get too close.

I can't help myself; I reach for her forearm and immediately electricity sizzles through me at the contact. "Sophie." She doesn't move out of my grasp, only meets my gaze. "I'll see you later."

She smiles politely. "Yeah." I hold her arm for a second too long and when she draws it back, I immediately miss it. "Bye, Liam." She walks quickly toward Doc's office door, and I am left feeling like I lost something, but I don't know what.

Chapter Nineteen

Sophie

I'm surprised to see Liam coming out of Dr. Stevens's office. Surprised, and intrigued. This guy keeps getting more intriguing. Every time I see him draws me in before I even have time to prepare for the effect he has on me. He makes me feel out of control of my body. My physical reaction to him is reflexive and I forget how to behave like a functioning adult. I am bewitched.

And I want to know why he is here; I want to know all about him. The rational part of my brain knows it's not a good idea. He has shown me his gruff side twice now, but both times he has redeemed himself. He completely surprised me the night after we met when he brought me food. I didn't even think he noticed me that day. That was my first glimpse at the softness he tries desperately to hide.

He does something to me that I didn't expect to feel for a man again so soon. The physical attraction is there, but it's more than that. Liam looks at me in a way that makes my skin prick, leaving me feeling exposed but unafraid. It's almost as if he can see my trauma and he seems to accept that it's a part of me, at least right now. And yet, he irks me, because I find him brash one minute and endearing the next. I want to know him. I want to find out what makes him tick.

ભ

My appointment with Dr. Stevens went well, but I didn't realize how exhausting it is to be the one doing most of the talking. I walk back to Ellie's, say a quick hello to her and Lucy, and then excuse myself to take a shower and lie down for a bit. My mind is a swirl of things I need to decide and plans I need to make, but it's overwhelming and I feel paralyzed.

I turn on the shower in my bathroom and while I wait for it to get hot, stare at myself in the mirror. I look tired, probably because I am. The past few months have been really hard. I had my last miscarriage in January, then I discovered James' affair, and now my entire life is uprooted. Truth be told, my body has been under stress for years trying to get pregnant.

I step into the shower, let the hot water run over my head, and the tension begins to melt. It's no wonder everything is catching up with me finally. I'm proud of myself for seeing Dr. Stevens. I truly believe I'll find my footing again with his help.

After I filled him in on the events of the past week, we talked about what's next. I told him how Liam offered me a job watching Lucy for him and that I'd be doing that for the time being. I explained to him that being with Lucy is healing for me because I worry I will never get to be a mother myself.

Dr. Stevens told me I should break my goals into short-term and long-term categories. If I'm planning to stay here for the foreseeable future, I should consider if I want to look for a job in the therapy field, take up a new hobby so I can start to build a social circle, and write down things that bring me joy. I can do all those, I think. As far as work goes, I can't imagine being anything *but* a therapist, but I know I need to give myself time to heal, too.

My mind wanders to what Dr. Stevens said about building a social circle here in Cape May. The only people I've met so far are him, Ellie, Liam, and Lucy. I don't even know how to go about making friends in this small town, but I do know that getting through hard times is easier to do with a support system.

I turn off the shower and towel off, letting my mind wander back to Liam. Maybe we could be friends. He doesn't let them show often but he has let me see some of his vulnerabilities. I bet he has a story to tell.

I wander out to my room and dig around for something to wear, choosing a pair of leggings and a loose T-shirt. I twist my wet hair into a knot on the top of my head. Dr. Stevens suggested I try to find some things to do unrelated to a career that would make me feel good. It could be anything I wanted but should be something that I feel happy doing and occupies my mind so I am not focused on the hard parts of my life.

I try to think of things I enjoyed doing before my life took a drastic turn—the gym and working out, or any physical activity really. I have been trying to walk everywhere I can in Cape May because I know the movement is good for me, but I probably need more than that. I open my laptop and then Google, but instead of searching for local activities, I find myself wanting to Google Liam instead. I can't get him out of my mind, and I am so curious why he was at Dr. Stevens' office this morning.

Against my better judgment, I type in "Liam Harper Cape May, NJ" in the search bar. Several results pop up spanning from the last twenty years. My eyes widen as I scroll the headlines.

Local Artisan Designs Custom Artwork for Millionaire's Beach House (6/31/21)

Local Artisan Promotes His Woodwork at Cape May Art Festival (4/14/22)

We Remember: 20th Anniversary of Teenage Car Crash Family & Friends Remember Cara Cote (9/15/20)

Celebration of Life Memorial to be Held for Lost Teen (10/1/00)

Two Car Crash Kills Teen Girl and Injures Two Others (9/16/00)

Driver of Fatal Crash Killing Teen Girl and Injuring Two Others is Sentenced (3/20/01)

I gasp, unsure where to click first. *Poor Liam.* I put my head in my hand and click on one of the tragic headlines. It's from the major newspaper in the area called *The Press of Atlantic City.* As I read, the sting of tears pricks my eyes.

September 16, 2000

Lower Township - *In an unexpected and horrific turn of events, a fatal car accident in Lower Township claimed the life of a 17-year-old girl and left two others injured. The accident occurred at the four-way intersection of Lincoln and Birch streets yesterday evening when a Dodge Ram pickup truck, driven by thirty-year-old Joseph Griffin, allegedly ran a stop sign at a high rate of speed. The victim of the accident has been identified as Cara Cote, a 17-year-old senior at Lower Cape May Regional High School. Cara was pronounced dead at the scene by paramedics. The loss of Cara has left friends, family, and community members grieving.*

Two other individuals involved in the accident sustained non-life-threatening injuries. Liam Harper, 18, was driving and Melanie Glick, 17, was a rear passenger in the vehicle struck by Griffin's truck.

I sniffle and bat away a stray tear. I feel nauseous. Liam's prickly exterior makes so much sense to me now. He suffered a major loss, and he was driving. *He probably blames himself.* My heart aches for him. I keep reading.

According to witnesses, Griffin's truck failed to stop at the four-way stop, leading to the crash.

"It wasn't his fault," I whisper to myself, using the back of my hand to wipe my cheeks.

The force of the impact was so severe that the Jaws of Life were required to extract the deceased. Police have noted that charges against Joseph Griffin are pending as investigations into the accident continue.

I exit the article, click on the next one from *The Cape May Chronicle* for the 20th anniversary, and scan it quickly. Friends and family talk about what a light Cara was. According to the article, she had a bright future as a soccer player and wanted to be a nurse. Her friends remember her as being very funny and always there when you needed someone. She was Melanie's best friend and Liam's girlfriend.

Melanie's face comes to my mind as I connect the dots. Maybe this is why I got such a possessive vibe from her the night she went out with Liam. I also probably should stop thinking about Liam entirely considering he literally just took Melanie out on Friday.

The article is really nice, but I have to skim the sentiments from Cara's parents and siblings because it's more emotional than I can handle right now. I look for mention of Liam, but I don't find anything until I get to the bottom where a footnote shocks me to my core:

Classmate Liam Harper, who was driving at the time of the accident, could not be reached for comment.

The articles leave me feeling somber. I cannot imagine being eighteen and having my world rocked like that. I want to run next door and throw my arms around him but clearly that would be weird. Unfortunately, now I can't escape the feeling that I somehow invaded his privacy. There would be no other way for me to have found out about the accident and Liam's involvement without Googling. I'm sure Ellie would never share that kind of information about him. The realization has me feeling gross and insensitive and I wish I could unlearn everything I just read. I guess the only thing I can do now is give Liam some grace.

I pick up my phone initially planning to text Claire and tell her what I've learned but instead, I type in Liam's name.

> **Me: Hi... I'm sorry I couldn't find my voice this morning. I didn't expect to see you there.**

It takes him a few minutes, but his reply is short and to the point, leaving me feeling worse than before.

> **Liam: It's okay. We all have off mornings.**

> **Me: Will we see you for dinner?**

> **Liam: Not tonight, unfortunately. You good for Lucy tomorrow, though?**

> **Me: Yes, definitely. Oh, and I heard you made Dr. Stevens' tables. I love them.**

> **Liam: :)**

I decide not to say anything back. I don't know him well, but maybe he isn't a big texter. Either way, this text exchange didn't go exactly as I had hoped. It's probably just as well. I don't need to be thinking about Liam as anything more than a temporary employer. I shut my laptop, toss my phone aside, and head downstairs. Maybe some Lucy snuggles will help lift this weight that has settled in my chest.

⚮

The next morning, I decide to put aside whatever preconceived notions I had about Liam Harper and do my best to be neighborly. I really enjoy my time with Lucy, and it's important for me to stay on good terms with Liam.

Ellie has said that Liam comes early because construction starts at 7 a.m. I set my alarm for six and take my time with my appearance. There is something about putting on makeup and nice clothes that boosts my self-esteem. Since mine has been in the toilet lately, I resolve to make an effort to look good each day. I take my time and use my good body cream, and I choose jeans and a tank top for this spring day. I scrunch my hair into its natural waves and apply a little lip balm before jogging down the steps. Just as I reach the last step, the front door opens.

"Good morning!" Liam roars before he notices me standing there. When he sees me, he startles. "Oh. You're right there."

I smile. "I'm right here. Ready for Lucy." I reach out to take her from his arms. "She looks like she's feeling so much better." Liam has tried to give her a Pebbles Flintstone hairstyle but she's still wearing her pajamas with remnants of banana stuck to them.

"She is," Liam nods. "I was so worried..." He stifles a cough. "But we made it through."

I'm speechless for a moment, thinking about the articles I read yesterday and feeling my heart tug. It takes everything in me not to reach out for Liam and hug him. I shake off the urge. *Silly girl.* "Does she have clothes in her diaper bag? I can get her dressed. Is there a stroller somewhere if I want to take her for a walk?"

"Yes...plenty of outfits to choose from in there." He gestures to the bag. "The stroller is on my front porch. Do you need me to get it down for you?" He turns toward the door.

I shake my head. "No, no. It should be fine. We'll be fine, don't worry." I start to usher him out the door.

"Okay, well, I'll be back at about three-thirty," he says. He kisses Lucy on the side of the head. "Bye, Lulu. Be a good girl." Then he meets my gaze and gives me a smile that makes my stomach flip. "Bye, Sophie. Thanks again." And he pulls the door shut.

I have to fan myself after that conversation. "Woo!" I say to Lucy. "Your uncle is like a Greek god."

From the kitchen, I hear Ellie bark out a laugh, and my face immediately reddens.

"He is quite handsome, isn't he?" She giggles as if she knows that I must be embarrassed.

"You weren't supposed to hear that!" I laugh as I walk into the kitchen. I bypass Ellie and set Lucy on the floor in the living room with some toys and books. "Besides, you can't blame a girl for looking."

Ellie nods her head in agreement. "No, that is for damn sure. But Liam is...well, he's not really a relationship guy." She pours two cups of coffee and sets them down at the table for us.

"What do you mean? What about Melanie?" I ask, fixing my coffee with cream and sugar.

"Oh, they've just been friends for years." Ellie waves her hand in dismissal.

"Oh. That's definitely not what I thought." I swallow the hope I feel in response to this revelation. "I thought for sure they'd have been together for years." I just assumed because of the articles I read, but I can't let on to Ellie that I Googled Liam.

This changes things.

"On and off for years, I suppose. But this time it's really off." Ellie pulls out her chair and sits down. "Now, I have already said too much. What should we do with Lucy today?"

I want to laugh about how much Ellie knows but pretends she doesn't. She seems like the lady you see in movies, always peering out her front window or listening to private conversations when people think they're alone. She knows it all. She sees it all. She seems to be very proud of it too.

Chapter Twenty

Liam

I work for Danny for the rest of the week and agree to work next week too. It helps me to go somewhere every day instead of putzing around my workshop and visiting with Ellie. It also helps me to stay away from Sophie. Every time I see her, I am struck by her beauty. She has been ready and waiting for me each day at 7 a.m., and each day I wish I didn't have to leave for work so I could spend a little more time with her.

The problem is, seeing her hold and bond with Lucy is tugging at my heart in an unfamiliar way. It's funny how much time I spent keeping Melanie away from Lucy, but when I see her in Sophie's arms, everything feels right. Then I start to imagine us as a little family, playing on the beach, walking around the town, eating ice cream. It's a very dangerous game I am playing with myself.

Somehow my attraction to her grows each time I see her. Sophie takes great care with her appearance, but even if she didn't, she'd still take my breath away. The spring sunshine is starting to give her a pink glow to her cheeks, with freckles dotting her nose. She looks much happier and healthier than she did just a few weeks ago when she arrived. Cape May agrees with her. And whatever lip balm she has on every day makes me unable to look directly at her because if I do, I'll only be looking at her lush lips.

So, I am in a jam. I don't trust myself to get involved with her. I also think she has her own shit going on and she doesn't need me wrangling up her headspace. The best thing I can do is keep my distance.

Friday evening, I pick up Lucy and take her home for dinner. I have plans to check out a yoga class at a new place downtown tonight for my therapy homework, and I asked Ellie if she would watch Lucy over here for me so she could put her to bed. Ellie arrives at 6:30 p.m. leaving me thirty minutes to get there.

I don't know what I was expecting with this yoga studio, but it's essentially one room with big glass windows and enough space for about thirty people to practice yoga. I wasn't aware that *anyone* could walk by and see me in the window looking like an inflexible fool, and I am already embarrassed. I try to keep Doc's message in mind about cooling my stress levels and getting out of fight-or-flight. I decide the safest option is to pick a spot up near the front of the room where I am least likely to be spotted from the street.

I open the front door and a young blonde receptionist, no older than seventeen, smiles at me. "Hi! Did you pre-register for the 7 p.m. class?" She reminds me so much of Cara that I think if it were twenty years ago, it could've been her.

My jaw opens and then closes. "Shit. I mean...shoot. No, I'm sorry, I didn't realize I had to."

"Of course you didn't." I hear a voice behind me, and I turn around to see Sophie grinning at me, her pink yoga mat tucked under her arm. "I bet you don't have your own mat either," she teases.

My cheeks heat up and all I can think about is how ill-prepared I am for this class. I duck my chin and scratch my beard, suddenly feeling shy.

The teen behind the counter says, "Hold on! You're in luck. I just had one cancellation. If you want to take the class, it's a $17 drop-in rate."

I was already nervous about yoga and knowing there were no spots left was enough for me to consider abandoning the mission. But Sophie is here, and she smells like cinnamon and vanilla, and she is giving me those doe eyes. I imagine she fully expects me to bail. Without a word I slap my credit card on the counter, not taking my gaze off Sophie, calling her unspoken bluff.

"Great! And you can borrow a mat. We have extras in the front left corner." She hands me back my card.

I turn to Sophie and smile. "Want to be my yoga partner?" I wink and walk toward the mats.

"In your dreams, Harper." She laughs but she follows me to the front of the room where I can remain incognito. "So how did you know I'd be here?" She casts a sideways glance at me, putting her mat on the floor. I can't help but think how presumptuous that sounds. Like Sophie believes I would stalk her out on a Friday night. I mean I definitely wondered what she was up to, but this here is serendipity.

I chuckle. "What are you talking about? I am here because Doc says I need to eliminate stress. But I've never taken a yoga class." I put my mat down next to hers.

She gives me a curious look with a playful smirk like she doesn't believe a word I say, "Okay, Liam." She gets down on her mat and starts to stretch. "This is called child's pose. Try it."

I follow her lead and attempt to get in the same position. "Oh my *god*," I say, as my lower back muscles fire. I catch the ladies on either side of me giving me a side-eye, and I realize I'm probably speaking too loudly.

"Welcome to hot yoga, everyone. My name is Rachel and I'll be your guide for the next sixty minutes." She smiles in my direction when I audibly gasp.

Sophie looks at me with a "What is wrong with you?" expression and I mouth "*Hot* yoga?" at her. I thought this was just a regular yoga class. I am in no way prepared for the amount of sweat that is going to pour out of me in the next hour.

"Remember, no matter what level you are, this is your practice, so do what feels right for you. You can modify or increase the intensity if you need to." Then Rachel is at my side, placing a hand on my shoulder. "If you are a beginner, I will be paying close attention to you to help you in any way I can."

Feeling the attention on me, I raise my arm. "That's me, beginner," and people around me chuckle. I am in way over my head.

An hour later, I survive yoga class, but as I expected, I was so not prepared for how inflexible I am—or how much sweat I would be leaving in my place. No one recognized me, though, so that's a plus. "Gross, Liam," Sophie looks at my mat when I stand up. "You need this more than I do." She chucks her gym towel at me.

I give her an embarrassed laugh. "Thanks, I really wasn't prepared for a hot yoga class," I say, wiping down my face and shoulders. I wipe off the mat as best I can and put it back on the rack. Then I head toward the front door with Sophie once most people have started clearing out.

When we get outside I beeline for the bench in front of the building. Sophie follows and plops down next to me, a class schedule in her hands. "So, what did you think of hot yoga?" She asks teasingly, a glimmer in her pretty green eyes.

"I wanted to take a yoga class to relieve some stress, but I'll be honest, that was pretty stressful for me," I admit with a growl.

"I think you need to try a yoga flow. Sunday nights they have an evening flow class you might like. It's much easier." Sophie pats my knee and it sends a jolt right between my legs. She doesn't move her hand away and our eyes lock as if she's daring me to pull away.

"I don't know..." I hesitate but I don't move.

"Come on," she urges. "We'll do it together. It'll be fun." She doesn't take her eyes off me when she says this. I am feeling that familiar buzz behind my neck that Sophie seems to invoke any time she shows me one of her genuine smiles. I tear my eyes away from her and force myself to stand up before I have a full-blown erection. *Cool it, bud. You're not in a good place right now to be this into someone.* I give myself a pep talk. But I am into her. I'm so into her and I want to spend every free second I have getting to know her. I haven't felt like this in almost too long to remember.

"It's a date then," I say. I look down at her and offer her my hand to pull her off the bench. As much as I want to keep holding hands, I let go and start walking.

"It's *not* a date. It's a yoga class." She rolls her eyes but she's smiling as she falls in step beside me.

"Hey, you know I had to try." I grin, playfully bumping into her.

Sophie eyes me carefully, she looks like she wants to say something but holds back, biting her lip instead. "Let's start with yoga," she murmurs but she lets her knuckles graze mine as we walk.

I bite back a grin. "Did you drive here?"

"No." She shakes her head. "I walked. It's such a nice night."

"Walk home with me?" I raise my eyebrows, feeling hopeful.

"I think I already am." She grins.

Then we're walking side by side on the main street in comfortable silence. It's growing darker out but stores and restaurants are still open. A decent amount of people are milling around, and everyone seems to be feeling the excitement of the first May weekend. Sophie looks wistful as she walks and watches people.

Then we're in front of a new smoothie bar called Sunset Smoothie. We both stop and look up at the sign. The store still has its Grand Opening banner hanging in the window from a few weeks back.

Sophie's closeness makes me nervous. She is flushed from the heat and her lips have a pink tint to them. I can't stop staring at her. She catches me and covers her face. "What? Do I have something on my face?"

I cough. "No. No, not at all." I want to tell her she is gorgeous in this golden hour light, but it's been years since I've flirted with a girl I'm interested in and I can't work up the nerve. Instead, I say, "I was just wondering if you wanted to get a smoothie for our walk back?"

She smiles. "I would love to."

Chapter Twenty-One

Sophie

Liam is not rebound material. I have to remind myself as we walk into Sunset Smoothie. We're in line behind a few other people, standing quietly and reading the menu. Liam clears his throat. He does this a lot around me before he speaks. I wonder if it's a nervous tick. "What are you going to get?" he asks me.

I smack my lips together. "I think...a Pink Pitaya," I say, licking my lips. "What about you?"

"A Kowabunga," he says laughing. "I used to love the Ninja Turtles."

I laugh too. "So did my brother Simon. Sometimes he would let me play with him."

Liam smiles and looks up. "Oh, it's our turn." He puts his hand on my lower back and guides me forward. My skin sizzles. The butterflies in my stomach from his touch are putting me in a dangerous headspace. I remind myself once again that anything more than a friendship with Liam is to be avoided. He doesn't seem bothered, nor does he remove his hand while he orders.

The teenager behind the counter takes our order and then takes note of my yoga mat. "Did you guys try that couple's yoga class down the block? My boyfriend and I have been wanting to try it."

"Oh...we're not a couple," I say hesitantly. "I mean...it was just a regular hot yoga class."

I glance at Liam who promptly removes his hand from my

back.

The cashier nods. "Too bad, you guys would make a cute couple. Let me get those started for you." She turns and walks away from us. I'm so stunned by her remark that Liam whips out his credit card and pays before I can stop him.

"Liam, I didn't want you to pay! Let me Venmo you," I tell him firmly.

He laughs, tucking his card back in his minimalist wallet. "Not a chance, Soph. I wanted to."

I feel my cheeks heat up when he calls me Soph, and it's not leftover from the yoga class.

The cashier brings our smoothies over to the pick-up counter and tells us to have a good night. We take them and some napkins and start walking toward our homes. Liam falls in step beside me, his knuckles keep grazing mine and it sends a chill up my spine. I glance at him while I sip.

"So..." We both say at the same time and then we laugh, glancing at each other. *There is something here.* I think to myself. *I can't deny it. I can see it in the way he looks at me.* "You first," I tell him, gesturing with my free hand.

"I was just going to ask what made you move here. But if you don't want to talk about it, that's fine too." He takes a long sip.

"Oh...well, I guess you might've figured by now that I am getting a divorce," I tell him, leaving out any sort of context.

Liam plays dumb. "I didn't figure that."

When I give him a knowing look he shrugs.

"Okay, I did see his picture come up when your phone rang. And the photos in your box. I'm sorry. I didn't mean to snoop." We come to a street corner and Liam darts over to the trash can to throw out his empty cup.

"Geez, you drank that fast!" I exclaim. "Didn't you get a brain freeze?"

Liam smirks and gives me a shrug. He's quiet, maybe waiting for me to continue.

I contemplate how much I want to share. I haven't been able

to talk much about James without crying, and I really don't want to cry in front of Liam. That would be embarrassing. "My husband had an affair."

"Jesus, Sophie. I'm sorry," Liam laments. "I didn't mean to bring up a painful subject. I'm such an ass. I just thought we were getting to know each other." He looks at me with such sincerity that I almost blurt out everything at once.

"It's okay. Anyway, I never really thought I'd be divorced, truthfully, but he got her pregnant." I exhale loudly and take another sip of my smoothie. "So here I am."

"Christ," Liam mutters. "You've been through it, huh?" He drapes an arm around my shoulder. The moment of affection catches me off guard but surprisingly, isn't unwanted. "I'm sorry I was such an asshole to you."

I shake my head. "Don't worry about it," I remember all that Liam has been through too and my heart swells. "We all have our shit, remember?" I give him a weak smile, trying to make light of the situation. "I came here to move on. And that's what I'm going to do." He peers down at me, a half-smile playing on his lips, and tugs me closer into the crook of his arm. I let my arm find his waist and curl into him. We finish the walk like that, neither of us wanting to pull away. I know something is happening here, but I can't bring myself to call attention to it.

Before we know it, we're in front of our two houses. He lets his arm fall from my shoulder, and I immediately wish he would put it back. I wish I could tug him close and feel his rock-hard abs against my soft middle while I wrap my arms around his back and tug on his T-shirt. I won't do that. But I am surprised at the longing I feel for someone I have so recently met. I think he feels it too.

"Well, here we are," he sighs. He turns and looks at me in earnest. "Want to walk to yoga together on Sunday?" He looks so hopeful that I don't bother to disguise my own eagerness. *I think I'm starting to like him.*

I grin at him. "I'd like that."

He nods and smiles. "Okay. Yeah. That's great." He steps aside and makes for his own staircase. "I better let Ellie get home. Goodnight, Sophie." He turns and waves as he walks away. I stand there watching him until he's inside.

~

Ellie doesn't come back from Liam's immediately, and I am a little too riled up to talk to her anyway. I'm certain she will be able to see what being in his presence does to me. I am flushed and warm all over. I want to text him, but I think that's a bad idea. It will start something I shouldn't be starting. I can still feel his touch across my shoulders and on my lower back. I should have wanted to pull away, but I didn't, quite the opposite, I all but sank into him.

I shower off as quickly as possible and put on some pajamas. I tiptoe toward my bedroom door but I still hear no movement from Ellie. I can't see Liam's house from my window, and it's probably better that way or I would be peeking over there all the time. I walk out of my room and down the hall to the window I can see him out of. Liam is on his back deck talking to Ellie while the sweet puppy runs in the backyard. He looks animated and Ellie is laughing at something he is saying. I feel something twinge in my chest and I recognize it as envy. I wish I were over there hanging out with them. I trek back to my room for my phone, I absolutely need to put Liam out of my head.

Picking up my phone, I FaceTime Claire. She answers on the third ring, but she isn't home. She's out somewhere with Derek and it's noisy.

"Hi Soph!" she shouts into the phone. She moves the screen away from her face and up to her ear so she can hear me, giving me a direct view down her shirt.

"Hey...where are you?" I can see that they are outside in a crowded area and she's holding an open beer.

"We're at a show for Derek's friend Josh. He's playing outside tonight. It's so nice out. What are you doing?" She's shouting into the phone, still not showing me her face.

I am suddenly feeling lonely and moody, and it's because I had hoped Claire would be home to talk me off the Liam ledge, but she's not. She's out having fun, as she should be. "I just got back from a hot yoga class...with Liam."

"*What!*" Claire shouts. "Hold on. I have to go somewhere quieter." Then to the people she's with, "I'll be right back guys, no one take my seat!"

I wait while Claire walks through the crowded outdoor area then in through the bar and finally outside to the front of the restaurant she is at. "I'm sorry, did you say you went somewhere with Liam?" she clarifies, holding the phone back up to her face.

I groan. "Well, I mean, I didn't go with him. He was just there, and we ended up doing the class together and then going to get smoothies on the walk home." I wait for her response. She's giving me a pointed look and chewing her lip but she doesn't say anything, so I continue. "He's not as bad as I thought...but it's a lot to tell you when you're out having fun. Maybe we can have a phone date tomorrow morning?"

Claire nods. "Yes. Definitely...we can. But Sophie, be careful. He isn't the nicest guy, and you are very vulnerable."

"I know, I know. We made amends though. I didn't get to tell you that yet. Gosh. I miss you. I know if I were home, I'd be out with you tonight," I whine, suddenly feeling exponentially sorry for myself.

"You are home now, baby girl." She says to me with a big smile. "Listen, I have to go. I will call you in the morning."

I say goodbye and fall back on my bed. Here I am, after a great yoga class and a fun chat with Liam and I am feeling sorry for myself because my best friend has her own life and cannot hold my hand through this moment. Then my mind wanders back to Liam and I wonder if he feels it too, this thing building between us. Surely he has noticed the electric energy we seem to have. I cannot be the only one feeling it. I pick my phone up and text Claire.

> **Me: What if I want him though?**

> **Claire: Only you know what is right for you, Soph. But you may just be lonely and it's okay to feel that too.**

She didn't tell me not to.

I take a deep breath in and exhale loudly. This is not what I should be thinking about. I cannot just jump from one relationship to the next. It's not healthy and it wouldn't be fair to him. I force myself off the bed and start puttering around my room, unpacking some more boxes while listening closely for Ellie's return. It's no use though. Thoughts of Liam and the way I felt in the crook of his arm tonight permeate my brain. I plop back down on the bed, resting my head against the pillow. I close my eyes and allow myself to imagine for just a moment, letting myself fall for Liam. Sure, neither of us have confessed any sort of feelings yet but it could happen. Against my better judgment, I pick up my phone to text him.

> **Me: I had fun tonight. Thank you for making me smile.**

His phone must have been in his hand because his reply comes at rapid speed.

> **Liam: If I could make you smile every day, I would, Sophie.**

Maybe he is feeling something between us after all. His response has goose bumps rising on my arms and a funny feeling develops in my belly. This is flirting, right? I mean, sure, it could just be a nice thing to say and maybe Liam really is a nice guy and I am reading into it too much. I hear Ellie bustling around the kitchen, probably making her evening cup of tea. I start to type back that he can probably make me do other things too but promptly erase it. That would be entirely inappropriate. Instead, I settle on this:

> Me: It has been a long time since I've done anything like that, and it felt really nice.

I am being forward now, but that's not stopping me from feeling hopeful that he feels the same way. His text comes through, and I can't tap on it fast enough.

> Liam: For me too...

I know a new relationship so soon is a bad idea. This will probably blow up in my face, but I can't help myself. I've got to curb it. As much as I want to say more, I settle on something simple:

> Me: Well, goodnight, Liam. :)

> Liam: Night, Sophie.

Chapter Twenty-Two

Liam

After I say goodnight to Ellie and peek in at Lucy, I fall into bed, but I'm restless. It was nice to spend a little time with Ellie tonight. We haven't spent an evening together without Lucy in a while and she seemed happy when I asked her to visit for a bit. In true Ellie form though, when I told her Sophie was at yoga too, she had to make sure she put a warning label on it for me.

Ellie means well; she doesn't want to see me or Sophie get hurt. In some ways she is right, I am not in the right headspace to start a new relationship. Based on what Sophie has shared with me, neither is she.

That conversation with Ellie is why I kept it kosher when I got a flirty text from Sophie a little while later. It would have been very easy for me to take the conversation a step further, but I stopped myself. Being near her tonight did something to me that I haven't felt in a long time, maybe ever. I just haven't figured out what it means yet.

"Ugh," I groan. My mind is jumbled with thoughts of Sophie, and I need to clear it. I prop my pillows up and reach for my phone, sleep eluding me. I go to my Perry Street Boys group text.

> Me: Boys, let's go out tomorrow night.

Jack: I'm in. Can wives come though because Steph isn't going to deal with me being gone a second Saturday in a row.

Danny: Same. I'm in if Kristen can come.

Miles: Wives suck.

I laugh. Nothing like Miles chiming in. He got divorced about a year ago and since then has nothing nice to say about women and relationships.

Me: Fine, Miles, I'll be your wingman.

Miles: Done. I'm in.

I fire off a quick text to Ellie asking if Lucy can sleep over at her house tomorrow night. I know I am asking a lot of her but tonight was only for about an hour and a half. If she says no, I'll bail out, but I could really use a night with my friends. I try to convey that to Ellie in the text and she writes back almost immediately.

Ellie: What are neighbor grandmas for? :D So long as you stay out of trouble.

Me: No promises.

❦

Saturday morning I decide I am going to be productive, especially if Ellie is helping me out again tonight. I wake up early and bring Lucy outside to Ellie's front yard with me and set her on a blanket with some toys. She isn't walking yet so I don't have to worry about her going too far. I decided late last night to weed Ellie's front garden. Once spring is really underway, she is usually outside doing it herself, but I couldn't help noticing she hasn't gotten to it yet. It's only 8 a.m., and her house is quiet. I get right to work, yanking the dead stuff, and using a shovel for the stubborn ones. I glance at Lucy every few moments who is happy just looking at her books and toys, hanging out in the shade of Ellie's weeping willow.

I've got a good number of weeds and branches cleared out and put in a pile when I hear Ellie's front door open. I wipe the sweat from my brow, and look up to see Sophie, looking cute as ever in a pair of black biker shorts, and a tank top. She notices Lucy first and is making funny faces at her. "Are you out here by yourself, Lucy girl?" she coos.

"Hi," I wave at her from the garden bed.

Hi," she gives me a wave and jogs down the steps. "You're working on Ellie's garden, that's so nice," she gushes.

I stand up and dust off my hands on my old jeans. "Yeah, well, she does a lot for me, and I have convinced her to watch Lucy again tonight, so I want to do her a favor." Then as an afterthought I add, "It's Saturday night. I figured you might be busy..." *Now I'm wondering if she actually is.*

Sophie nods. "Got it. Well, that's nice. Listen, I wanted to ask you... Since yoga isn't your usual thing, is there a gym you belong to that you like? I think it's time I get some regular exercise."

"Yes, of course. I go to Local Fitness on the main strip, not far from where we were last night. You can probably walk there." I point up the road. "If you wanted to wait for me, I could take you..." I trail off.

"Oh, no. I'll be fine." Sophie waves her hand. "You've got your hands full right now anyway."

"If you're sure," I say, feeling desperate to spend time with her.

"Yep! I'm good," she chirps enthusiastically. "I am going to go see about signing up then." She turns and starts walking quickly away from me leaving me wondering what in the world is going on in her head.

જી

A little while later, Ellie comes barreling down her front step. "Liam! I was going to do that," she huffs. "I just haven't gotten to it yet." She bends down to pick up Lucy and for a moment I think how grateful I am to have this relationship. I think Ellie must be grateful too. It's amazing how natural it is for her to love on me and Lucy. We're the children she never got to have herself, and she loves nurturing us.

"I know, El." I stand up from my position on the opposite side. "I just wanted to do something nice for you since you have been taking great care of literally everyone lately. Now it'll be ready for you if you want to go get some new flowers."

Ellie hugs Lucy and plants a kiss on the side of her head since I'm filthy. "Oh, Liam! Thank you. That means so much to me."

I wink at her. "You got it."

"How about I take Lucy inside for a bit? It's getting warm out here and I am betting you didn't think to put any sunscreen on her." She gives me a knowing look, but the corners of her mouth curl up into a smirk.

A light breeze blows through the yard, and it makes Lucy giggle. Ellie and I smile at Lucy and then at each other. It's the first time in a while that I am feeling optimistic. I know with Ellie's love and support, Lucy and I will always be okay. It hurts me on some level that my own parents don't reach out to me to see how we are doing. In some ways, I think my pain caused them so much pain that they don't know how to look at me anymore. Losing Leah was the icing on the cake, and it's just too hard for them to be close to Lucy and me. I wish it were different but I am so thankful for Ellie and my friends here.

"She seems to like it out here, but if you miss her company, you're welcome to take her." I steer the wheelbarrow full of topsoil and dump some in my now weeded garden bed. Then I get on my hands and knees to spread it.

"I think I'll just take her in for a little while. I would hate for her to crawl away and you to miss it." She stares at me, looking for my reaction.

I roll my eyes and smirk at her, "Ellie, I'm not going to let my toddler crawl away and somehow miss it," I laugh. "Glad to see you have so much faith in me though."

Ellie starts to walk back inside and then whirls around again. "Where is it you're going tonight?" She cocks her head curiously at me.

I stand up, dusting my hands off on my jeans. "Probably just The Rusty Nail." I raise my eyebrows with a slight uncertain tilt of my head. "It won't be anything crazy," I assure her.

Ellie looks like she wants to say something but then she closes her mouth, hesitating.

"Did you have something you wanted to add?" I bite back a smile. "You look like there is something you're not saying," I smirk, raising my hands innocently.

"It's just... What did Doc say about alcohol and your stress levels?" Ellie winces as she says it and shifts Lucy to her other hip. Lucy pats Ellie's cheek, cooing, and Ellie smiles down at her.

I'm quiet for a moment. I know she's right. I shouldn't be going out drinking when the nightmares are back and I'm under so much stress. I suck in a breath and nod. "Yeah. You're right. He did," I pause. "I just want to hang out with the guys a little." I chew on my lip thoughtfully.

"You can go out and not drink, Liam," Ellie says as if it's the most obvious thing ever. "Go listen to the music and see your friends but hold back on the drinking." She pauses and then, "It's the only thing that is going to make it better right now," she says quietly.

I groan and drag my filthy garden hand down my face. "You're right. I'll think about it," I promise.

"Please do." She gives me a smile over her shoulder as she walks away singing a song with Lucy's name in it.

The thing is, she's not wrong. I want the nightmares to stop, and I want to move forward in my life. For the first time, I want to get to a place where I can be in a relationship. Not just for me, but for Lucy too. I'm still not entirely convinced that I deserve it, but I know improving my well-being is the best way to get there.

I just have to prove it to myself.

Chapter Twenty-Three

Sophie

I walk quickly up to Lafayette Street, where we walked together last night, in search of Liam's gym. It doesn't take me long to spot the sign with black lettering that reads *LOCAL* outlined in red. I am frozen on the sidewalk for a moment, taking it in. This is not your typical gym where you may find group exercise classes, a sauna, or a locker room. No, this is entirely open air with nothing but groups of bulky men lifting, not a woman in sight. I am not sure if this place is exactly what I'm looking for. I'm busy hesitating out front when I see Melanie walk in through the open front doors.

She notices me too because she turns around, shades her eyes and says, "Are you just going to stand there or are you going to come in and work out?"

This is the push I need, so I follow her inside. She's signing in at a kiosk at the counter when I walk up. The older gentleman working sizes me up. "Can I help you?" he asks.

"Hi... Yes. I just moved here. I'm looking for a gym membership." I pause and look around. To my right is an assortment of cardio machines, ellipticals, stationary bikes, treadmills, and stair climbers. Further back where the meatheads are assembled appears to be various free weights and machines with bigger weights that I don't know the names of. There's a staircase to a smaller loft area where, when I look up, I am surprised to see a few women. I exhale and raise my eyebrows. "I guess you don't have any group exercise classes here, huh?" I laugh nervously.

The man doesn't laugh back but Melanie cackles from her place at the counter where she's watching our interaction all too closely.

"Listen, lady, have you tried the yoga place up the street?" he offers.

"I have. I need something...different," I say, looking around again.

"Well, this gym ain't fancy. What you see is what you get. Take it or leave it," he says. He turns away from me to answer the phone. I'm looking at the membership options and silently mulling them over when Melanie interrupts my thoughts.

"Sophie, right? Liam's new neighbor?" She cracks her gum and leans on the glass countertop next to me.

"Yep...that's me." I blow air out of my mouth and don't meet her eyes.

"If you decide to join, I could take you through my routine. Maybe help you navigate the weights," she offers. She seems genuine but since Liam just permanently friend zoned her, I don't know what to think. I don't have time to answer her before the man hangs up the phone and turns back to me.

"So, what'll it be?" He leans on the counter opposite me and now I'm sandwiched between him and Melanie. "You two know each other?" He's talking to Melanie.

"Yeah, Duke, we do." She cracks her gum again. "Sophie here just moved in next to Liam. What do you say we let her try it out before she joins?" Melanie asks, and if I'm not mistaken, bats her eyes at Duke.

Duke drops his hands in defeat. "Whatever."

Melanie smiles big then turns to me. "Let's go!"

◌੪

I'm not sure what I'm doing or how I got here but I am sitting at a chest press machine pushing the lightest amount of weight possible and Melanie is next to me talking my ear off. So far, I have learned

161

that she has lived here all of her life and that Liam is...or was...her best friend. She told me about the car accident and how Liam is fucked up from it and can't sustain normal relationships. I don't know what to say to all of this, so I just listen to her and react in short answers. She doesn't ask me anything about myself or why I moved here and that much I appreciate.

"Liam just doesn't *know* what he wants. I just feel so sorry for what he has been through, so I keep going back to him. But like, it's so *stupid*. Not anymore." She snaps her gum.

We switch spots so Melanie can take her turn. She adjusts the weight up twenty pounds from what I did, and I want to laugh but can't because I'm too busy digesting this information. Hearing Melanie talk about Liam in this way should scare me. After all, she's another woman and she's been scorned by him. Instead, it only makes me want to know him more. I want to peel back his layers and uncover the broken man that I know is hiding underneath his prickly exterior. *Fix him?* I shake the thought away immediately.

"That's...really sad," I tell her, meaning it. "Liam hasn't told me anything personal about himself." That much is true. We made it home from our walk last night before he could share anything. I like to think maybe he would have if we had more time.

Melanie finishes her set, and we move on to another machine that says chest fly. Melanie hasn't explained anything to me about how to use these machines. She is just waiting for me to sit down and figure it out. I let her go first this time. "And all my friends are married to his friends which is super annoying. So, he makes me mad and then I can't even really avoid him. I'm tired of waiting for him to figure things out though."

"Mmm." I nod. "I can see why." It's my turn now and I sit down and start to mimic the same motion I watched Melanie do moments before.

"Anyway, you should totally come out with me tonight. You're new in town, you look single. Why don't we go out and try to find some men?" She snaps that gum again.

I stop what I'm doing. *How did I get here? I look single? And why is she being so friendly?* "I don't know..." I trail off.

"Oh come on, girl! Live a little. Be my wing woman. I promise, I'm a ton of fun." Melanie does a little dance that reminds me of something Claire might do. I really don't have a good reason not to go, other than it would probably irk the hell out of Liam. But why am I worried about what Liam thinks? It wouldn't hurt me to have a girlfriend here since my best friend is four hours away, and Ellie is not exactly in my age bracket. "I will introduce you to some locals. You'll fit right in."

Work on building your social circle, Doc's words echo in my head.

I stand up, ready to move to the next machine and take a sip of water. Melanie has stopped talking now and is eyeing me suspiciously. I know she's waiting for me to give her an answer.

"Okay, okay. Yeah, why not?"

"Yes! That's my girl." Melanie claps. "We're going to have a great time."

"Okay. Where are we going?" I ask, following her over to a flat bench and some free weights.

"You ever heard of The Rusty Nail?"

ॐ

I call Claire on my walk back from the gym and neither of us knows what to make of the interaction with Melanie.

"That's so weird!" Claire says. "And last time you saw her she acted like you didn't exist?"

"Last time I saw her it was super contentious and awkward. Like she didn't like me babysitting for Liam." I stop at a Do Not Walk and take a swig of my water. The streets are filling with people walking to get breakfast or coffee or on their morning jogs. The Saturday morning air is salty and sweet, and I can hear the sound of the ocean. I *want* to be optimistic. "Maybe she just needs a friend?" I suggest. "She did say all of her friends are married to Liam's friends."

Claire makes a tsk sound. "I don't know. It's fishy to me. Be careful. Maybe take your own car." She sounds like a mama bear. "I wish I was there to go out with you again. That place was fun."

"Maybe you and Derek can come for Memorial Day?" I suggest. "And I will be careful. I don't have anything to lose by trying to make friends. And she doesn't know anything about me. Nor did she ask."

"See, that's what makes it weird to me," Claire says thoughtfully. "Why wouldn't she want to know more about you?"

"Maybe she is thinking she'll find out tonight? How about this... You call me at 9 p.m. and if it sucks, I'll make your call an excuse to leave." I laugh. "Just like our bad dates in college."

"Okay. I will do that. And Sophie, I mean it... Be careful."

"I will, Claire. Thanks for always looking out." We hang up and I am left alone with my thoughts. Maybe I should tell Liam I am going out with Melanie tonight? I don't want to upset him when things appear to be going well between us. I think I like him and I hope maybe he likes me, too. *I'll just see how tonight goes. Anyway, he already told me he has plans tonight, too.*

As I come up on the house, I see him in the garden still looking like an Abercrombie model straight out of the early 2000s catalog.

Liam stands up when he sees me coming, grabbing his water bottle and taking a swig. He grins at me. "I thought you got lost," he jokes.

I force a laugh. "No, not lost. I did get a good workout in though, so thank you." I push my lips together eyeing him carefully. "You got a lot done out here," I muse, assessing his progress.

"I'm glad," he says, raking a hand through his hair. "I'm just finishing up. Do you want to have some lunch with me and Ellie?"

Yes. But I'm afraid to tell him I'm hanging out with Melanie tonight. "I can't," I hesitate, chewing on my lip. "I haven't finished unpacking and I'm going out tonight, so I need to find something to wear in those boxes." I laugh half-heartedly.

Liam looks like he wants to say something else to me, but he swallows and remains quiet for a moment, surveying the garden. Then he turns back to me with a tight smile. "Well, have fun... I'll see you tomorrow for yoga, right?"

I grin. "Definitely."

ℭℛ

I'm getting ready a few hours later when I get a text from James. A realtor is coming to assess the house on Monday and he'll let me know what they think is a good listing price. The realization hits me that we're not just selling our house, we're selling dreams we built together when we bought it. My eyes well with tears and I angrily bat them away. In no universe could things have worked out for us, but the loss of the hope I had when we bought the house, well, that hurts almost as much.

I try to focus on getting myself ready. I blow out my hair straight, which is something I don't do often. I wear a pair of loose white boyfriend jeans and a blue top with a plunging neckline. I cuff the ankles and slide on a gold pair of gladiator sandals. Just for fun, since I don't wear it often, I put on some jewelry—little anchor earrings and a shell bracelet. I put on my favorite guava color lip gloss and perfume, and I am ready.

I head downstairs to find Ellie sitting on the couch with Lucy reading a book. "Wow, Sophie. You look great, dear." She smiles. "Who are you going out with? Not Liam?"

I would assume Liam had told her where he was going but I don't ask because I don't want to seem too interested. I'm being very careful with how I act around Liam and how I talk about him to Ellie. I'm not sure how she would feel if she knew I might be interested in him.

"Actually...Melanie. I met her at the gym today and she convinced me." I put my hands in my back pockets.

Ellie can't hide her surprise. "Oh...well, then. Have fun. And be careful. Are you driving?"

"I have an Uber coming in just a minute," I assure her. "I

never drink and drive. And I just got a text from James about a realtor coming to the house, so I have a feeling I'm going to need a few drinks tonight." I sigh. My phone buzzes letting me know my ride's here. "Don't wait up." I smile and turn to go.

"Bye Sophie, and please be safe!" Ellie calls after me.

೮

I text Melanie when I get to The Rusty Nail, and she meets me at the door. I can already hear the band getting started. It's a different band from last weekend when I came with Claire. This one is playing early 2000s pop-punk hits. I feel a rush of excitement as we walk in. Melanie seems to know everyone and is saying hi to people left and right as we make our way to the back corner of the wrap-around bar to a few other girls.

"I'll introduce you to my friends," Melanie says. "They're married so they aren't much fun." She laughs at her own joke, and I pretend to laugh because I like to think I was still fun when I was married. We get to the corner, and I can see the other women sizing me up. One of them is tall and thin with curly blonde hair and clear blue eyes. The other one is shorter and rounder with a long brunette bob and eyelash extensions that I can't unsee. "Ladies, we're here!" Melanie sidles up to the girls and leans on the bar to get the bartender's attention. "Sophie, these are my friends, Steph and Kristen. Girls, this is Sophie. She is staying with Ellie."

"Ohhhh." The blonde gives a knowing look. "So, you're Sophie."

I instantly feel awkward. *How has she heard about me?* I laugh, nervously. "How do you know of me?" I ask, trying my best to play it cool.

Once Kristen explains that she's married to Danny, Liam's friend, it feels less nefarious. But I can't help feeling funny about being out with Liam's people right now.

The same jolly bartender from last Saturday comes over. "What'll it be ladies? And what are we celebrating?" He smiles the same effervescent smile I remember from the week before. Then he notices me. "Oh, hey! Divorce girl. I remember you from last week."

I grit my teeth through a smile. "Hi...yeah. It's me. Sophie," I remind him. Then to the girls, I explain how we met the last time I was here.

"That makes so much more sense now," Steph says, taking a sip of her mixed drink.

"So, what are you having, Sophie, Melanie?" he asks, expectantly.

"I think...I'm going to do a margarita on the rocks again," I say.

"Oooh that sounds good, me too!" Melanie says. "And how about four shots of tequila to go with it?"

Our happy host, whose name I find out is Bobby, comes back with our drinks and in no time, I feel relaxed. Stephanie and Kristen seem kind enough and no one has asked me anything super personal, since we moved past the divorce thing. We take our shot...and then another, and I am feeling proud of myself for taking an Uber here. All feels right until I look up and see a group of guys headed our way. Two with wedding rings and two without. Trailing at the back of the pack is none other than...Liam. And he's as surprised to see me as I am to see him.

Chapter Twenty-Four

Liam

I spot her from across the bar where I am playing pool with the guys. What I don't expect to see is her walking in with Melanie. I was kicking myself after I recommended Local to her because I knew Melanie went there. My fear was that Melanie would be nasty to her, not befriend her. Melanie is going to ruin this for me, if she hasn't already. It's eating at me, and I'm distracted.

"What's with you, man?" Danny nudges me as we finish the pool game with a loss to Jack and Miles. "You're out of it."

I drain my coke, but don't meet his eyes. I can't take my eyes off Sophie. I made the right decision to stay sober tonight because I feel a protective urge to get her away from Melanie immediately. "I'm cool. I'm cool. Let's get another drink."

"Hey, is that Sophie over there with the girls?" Miles drops his cue in Jack's hand and makes his way to the corner of the bar, not bothering to wait for a response. My "wingman" has my blood boiling.

"With Melanie?" Jack raises his eyebrows. "That looks like trouble."

We all follow Miles over to the corner of the bar. Sophie is already looking relaxed, and she is smiling while talking to the ladies, but when she sees Miles her face really lights up. He puts his arm around her, and she gazes up at him.

"Is this the beautiful girl I danced with last Saturday night?" Miles' boisterous voice echoes through our corner of the bar.

Sophie laughs and eyes me cautiously as I approach.

"I hope you're ready for some more dances," Miles adds.

Sophie doesn't respond to Miles directly, but she picks up her drink and drains it in one sip, watching me the entire time.

I am working hard to control the expression on my face to not give away my change in mood. I lean down over Melanie and whisper in her ear. "What are you doing?" I make sure my tone reflects my suspicion about her motives.

She looks back at me, teasing eyes glowing in the bar light. "Whatever do you mean?" She laughs and waves the bartender over. He comes quickly. "Bobby, can we please get eight shots of tequila?"

"Seven," I correct. "I'm not drinking." Melanie and Sophie simultaneously whirl around and look at me when they hear me say that.

"Seven shots of tequila, coming right up." Bobby jets to the other side of the bar.

I take a breath and turn around to face the wall. Running my fingers through my stubble, I'm trying to get a hold of myself—but I am seething. Melanie knew exactly what she was doing, bringing Sophie here and introducing her to our group of friends. She's making it so if I ever wanted anything romantic with Sophie, it would be impossible to achieve because of their friendship. I hear Sophie laughing at Miles' stupid jokes behind me. He grabs my shoulder.

"Yo man, since you aren't taking a shot, take a picture of us," Miles thrusts his phone in my palm.

It takes everything in me not to growl at him. They all clink their glasses together and I snap the photo. Everyone puts their shot glasses on the bar, just as the band starts playing "Mr. Brightside" by The Killers.

"Let's go dance!" Kristen shouts and all the girls get up and beeline toward the stage. I'm trying to tell myself to relax and have a good time, but Miles' obvious interest in Sophie is making it nearly impossible. I need to get her alone before he does. I have never wanted a drink so bad. I wave Bobby down and ask him for water instead. He's quick about it, and I down it before heading up to the front of the stage to join my friends. I stay far away from Melanie and stand right next to Miles who is dancing behind Sophie. I've known Miles my entire life but for the first time in thirty years, I want to punch him in the face.

"Miles, I thought I was your wingman." I elbow him just as he puts his hand on Sophie's waist.

"You are, my dude," Miles laughs. "I gotta take a leak." He walks away and I take this as an opportunity to stand in his place.

I step behind Sophie, leaning down to whisper in her ear. I can't ignore the blush creeping up her neck or her obvious physical reaction. "Stay away from Miles, Sophie. He's no good for you," I murmur, my breath lingering on her neck a moment too long.

Sophie remains perfectly still but cups her hand over her mouth and says, "Why? Are you jealous, Liam?" The way she says my name is riddled with tension.

I feel my desire grow against her backside, and I am certain she can feel it too. I'm standing too close to her, and it's doing things to me that both scare and thrill me. I can't hold back. "Maybe," I whisper in her ear. It's this remark that has her turning and meeting my gaze. Her cheeks are flushed. Either she is turned on too, or she's mad. I can't tell which.

"I need a drink," she says and pushes away from me. I don't follow her. I am trying not to draw attention to the fact that I am raging with jealousy and want. If Sophie hooks up with Miles, I will lose my mind. I know there is something between us, and if she hooks up with him, we'll never get to figure it out.

I give it a few minutes before I walk over to her. She's still alone at the bar waiting for Bobby to bring her drink. I flag him down and then go stand next to her.

"Here you go, pretty lady." He smiles, placing another margarita in front of her. "Liam?"

"Just water. Thanks, man," I say. I lean next to her waiting for her to speak.

When Bobby walks away, she turns to me and says, "What the hell was that?" *Ok, she's definitely mad.*

"I just... I don't want you to hook up with Miles," I tell her. Honesty is the best policy.

"I'm just having fun." She throws her arms up dramatically. "I am getting divorced. It feels like I haven't had fun in years," she huffs.

"Just...not Miles. He's not going to be good for you." I let my forearm graze hers and we both look at each other when we feel it. That electric charge that is growing between us with each passing moment.

Sophie seems to ignore it. "You're going to have to do better than that, Liam. I want to have sex." She pushes off the bar and wobbles. I grip her arm to steady her and our eyes lock. She's had too much to drink.

I pass my water to her. "Maybe it's time you have this instead."

She glares at me indignantly. Then she lets out a defeated sigh and takes a sip of the water.

"I don't want to see you do something you will regret later," I tell her sincerely.

She narrows her eyes. "I think you're just jealous." She leans forward on the bar and takes another long sip of water. I glance at my watch. It's only 10:30 p.m. If we stay here, there's plenty of time left for Miles to pursue her, and by the way she is talking, he may just succeed.

Miles is my buddy and has been since third grade...but I saw his divorce. I know how nasty it was. His ex-wife was a transplant who moved here for him and had no friends or life of her own. That divorce broke both of them, but from the outside looking in, Miles wasn't exactly compassionate. She moved home to be near her family, and I can't help but think she's better off.

"I already told you, I am." I let my fingers graze her arm and she reacts by touching my hand. Our eyes meet and for a minute, all I can think about is kissing her. I want to grab her face and ravish her mouth with that stupid pink lip gloss. I want to taste her cool margarita flavored tongue and feel her hands moving up my back and under my shirt.

She sighs. "Can you take me home? I think I've had enough." She lets go of my hand and throws some cash on the bar.

"Sure. Go wait outside while I close the tab." I gesture toward the side door. "I'll tell everyone you aren't feeling well."

She gives me a rueful half-smile and walks toward the door. I wish I was taking her home to my bed, but I am just glad to be taking her away from Miles.

∝

It's a Saturday night at the height of spring, so we have to wait about ten minutes for an Uber. Sophie is pacing around outside in the front of the bar, hugging herself and ignoring me. I should have just driven tonight but I didn't make up my mind about not drinking until I got here. I can tell by the way she's walking that Sophie has had more than she realized and her furrowed brow tells me she is upset with herself. She looks my way, glaring angrily. *Or me. Maybe she's upset with me.*

"What is going on here, Liam?" she antagonizes me, as if she's looking for a fight.

"What are you talking about?" I play dumb. I know what she's talking about. I let my hands linger a little too long more than once tonight. I told her I was jealous. But now, I am standing way over here. I am giving her mixed signals because I am trying to avoid the inevitability of falling into bed with her and thus making everything weird.

"You couldn't just let us all hang out and drink and be carefree? Why are you so worried about what *I'm* doing? I wanted to have a good time tonight, but you have to march in and save the day in your big stupid macho way that makes me nervous and infuriates me at the same time." She exhales deeply and drops her arms, then she continues pacing.

I swallow what I really want to say about how much I want

her and instead say, "Okay, Sophie. I can see that you've had a lot to drink, and I know you're in a vulnerable spot right now. Sure, I don't know the details surrounding your divorce, but I don't want you to make a mistake." I plop down on the bench in front of the bar just as "I Want You to Want Me" starts playing. The timing is impeccable. "And yes. It made me jealous because I would hope if there was anyone in there that you'd have danced with like that, it would've been me. There, I said it. Okay?"

Our Uber pulls up then and I gesture toward the car before she can speak. I let her slide in first and I get in behind her. Both of our hands rest on the middle seat. Neither one of us is speaking so instead of making the situation worse, I put my head back and close my eyes. A moment later, Sophie's hand grazes my pinkie finger. I pick my head up and meet her gaze. *I want her so bad. I'm inches away from tangling my fingers in her hair and tasting that last margarita she drank*, but I can't and I know I can't for all of the reasons I just gave her about Miles. I can't say I am looking out for her vulnerability with my buddy and then go and do the same thing he was trying to do, no matter how much I want her. Especially not when she's drunk and I'm sober. But maybe I could hold her hand. I lace my fingers through hers, and she doesn't pull away.

She's looking at me with a longing that I haven't ever seen from her. Her breath quickens, matching the pounding of my pulse in my chest. Sophie wants me. Her eyes lock with mine and I see the same desire in them that I feel low in my gut, which makes it harder to resist. I want to give in to this careful control, but something inside me says no, not yet so, I keep holding her hand. I pick it up and trace my thumb around her palm. I see goosebumps rise on her biceps, and I know she is feeling the same tingling in her body that I am. My erection grows beneath my jeans, and I am grateful for a dark back seat and the twelve inches of space between us. But I keep holding her hand because I don't know if there will be another chance to.

The car pulls up in front of our houses and I open my door,

slide out, and pull her out behind me. The driver leaves us facing each other on the sidewalk. Sophie steps closer to me and runs her hands up my forearms. "Liam," she whimpers my name, prompting me to meet her eyes. She moves her hands to my chest and pulls me down to her so our foreheads are touching. She's practically begging me to take her upstairs. She moves one hand to my cheek and strokes my beard. "Liam," she says again, more forcefully, willing me to feel what she feels. "I know you feel what I feel," she whispers, glancing down at our hips flush together. Caught.

I feel it too, the electricity between us, but I will not be the next person who hurts her. Sophie is too good for me.

"Sophie," I breathe, pressing my forehead harder into hers. "I can't."

At these words she drops her hands and backs away from me, her jaw open in shock, embarrassment, I can't say for sure. She covers her own face and lets out a cry that makes my heart ache and then she turns and runs into the house.

I should get a fucking medal for that.

I groan and trudge up the steps and pull out my phone. There's a single text in my Perry Street Boys group chat. I open it.

Miles: You fucking cockblock.

Chapter Twenty-Five

Sophie

It takes me a few minutes on Sunday morning to realize what I have done. First, I'm greeted by the familiar migraine that comes with too much tequila. The bright sunlight is assaulting me because I never closed my shades last night, making everything worse. I am lying in my bed, trying to remember how I got home. There was definitely an Uber ride. Liam was there. I remember being annoyed when he showed up at the bar. In my drunken state, I thought Miles would be the perfect rebound hook up for me to forget about James and selling our house. As soon as I saw Liam, I knew I couldn't hook up with Miles.

I remember Liam standing extra close and moving in when Miles left for the bathroom, making damn sure he marked his territory. After that is where things get hazy for me. I recall asking him to take me home. I even recall being angry at him while waiting for the Uber. Then in the Uber we were holding hands. *Did I kiss Liam last night? Or did I just dream that? Wait. Liam wasn't drinking last night. So, what happened when we got out of the car?*

Then it all comes rushing back to me. We were facing each other. I touched him first. I leaned into him and could feel his arousal. I don't think anything happened though. Why not? I am pretty sure I remember how close we were to kissing. I all but threw myself at him and he turned me down. *He turned me down.*

The realization stings more than I expect it to. I was

practically begging him to put his mouth on mine and he said no. Actually, I think he said, "I can't." *Why, Liam? Why can't you?* The rejection embarrasses me and makes me angry. I could have had a fun, easy night with new friends. Now I am mortified. And hung over. I groan and turn to face the wall, putting a pillow over my head.

There's a knock at my door. It's a soft knock so I almost don't hear it. Before I answer I glance at the time on my phone. 9 a.m. "Come in, Ellie," I moan. Surely, Ellie is ready to go flower shopping. Yesterday I told her I'd go with her.

A throat clears. "I'm not Ellie."

I bolt upright and pull the covers up over my chest. Standing in front of me with two lattes is a tentative looking Liam, awkwardly shuffling his feet, his eyes darting anywhere but directly at me. I wonder if he slept at all. He looks as bad as I feel, with dark circles under his eyes and a pained expression, but he took the time to get me a coffee.

"I brought you coffee...and some Advil." He sets both down on the nightstand next to my bed. "I thought I'd stop in here before I grab Lucy from Ellie. They're out on a walk." Then he gestures to my bed. "May I sit?" He is so gorgeous even when he's clearly exhausted.

I shrug humbly. *I'm a goner for this man.* Coffee and medicine, but the jerk wouldn't kiss me last night when I was basically begging him to? *Maybe it's a peace offering so I'll still be his babysitter.* I can't look at him when I speak. "I'll still watch Lucy for you, Liam, if that's what this is about." I force myself to meet his gaze.

His brow knits together. He opens his mouth to speak and then closes it again. Then he sits down by my feet. "That's not what I came here to talk about."

I look down at my hands. "Oh," is all I can get out.

"Sophie, look at me." He pats my foot. I raise my eyes to meet his gaze. "Last night...I should have probably minded my own business, but the thing is...I feel like you are my business." He sighs and runs his fingers through his hair, possibly a nervous tick.

I don't know what to say so I wait for him to continue.

"The thing is, I am so attracted to you, Sophie."

Well, that makes me feel better. Blood rushes to my cheeks. I want to grin like a lovesick fool, but I don't; I bite my lip to hide it.

Liam continues, "But look, you've just been through something hard. And I have never been in a serious relationship. Like...never. I don't know how to do it." That must be hard for him to admit because I notice the tips of his ears turning pink. "I don't want to hurt you if I start something before I'm really ready."

My surprise must be evident because he smiles.

"I'm serious. And I really like our friendship, and I like spending time with you. I liked yoga so much the other night. I've never spent time with a woman and had it be so easy." He stands up and begins walking in circles around the room, like he's having an argument in his head that I'm not privy to.

"What about Melanie?" I ask, genuinely curious.

"Melanie is...that's different. I spent so much time with Melanie because everything was hard, not because it was easy. I know that won't make sense to you... I don't know what she told you." He runs his hands through his messy hair again, and I want to pull him onto the bed with me. Before I can say anything else, he continues. "I just think if I hooked up with you now, it would be for the wrong reasons... Sexual attraction is obviously present between us. But you're not in a good place and hooking up with you because I'm jealous is exactly what the old Liam would do." He sits back down on the bed and looks at me earnestly. "I am not rejecting you," he says softly. "I just think it's not the right time. Does that make sense?"

Tears burn the back of my eyes, and I don't know if it's because I still feel rejected, if I am sad that my marriage is over and I'm actually in this position, or if I am happy to have found a friend in Liam. I sniffle and the ugly cry is threatening in the back of my throat. All I can do is nod. I sniffle again and Liam reaches for a tissue from the box on my nightstand. *Was this man sent from heaven? I* may *have misjudged him.*

"Can we be friends?" he asks, and he is so hopeful I can't resist him. "Please. I need someone to go to yoga with today."

I laugh through my tears and it comes out as a snort. I still want to tear his clothes off, but I think he's right about the timing. I suddenly feel anxiety creep up in my chest when I remember my Irish goodbye. "Melanie is going to hate me now if she thinks I left with you."

Liam rolls his eyes. "Melanie is a pain in my ass. But you're fine. I told everyone you were sick from all the tequila." He gives me a wry smile.

I lay back on my pillows. "That's not far from the truth." I moan, reaching for the Advil he brought. He hands it and my bottle of water to me, then he stands to go.

"Why don't you go back to sleep, and I'll see you later for yoga?" He walks to my windows and closes the shades, then makes for the door.

"Thanks, Liam," I say, pulling my blankets up higher. I feel much better than when I initially opened my eyes. I close them again and start to relax.

"And Sophie?" Liam's voice prompts me to look his way. "Please don't hook up with Miles. It would kill me to find out that nothing could ever happen between us."

My voice comes out as a whisper. "Okay."

I can't wait to call Claire.

❦

Hours later, I am feeling much better. I slept an additional two hours before I dragged myself out of bed and downstairs to see Ellie with my tail between my legs. I find her in the kitchen fixing brunch. She looks up at me with a gentle heartfelt smile. "Are you feeling better, Dear?" How can one woman give a virtual stranger so much grace?

"I am," I rasp. "I'm sorry I missed flower shopping." I grimace in embarrassment.

Ellie waves her hand. "Nonsense! Liam said you weren't feeling well. I went with him and Lucy instead. Whenever you're ready, we can start planting." My heart swells at the thought of him doing all of that. After I threw myself at him last night and he turned me down, he still finds it inside himself to take care of Ellie and me. My neck heats up and I feel myself blushing just thinking about Liam. *How will I ever stay in the friend zone with him?* If Ellie notices, she doesn't say anything. She busies herself making me a plate much like the one I had the first time we shared a meal.

"Thank you so much." I didn't realize how hungry I was and we eat in relative silence. I pop the lid off my coffee and reheat it in the microwave. Then I rinse my plate and load it in the dishwasher. "I have to make a call. Can I meet you out front in a bit?"

"Sounds perfect." Ellie radiates kindness and I get the sense that even if she wanted to judge me for last night, she couldn't. She only sees the good in people.

Once I'm upstairs I FaceTime Claire. She answers almost immediately, and I fill her in on the events of the previous night. I make every effort to keep her on the edge of her seat.

"Wow, I might actually like this guy, now," Claire ponders. "He had every opportunity to do you last night and he said *no*? Do you think he finds you attractive?"

"Well, when we were standing close together, I got that impression if you catch my drift," I mutter. "My confidence was in the toilet this morning, but then..." I trail off, teasing her.

"*What?!*" she screeches. "Sophie Lynn, you tell me right now."

I cave and fill her in on Liam showing up at my door this morning making me swoon. If he was trying to get me to stop wanting him, he failed. Now I want him more.

Claire physically takes her hand and pushes her mouth closed. "Wow. That's pretty intense. But hold on. He's *never* had a serious relationship? Isn't he like forty? What does that tell you?" She looks doubtful and she's not wrong. I suspect it's because of the teenage accident but since Liam didn't tell me about it himself,

I feel funny telling Claire.

"Maybe he hasn't met anyone worth settling down with," I shake my head helplessly.

"I'm going to Google him, Sophie. You should have *already*," she scolds with a warning look.

"Okay, okay. Let me know what you find out." I know if I don't agree to it, she won't let it go. Like I said before, Claire means well but she can be very pushy. "I just wanted you to know I am alive but I am supposed to be planting flowers with Ellie now, so I am going to call you later."

I hang up and I jog down the stairs to meet Ellie outside. Sunshine and girl time with Ellie is just what I need.

Chapter Twenty-Six

Liam

After I take Ellie to the garden center, I decide to put Lucy down for a morning nap and make myself scarce. As much as I would like to help and be around Sophie, I know it's best if I stare out the window at her instead. I think I am going to really have to work hard at staying just friends with her. I haven't ever been this enticed by a woman before. I am sure Doc would say that's because I haven't let myself, but I don't think that's true either. I like to think after all this time, I would have been open to a relationship with the right person.

Is Sophie the right person? I don't know. I can't imagine she is ready to be in a relationship with anyone if she's getting divorced. The sexual tension is obvious, neither one of us can stop looking at each other when we're together. I know Ellie must see it, but she hasn't said anything to me—which is very unlike her. I am sure my friends see it too or Miles wouldn't accuse me of being a cockblock. Speaking of Miles, the very fact that that's what he called me makes me angry. Just what was he planning to do after a night with Sophie?

My heart twinges as I think about someone hurting her. I wasn't prepared for the emotions I felt last night, standing in front of our houses. Sophie couldn't stop touching me. She was running her hands up and down my forearms, touching my chest. When she pulled my neck down and pressed her forehead to mine, I thought I was done. I don't even know who I am anymore because

Old Liam would've flung her over my shoulder and carried her to bed, but all I could think about was how she isn't in the right headspace to go to bed with me. For one, she was totally wasted. I don't even know if she'd have been that forward with me if she wasn't. And two, I suspect she couldn't be ready for anything serious with anyone else given that she's going through a painful divorce.

Now that I'm home and reflecting in the quiet, I realize how much I don't know about Sophie. I need to keep my distance, so I don't move us out of the friend zone, but I also feel an overwhelming desire to protect her. I pick up my phone and look at the muted Perry Street Boys text thread. There are several missed messages that I know I need to respond to.

> **Danny: Not cool, Liam.**

> **Jack: I wonder if they're still in bed.**

> **Miles: Liam, you are such a dick.**

> **Danny: Taking Sophie home when you knew Miles wanted her is low even for you, Liam.**

> **Jack: I don't know, I saw how she was looking at Liam. Maybe Sophie made her choice.**

> **Miles: Shut up Jack.**

I groan. I think about how to word this delicately.

Me: Yo. Lay off. I didn't take her to bed. I took her to her house. She had too much to drink.

Miles: Oh, so you took her to her bed.

Me: No. I didn't go to bed with Sophie, Miles, and neither should you.

Miles: And just why the fuck not, Liam? You want her? Just say the word and I'll back off.

Me: Sophie and I are friends.

Miles: Okay then.

Me: No. Not okay. She's just been through a nasty divorce. You remember what that's like. And it's only been a couple of weeks for her. Be her friend.

It takes Miles a few minutes to answer and no one else says anything either, making me think they know I'm right.

Miles: Fair enough. I'm sorry I called you a cockblock.

Me: All good, buddy. Hey, Melanie's available now. LOL

Miles: Sloppy seconds ain't my style.

Danny: Can you assholes continue this love fest in a private text? My phone won't stop vibrating.

I decide not to answer after that, but I do feel better. I think the Miles issue is over for the foreseeable future.

I text Sophie late in the afternoon and we meet out front to walk to the yoga class. Once again, her radiance leaves me momentarily speechless. She's wearing hot pink workout leggings and a blue sports bra looking top that shows a peek of her midriff. Her hair is piled up on her head and there's that lip gloss again, driving me wild. She greets me with a big smile. "Ready?" She asks, falling into step beside me.

"I guess so," I admit. "I hope flow yoga is easier than hot yoga." I laugh.

She shakes her head vigorously. "Oh, it is. I promise you'll be fine. You may even relieve some stress." She elbows me teasingly.

Being with Sophie is so easy, I want to be with her all the time. I can't help but notice how close she is walking to me, like she did the other night. Our knuckles brush against each other, and I am remembering what it was like to hold her hand. My stomach flutters at the memory of our almost-kiss and my dick moves. I need to distract myself. I take a small step to my right and if Sophie notices, she doesn't react. I already miss the closeness, but I need to keep my head in the game.

I force my mind out of the gutter. *Think about your grandma. Now is not the time.* I stifle a cough and catch Sophie looking at me curiously.

"So...are you happy to be living in Cape May?" I blurt. That came out weird.

She raises her eyebrows, and I am sure she's thinking that I am a moron. "Under the circumstances, not really," she admits. "I feel like I'm having to start my whole life over again. But I do love it here. I came here every summer weekend as a kid." She must feel the spring chill because she wraps her arms around herself.

I raise my eyebrows in surprise. "Oh, really? Did you have a house here?"

"I did. It was my grandparents' house on Jackson Street. We used to stay there when we visited." She seems wistful with a faraway look in her eyes. "My parents made friends with some locals and other out-of-towners and we kids would play on the beach until sunset. Then when my mom died, we stopped coming."

Her revelation throws me off balance. "Oh, Sophie, I'm so sorry." I want to touch her, god I want to touch her, but I don't. "I didn't know your mom died."

"It's okay." She offers me a grim smile. "It was a long time ago." Her voice drifts off. We stop to wait for a walk signal as we approach the next block.

"What happened to the house?" I ask, genuinely curious whether a developer knocked it down and built two in its place.

"My grandparents sold it. They were getting old and couldn't manage the upkeep. And it was just too painful for my dad to come visit here anymore. He never saw the house again before it was sold. It's still there though." Sophie looks sorrowful, but I am sure that this conversation about her past isn't easy.

"I know that feeling. My house is the one I grew up in, and my sister Leah's imprint is on everything. When she died, I started going through her things, but it was so hard for me. My parents went back to Florida, and I got tired of crying every time I looked at her stuff. So now I just ignore it and leave it stacked in my living room taking up space. That may be just as bad." I smirk.

"Maybe one day I could go through it with you. I think it helps when you have a team. That's how my brother Simon and I went through the mementos in our house." She touches my bicep, and I immediately feel heat.

We share a tentative smile as we approach the yoga studio.

"I'd really like that," I tell her, and I mean it.

❦

This yoga class is much better. The room is dim and cool, but not too cool. The moves are slow and sequential. I feel deeply relaxed when it's finished, and ready for bed. Being this close to Sophie is a peculiar feeling. I feel bonded to her in a way I cannot explain. I feel as if I have known her my entire life, yet, I don't even know what hand she writes with. I know the more time I spend with her, the harder it's going to be to keep my hands to myself.

We walk up to the desk together and the front desk girl is the same, though someone else taught the class, a guy named Russ. He smiles at us.

"Did you enjoy the class?" he asks, looking at Sophie. I instantly feel annoyed by the attention he's giving her. *Check your jealousy, bro.*

I am standing behind her and box her in by putting my right hand on the counter. It's the only way to tell Russ to back the fuck off but still keep my hands to myself. Sophie looks up at me with a curious expression, but her eyes are twinkling.

Here I go again with the mixed signals. I can't help myself though, Sophie feels like she belongs to me.

"I loved it," Sophie smiles. "I am so relaxed, I could fall right into bed."

I wish she could fall right into my bed.

I clear my throat loudly. "Yeah. I liked it too. Is it always at this time?" I ask, shooting Russ a warning look.

"It is." He laughs nervously. "It's not always me who teaches it though."

"These are the class packages." The desk girl shows us a laminated flier with various tiers of class packages.

Sophie and I agree on a ten-class package each and sign up. When we're walking home, she gives me a nudge. "What the hell was that, Harper?" She grins.

"What?" I ask her, playing dumb even though I know exactly what she's talking about.

"I thought we're just friends? So why did you try to scare away Yoga Man?" She is being direct but smiling at me, so she can't be too annoyed.

"Yoga man?" I raise my eyebrows and avoid her question.

"I give everyone nicknames." She laughs and takes a sip of her water, side-eyeing me.

"What is my nickname?" I narrow my eyes at her and smirk.

"Hunkle Liam." She says it so fast I know she didn't even have to think about it. "You know...like you're an uncle, but you're also a hunk?" She barks out a genuine hearty laugh and covers her mouth.

I have no choice but to laugh with her and roll my eyes. I am so far gone for this girl.

ଔ

The next few weeks are considerably quiet. I work for Danny every day, and I've picked up two side projects for summer homeowners. I drop Lucy off each morning to Sophie and Ellie. I am so intrigued by Sophie's every move, but I must put some distance between us if I'm going to behave myself and keep things friendly. The only exception has been our weekly yoga date that's not a date. We meet out front, walk up to the yoga studio, and walk back, sometimes stopping for a smoothie. I allow myself to enjoy these moments with her, and she seems to enjoy them too.

I am still seeing Doc every week. I kind of let him in on the Sophie stuff. He's proud of me for respecting boundaries and being a gentleman. Such an old dude. I can feel myself changing for the better. Comfortable in my role as a parent now, I devote all my free time to Lucy. I am working hard on myself so that maybe, when Sophie is ready, I will be too. I feel like she has lived here forever, but it's only been eight weeks. Now, Memorial Day weekend is approaching, and it will be the official start of summer.

I know how busy that time of year gets for me with work, and this is the first summer that I'm parenting Lucy on my own. It's important for me to stay steady, but all I can think about is that if I let myself, I'd be falling.

Chapter Twenty-Seven

Sophie

The end of May is approaching, and I have started to find my groove here in Cape May. I watch Lucy every day for Liam, most days Ellie helps out too. He has tried to pay me, but I haven't cashed any of his checks. I love spending time with Lucy and in many ways, I think she is helping me feel like I can move forward. Lucy may not be mine, but the bond we've developed has healed the gaping hole in my heart left there by years of infertility.

Liam works every day and only joins us for dinner a couple of nights a week but being with him is easy. Sunday yoga is the highlight of my week because when I am with Liam, I feel like it's a different time in my life, before I was calloused with heartbreak. Liam makes me feel free from the burden of past hurts. I don't tell him much about James or my divorce because he doesn't ask, and it's not exactly an easy thing to bring up out of thin air. It's almost like I get to be someone else entirely.

A week ago, James called to tell me that the house is officially listed and the realtor thinks it will go fast. This should have made me happy but as soon as I hung up the phone I had a good cry. I haven't cried over it in weeks.

I still haven't thought about whether I want to open a practice of my own or if I just want to be Lucy's nanny forever. I know that can't really happen because eventually my money will dry up, but a girl can dream.

I keep seeing Dr. Stevens who tells me not to rush healing.

This is something I know, obviously, however, I can't help but push myself. My attraction to Liam grows every time I spend any amount of time with him, but lately, it seems like he's avoiding seeing me at all. I find myself desperately looking for a reason to text him or see him more beyond the usual drop-off and pick-up.

I feel ready to move on, but now I worry that the moment has passed for us. As time goes on, I am getting impatient. I have never been good at sitting still but the more time that passes without being able to move on to something new, the more antsy I am. I'm trying to tell myself that Liam is giving me time to heal from my divorce and that he'll be there when I'm really ready, but I'm still in a funk.

Today, Liam is trying to bring me out of it. It's the Sunday of Memorial Day weekend and the town is buzzing with summer excitement. There are tourists everywhere, and now that I'm kind of a local, it's really annoying me. Our evening yoga class relaxed me enough but as soon as I step back out onto the street, I feel grumpy again.

I huff angrily at having to wait to cross out onto the sidewalk.

"What's with you, Soph?" Liam bumps his shoulder into mine. "You're crabby." He gives me a lazy smile that makes my heart do somersaults.

"I'm just cranky, I guess. I'm stuck. I'm not moving forward." I pout. "I'm tired of healing. I want to *be healed*."

"Come on, you know as well as anyone that takes time, Sophie." Liam touches my arm. Then he gestures ahead. "Come on, I'll get you a smoothie." We fall into step together and once we're outside the smoothie place, he stops. The line is long. I roll my eyes.

"Look, why don't you save this bench for us, and I'll go in and get the smoothies," he says.

"Okay." I plop down on the green metal bench directly behind me and put my yoga mat next to me so no one thinks they can join me.

"Your usual Pink Pitaya?" he asks with a grin.

"Don't act like you know me," I pout with a scowl.

Liam just smiles and shakes his head, waiting for confirmation.

I let out an exasperated sigh. "Yes, please," I mumble.

Amidst my people watching, an entire wedding party comes walking down the street with the bride and groom, making my bad mood worse. The bride and groom look to be in their late twenties, and they are elated. The wedding party follows along behind them with their respective dates and the photographers are catching candid shots. As bad luck would have it, I'm scanning the happy faces in the group just in time to see one so familiar to me, I would recognize it anywhere.

James.

In Cape May.

He isn't dressed like the groomsmen. He's wearing a pair of tan chinos and a pale blue button down with an open collar. And those damn blue light glasses he thinks make him look smart. But he looks good.

I'm still sweaty from yoga and walking. I imagine my wild hair is a complete disaster.

On his arm is none other than Brittany, in a pale peach chiffon dress that matches the bridesmaids, with an empire waist that accentuates her newly swollen belly. My heart catches in my throat.

I make every effort to look away but it's too late. James sees me, and he stops right in front of me. Brittany keeps walking until she realizes he stopped and then she comes marching back over.

"Sophie," he says. His voice comes out like the water went down the wrong pipe and he's trying to find it again.

I slowly stand and meet his remorseful eyes. Brittany is by his side now and grasps his arm. "Hi," I say, uncertainly.

James doesn't say anything else, but he doesn't take his eyes off me. I'll admit, that feels kind of good. Brittany obnoxiously clears her throat and rubs her belly. James looks down at her and says, "You go on ahead with the wedding party. I'll catch up." She looks up at him as if she wants to argue but he gives her a look that says *please*, and she huffs away.

"H-how are you?" he asks, reaching for me. A hug feels superficial at this point, so I don't reach in return. His hand grazes my arm and he lets it fall. I notice when he touches me that I don't feel anything. It's nothing like when Liam touches me. There is no electricity, just too much pain.

"I'm okay." I shrug. "Good, actually." I force a smile. I can't let him see what this is doing to me. "What are you doing here?" I ask, remembering how when I brought him here, he thought it was nothing special.

"Brittany's friend from college got married today. She's in the wedding party." James looks over my shoulder, and I know he's looking for Brittany. She must catch his eye because a moment later, she's back at his side.

I nod in understanding just as Liam comes out of the shop. I can feel his presence before he's even at my side. Thank god for Liam because at the exact moment he hands me my smoothie, I catch a glimpse of a sparkling engagement ring on Brittany's finger. My jaw drops. James catches on to what I have noticed. Liam is standing next to me, trying to figure out what it is that he just stepped into. He moves closer and I lean into him for support.

Liam holds out his hand to James and says, "Hey, I'm Liam."

James, a few inches shorter and several pounds lighter than Liam, seems to have a realization of his own and grips Liam's hand in return.

Is that jealousy I am detecting?

"James." Then, gesturing to his fianceé, he says, "This is Brittany."

I am still trying to find my voice, and when it comes out it sounds like an incredulous sob. "You're engaged? Our divorce isn't even final." I feel myself becoming hysterical. My throat tightens and my sweaty hands are trembling with rage.

Liam puts his arm around me to steady me. He kisses the side of my head and rubs my back, but he doesn't speak. We both wait for James to respond.

"Well, I mean, Brittany's parents were really upset about a baby out of wedlock." James fumbles his words. He looks at his feet, then at Brittany, then finally back at me. He never once looks at Liam. Liam tenses beside me. He must be seething on my behalf.

"Out of *fucking* wedlock? Do her parents know what a trampy little homewrecker she is? That you were very much *in wedlock* with someone else when you knocked her the fuck up?" I sputter. I am unhinged, sucking in rapid, angry breaths. I take a step closer to Brittany and narrow my eyes. I feel Liam's hand on the small of my back, a warning to pull back. "You are a nasty human being to steal someone else's husband." I spat at her and then back to James. "You are a disgrace of a man." Neither one of them can meet my eye. "I wish you the best. You deserve each other," I snarl and stomp away.

I am around the corner, in an alleyway, leaning against a cool brick wall and heaving huge uncontrollable sobs when Liam finds me with my yoga mat tucked under his arm. He doesn't say anything, but he pulls me into a hug that would rival Simon's and lets me cry. I'm not sure how long we stay there. When my sobs turn to hiccups, I pull back and glance up at Liam, ashamed of my outburst, but he is only looking at me with compassion.

Liam takes his big, calloused thumb and wipes the tears off my face. He puts his hands on either side of my face and kisses my forehead, then wraps me in another tight hug. "Can I take you somewhere?" he whispers. I nod, burrowing further into his chest.

❧

Fifteen minutes and an Uber ride later, Liam and I are at Sunset Beach. The sun is beginning to set and there are still a few beach dwellers watching the water ripple at the shoreline. Children at the water's edge are scouring the sand for diamonds like I used to do. A couple of catamarans sail in the distance.

My heart contracts with nostalgia as we take a seat on an empty bench on the high sand.

"I used to come here a lot when I was a kid. Leah loved finding Cape May diamonds," Liam says, interrupting my memories. "When she died, I brought Lucy here nearly every day for a month. I let her crawl around while I sat here and cried." He exhales and looks over at me. My tears are falling again. Liam reaches for my hand and squeezes. "Do you want to talk about it?"

I sniffle and shrug, but I don't drop his hand. "James and I were married for thirteen years. We were steady, or so I thought. Maybe not madly in love but steady, comfortable. We waited a while to try to start a family—both of us wanted to get our careers established first. But turns out, I can't get pregnant on my own, and even with help, I miscarried. I couldn't have a baby in the seven years that we tried. I was grappling with never getting to be a mom. We weren't in a great place, but I always thought we'd get through it, you know?" I look at Liam and wipe my eyes.

Liam nods and squeezes my hand again, urging me to keep going.

"Then on my thirty-eighth birthday, I found him in our bed with her. She is his TA." I hold back another sob.

"And on your birthday? Jesus, Sophie," Liam mutters. "I'm so sorry."

I hiccup. "Yeah, and I thought maybe I would forgive him. He said it was a one-time thing, and he made a mistake. He seemed *really* remorseful. I took about a week to think about it. I mean, I'm a therapist. I help people through these kinds of things, you know?" I pause as the tears start flowing again. "But then she turned up pregnant. Can you believe she's pregnant?" I wail. "I couldn't get pregnant if I was standing on my head, and she swept right in and stole my life."

"Christ," Liam says, voice barely above a whisper.

My tears begin falling aggressively again, as he wraps his arms around me. I feel him kiss the top of my head.

"That engagement ring put me over the edge. I was doing okay, you know? And now I feel like I went backward." I sit up and wipe my eyes, Liam turns to look at me and takes my hands in his.

"You didn't go backward, Soph. You told them off in front of a street full of vacationers. It was awesome." He smirks.

I manage a small laugh and then I shrug. "I guess now I have closure."

Liam brushes a tear from my face and then lets his thumb linger over my bottom lip, rubbing soft circles with it. He looks me in the eyes and then I feel it. The buzz, the tingle, the desire, whatever you want to call it, rumbling in my belly. I know I am vulnerable and exposed right now. Liam can see all my open wounds, and he's still sitting here. I want nothing more than to kiss him. Before he moves his thumb away, I nuzzle my face on his hand and kiss it. It's such an intimate moment that it allows me to fully drop my guard.

"Anyone who would hurt you like that doesn't deserve you, Sophie. You are...everything," he rasps, barely above a whisper.

Liam leans in and I meet him there. Our lips brush lightly against each other at first, but his lips are soft and warm, and I open for him. I can feel the gentle tickle of his breath beneath my nose. He brings his hand to the back of my neck and pulls me closer, deepening our kiss. He's teasing me with his tongue, softly biting my lower lip, as our foreheads press together in hunger.

The familiar deep desire starts to blossom in my belly when Liam abruptly pulls away. He looks at me, bereft, and runs his hands through his hair. "I'm sorry, Sophie. I should not have done that when you're so upset. I was totally out of line." He puts his elbows on his knees and his head in his hands.

I reach out and touch his back, tickling his shoulder blade with my fingertips. "It's okay, Liam. I have been wanting to do that for a long time." Liam sits up and looks at me with longing.

He cups my cheek, and I lean into it. Then he moves in and plants another soft kiss on my lips that is entirely too short-lived. He looks me in the eyes, and I realize his own eyes are glassy. "I have wanted it too. But, I don't know how to do this, Sophie. I told you I have never been serious with anyone before. And seeing the hurt on your face tonight made me hurt. I never want to be responsible for making you cry like that." He pauses and I feel a letdown even though he hasn't said anything bad yet. "You're becoming my best friend. Let's just take things slowly, okay?"

I swallow another hard lump that forms in my throat. *This isn't rejection.* I tell myself. *Liam just saw you ugly cry and he still kissed you.* I nod and reach for his hand. He plants one more soft kiss on my wanting mouth and stands to go.

"Come on, let's go home."

Chapter Twenty-Eight

Liam

As soon as Sophie and I get back from the beach, I sense something is off. She was quiet and pensive on the Uber ride back and even though we held hands, she barely looked my way. When we get out of the car, it's noticeably cooler outside and starting to drizzle. I walk up the steps with her to get Lucy from inside, but I notice that she keeps her distance. *Maybe she doesn't want Ellie to know anything happened*, I try to reassure myself.

Ellie meets us at the front door with a freshly bathed Lucy in her PJs. "It's a little late for her. I didn't know if you wanted me to put her to sleep or not," she says, handing Lucy to me. She rests her head on my shoulder, my sign to get her home, but I don't want to leave Sophie.

Ellie turns her attention to Sophie, her brows knit together and a curious look of concern on her face. "Did you want to have some tea with me, Sophie dear?" She tilts her head slightly, offering Sophie a faint smile.

Sophie shifts uncomfortably. She *looks* like she's been crying—her cheeks are rosy and her eyelids are pink and a little puffy. I'm sure Ellie can see it too. "No, thanks, Ellie. If you don't mind, I think I'm going to just go up to bed." She feigns a yawn. "That yoga class will put you right to sleep."

"Okay, yes," Ellie says softly. She meets my gaze as Sophie starts for the stairs. "Rest up. Tomorrow is Memorial Day!" She clasps her hands together. "Shall we invite some people over for a barbecue?"

Sophie nods half-heartedly. "Sure, whatever you want." She tries to smile but I can tell she just wants to get out of here. I'm trying not to take it personally. "Goodnight, everyone," she says as she retreats up the steps.

When we hear Sophie's door close, Ellie whacks my forearm. "What did you do?" she scolds in a hushed voice.

I roll my eyes and mimic her volume so Sophie doesn't hear us. "What makes you think I did something? I am not a bad guy, Ellie."

"I'm sorry. It's just... I see those moon eyes you have for that girl. Can't say I've ever seen you look at *Melanie* like that," Ellie murmurs.

I ignore that last remark and give Ellie a little bit of the information I know she's craving. "When we got out of yoga, we ran into James." This time I really whisper so Sophie can't hear me.

Ellie picks up what I'm putting down and whispers back, "James?! Ex-husband James?"

My jaw ticks remembering that guy and his shamefaced expression. I shake my head in disgust. "It wasn't good. I think Sophie is exhausted from it." *At least that's what I'm telling myself.* I raise my voice to a normal level, so Sophie doesn't pick up that we've been down here whispering. "Well, I'll see you tomorrow. I'll help grill whatever it is we cook." Lucy is falling asleep on my shoulder. "Say, night night, Lucy." Lucy flaps her hand in a sleepy wave and we're out the door.

❧

Luckily, Lucy goes right to bed for me. I'm sitting out on my deck, wishing I could still look over the fence and see what Sophie is up to, but now her bedroom is on the other side of Ellie's house. I throw the ball for Maggie and then glance down at my phone. No messages. My friends have been quiet this week, and I was hoping to see a message from Sophie but nothing is there. I can't hold back anymore, so I decide to text her.

> **Me: I have been wanting to do that basically since you got here.**

It takes her a minute and I think maybe she's sleeping but then my phone buzzes in my hand.

Sophie: :)

I'm a little thrown. She has been flirting with me since we've established a little friendship. She came onto me after she'd been drinking, and I was a gentleman and resisted. Now I just get a smiley face? After I held her while she got snot and tears all over my shirt? I've been practicing being more upfront with Doc and I know if I don't talk about it, it's going to eat at me. I need to make sure she's okay.

> **Me: Sophie, are you ok?**

Sophie: I'm good.

Okay. What is going on here? I know people say you can't tell tone from text but this feels off.

> **Me: Come on, don't go cold on me, Soph. I thought you wanted this too.**

This time several more minutes pass. Maggie is nudging me with her ball. I pry it out of her mouth and throw it far to buy myself some more alone time. I am pacing the deck and running my fingers through my hair. I probably fucked this up somehow already. Finally, after four minutes that felt like forty, my phone buzzes.

> **Sophie: I did. I do. I am just emotionally exhausted tonight. I'm sorry.**

I sigh. Now I feel like I was insensitive, so I don't push anymore.

> **Me: I'm sorry. Sleep well.**

Then I call Maggie inside and decide to go to bed myself. I don't sleep though. I toss and turn, thinking about Cara, Melanie, and Sophie, comparing my feelings for them all and trying to figure out which ones are real.

C33

Around noon the next day, I venture over to Ellie's house and find her and Sophie sitting at the kitchen table. Lucy reaches for Sophie with a gleeful squeal, so I hand her over and we are all smiling down at Lucy.

"I think she's going to walk soon," I tell them, trying to keep the subject light. "She's been pulling herself up more.. Isn't fourteen months about the time?"

"I think as long as she walks before eighteen months. Babies do things at all different times. She's doing great." Sophie gives Lucy a motherly squeeze and I feel my chest contract.

"So what are you girls up to on this Memorial Day?" I ask. "Should we get some food to cook tonight?"

We're interrupted by a knock at the front door. We all look at each other to see if anyone knows who it might be. Sophie looks nervous and I am nervous for her. *Does James know where she is? Would he come here?* She stands and tells Ellie that she'll get the door and hands Lucy to her. I follow behind her in case it is James. I put my hand on her lower back, so she knows I'm here for her. She doesn't shake it off, so that's a good sign. The nervousness in her face and body language shows me she is expecting the worst. There is a second knock and then voices talking to each other from behind the door.

I reach for the handle and swing it open and Sophie immediately relaxes. "Claire!" she screams.

"Sophie!" Claire throws her arms around her friend and they rock back and forth. There is a guy standing behind Claire who I assume is her husband. He's about my height, with sandy brown hair and light brown eyes. Like me, he has a scruffy beard.

I hold out my hand for him to shake. "Liam," I introduce myself.

"I'm Derek, hi." He shakes my hand. His grip is firm, unlike James' who was clearly trying to give a firm handshake last night and failed miserably.

"Come on in," I open the door wider.

Now Ellie is making her way with Lucy into the foyer from the kitchen just as Sophie is saying, "This is such a surprise! I didn't know you were coming. This is Liam, and Ellie—it's her house—and sweet baby Lucy."

Claire squeezes Sophie again and then pulls away. "We can't stay more than one night but I remembered you mentioning it and I wanted to surprise you. Are you surprised?"

Sophie takes her best friend's hands and pulls backward to get a look at her. "Of course!" Then she moves to hug Derek. "Hi, D!" She squeezes him tightly. I like getting to see who Sophie is and meeting her people. It gives me a glimpse of the happy side of her. "We were just planning a barbecue for tonight. You have to stay."

"Of course!" Ellie interrupts. "You can stay in the peach room. We would love to have you." Ellie is beaming. I know she is so happy to have her house filled with life.

We move back into the kitchen and Ellie fixes us all coffee. I urge Sophie to take Claire and Derek out and show them around. Ellie and I can handle the meal. I make sure to text the Perry Street Boys and, I guess, Melanie to join us for dinner. I don't know that everyone will come since it's a bit last minute, but I see how happy Ellie is with people around. Danny and Kristen will bring their three kids. Jack and Steph will probably bring their two as well. It'll be a nice Memorial Day.

While Ellie is showing Claire and Derek their room for the evening, I grab Sophie for a minute alone. We're standing face to face in the corner of the kitchen, while Lucy is toddling around at our feet. I am rubbing Sophie's arms, and I brush her cheek, willing her to look me in the eyes. "Sophie," I say, my voice low. "Are you okay?" She hasn't looked at me any differently this morning, but she hasn't given me an indication that our kisses last night were as earth-shattering for her as they were for me.

She meets my eyes and simply nods. She doesn't pull away from me, but I feel exposed, like I have let her in and now she could hurt me. I don't like it at all. "Are we okay?" I don't move my hand away from her cheek and now she nuzzles it, giving me a little hope.

I lean in to kiss her just as we hear Ellie coming back toward the kitchen. Sophie jumps away from me like I have the plague. She shoots me an apologetic look but I can't help feeling rejected.

Ellie looks back and forth between us as if she knows she interrupted something. Then she reaches down to pick up Lucy. "Sophie, Claire said to tell you she is ready when you are." Ellie's eyes sparkle, crinkling slightly at the corners. "I'm just so excited. Liam, shall we make a grocery list?"

A few minutes later, Sophie, Claire, and Derek are gone. Ellie and I make the grocery list. I decide to go to the store alone so that I can pay for it all and so that Ellie and Lucy don't have to fight the crowds with me. We settle on a 4 p.m. party time and I send a text to Sophie letting her know. She responds with nothing more than a simple "okay" and my heart sinks. It doesn't even feel like we're friends now. We went from feeling like good friends, to almost lovers, and now what? Acquaintances? Neighbors? I am moping around the produce section when someone taps me on the shoulder.

"Hey, stranger." It's Melanie, and she's smiling like she's happy to see me.

It's been a few weeks and the air between us feels clearer. I try to manage a smile, but it feels forced. "Hey there. You going to make it over for dinner?" I ask, throwing some zucchini and peppers in my cart.

She nods, gesturing to a carton of strawberries she is holding. "I am. I'm going to make strawberry shortcake." She puts the strawberries in her basket and then catches my arm. "Thanks for inviting me, Liam. I don't want things to be weird with us."

I shrug. "Mel, we're friends. We'll always be friends." I reach to give her a hug, mostly because I feel like I need one.

When she pulls away, she meets my gaze and hesitates. "Is... Sophie going to be there?" She winces as she asks, and I wonder if it's because she suspects something is happening between Sophie and me.

I nod. "She is. Her best friend and her husband are down from Pennsylvania. They surprised her this morning." Best to avoid any indication that I have any sort of feelings for Sophie.

Melanie smiles. "Oh, that's great! Well, I think all the guys are coming. Danny and Kristen have to stop by his parents' house first but then they are coming." As she fills me in, I realize I haven't even looked at the group text. I've only been checking every five minutes to see if I have a message from Sophie.

"Would you like to help me shop?" I ask Melanie. I am trying to be friendly, break the ice, but I also need the distraction. I can't keep obsessing over what Sophie is doing all day. My heart hasn't left my throat since we were interrupted in the kitchen.

But Melanie declines. "I really should get home and start making this cake," She gives me half of a regretful smile. "I'll see you in a couple of hours." And then she's gone, and I'm left alone with my intrusive thoughts telling me just how not good enough I am for Sophie.

Chapter Twenty-Nine

Sophie

Having Claire here has improved my mood dramatically. It's been a challenge jumping from an old life to a new life and even though I really like everyone I have met here. Claire and Derek are my people. They are in my corner. They know me well and they love me hard.

"I am so surprised to see you," I say as we plop down on a beach blanket and settle in to relax.

"It was all Claire's idea," Derek grins. "She misses you."

Claire leans into my shoulder and rests her head against mine. "I do," she says, wrapping me into a squeeze.

I am surprised to feel the sting of tears, once again. I don't know why it surprises me so much because all I have been doing is crying lately. After I left Liam last night, I cried myself to sleep. I am sure he is taking my cold shoulder personally, and I feel awful about that.

I loved kissing him. I have been wanting to since the day I met him. His scratchy beard on my lips was everything I imagined and so much more. But it's complicated, and seeing James and Brittany—seeing that ring on her finger—it wrecked me. I can't just come here, pretend everything's fine, and this is my life now. *James* was my life. I really saw us having a family and growing old together. To see him planning to do that with someone else all but destroyed me. I need to explain this to Liam so he doesn't take offense to my mood swings. I loved kissing him, but I'm scared.

What if he dumps me like he dumped Melanie? I can't take another bruise to my heart. When I meet Claire's gaze, she is concerned.

"Sophie, what's wrong?" She squeezes me tighter.

"Nothing," I shrug. "Everything." I throw myself back on the blanket, thankful for the overcast sky. "I don't know where to start."

Reading the room, Derek stands up. "I'm going to go feel the water," he says awkwardly. No one answers him.

Claire lays back next to me and leans on her elbow facing me. "Just start."

I take a deep breath and tell her about my weekly yoga, how much I enjoy Liam's company, and how, in many ways, he and Lucy are bringing me back to life. I tell her how we get a smoothie after each yoga class, using the time to really get to know each other. Then I tell her about James and Brittany and how Liam handled my tears last night with such gentle compassion. And that I might be falling in love with him. Then I shake my head because that sounds crazy to be falling in love with someone else so soon. Claire listens intently the whole time and when I finish, I realize I have been crying yet again. I lay back with my hands behind my head and sniffle.

"James sure is a douche canoe," she says, looking at me with complete seriousness. We both explode into a fit of laughter just as Derek is walking back up toward us.

"Is it safe to come back?" He treads lightly in the gentle way that Derek does. I would have said this about James, even three months ago, but Derek really is an awesome husband. He knows exactly what Claire needs and by extension, her best friend too.

We sit up and I motion for him to come back, but Claire isn't finished discussing. "So, do you think Liam is as into you as you are into him?" she asks. "He certainly has shown you a lot of care these past few weeks."

"That guy that was at Ellie's?" Derek interrupts.

I sniffle and nod my head.

"That guy is in deep, man," Derek makes a face that says,

"Hello, are you blind?"

Claire juts her thumb in Derek's direction. "There you have it, a real man's opinion."

"You think so?" I ask, feeling hopeful. I wasn't super warm to Liam all morning. What if I already ruined things?

"Oh yeah. He's head over heels," Derek says, nodding. "He couldn't stop looking at you the entire time we drank our coffee."

I hug my knees to my chest, mulling this over. Maybe I didn't ruin it after all. Maybe I am the girl that Liam can see himself settling down with. "He's got baggage though," I tell them, doubtfully.

"Whatever it is, it's not worrying him. Trust me." Derek says emphatically.

"He does have baggage though. You know, the accident." Claire nudges me. "I Googled him like I told you I would." She looks proud of herself. I ignore it.

"He definitely keeps himself guarded, but he's let me see some glimpses. I know he's a good guy." I bat at a tear threatening to fall again. "But is it too soon?" I ask, worried they will judge me for wanting someone other than my ex-husband.

Claire makes an incredulous face. "Too soon? Was it too soon for James to get engaged?" She whips her red hair over her shoulder. "Absolutely not, girl. You go get yours."

I don't say anything else for a few moments and we sit together looking at the waves crashing. I'm lost in thoughts of Liam and his lingering lips.

Claire nudges me. "Can we go for a dip?"

And just like we did during that early April weekend visit, we charge for the icy waves.

❧

Ellie's barbecue is in full swing. Guests are settling on her back deck enjoying a summer breeze cocktail that Claire insisted we make as our contribution. The older kids are playing with Lucy in the grass, trying to get her to walk, Liam is grilling down on the patio and Maggie is sitting at his side waiting for him to drop a hot dog. It feels like home. I walk out onto the deck with a tray of glasses and another pitcher of drinks that Claire prepared. I am sure they're dangerous because they're pink and full of fruit, vodka, and I'm not sure what else.

Sitting around the table on the deck are Ellie, Dr. Stevens (I still can't call him Robert), Claire, Derek, Steph, and Jack. Hanging on the patio and keeping an eye on their kids are Danny and Kristen. Miles and Melanie are there too, and I think I sense a bit of flirtation between them that fills me with relief. The conversation is flowing easily, and everyone is enjoying the appetizers Ellie made and the light breeze. Dr. Stevens is talking to us about retiring this year, and I am definitely not mistaken when I catch him giving Ellie a few sidelong glances. Ellie doesn't let on to anything. I know they are great friends, but I may be detecting a little more.

I'm certain no one in this group besides Liam and I, and now Claire and Derek know about our kiss last night, and I have purposely been steering clear of Liam so as not to let on to anything. Claire thinks all anyone has to do is see us interacting with each other to pick up on how smitten we are. I definitely can't give any clues to anyone until Liam and I have had a chance to figure things out. I don't even know where his head is at. For all I know, he's had enough of my bullshit. There's also the fact that he said he's never been in a serious relationship. Part of me thinks there has got to be more to that, and of course, I want to find out. The other part of me wants to protect my heart and keep anyone away from me that could further fracture it.

I head down the steps and out onto the patio where Liam is moving some burgers from the grill to a plate. He takes a long pull of his water bottle and listens intently to a story Miles is telling. I can't help but notice he isn't drinking again.

I go over to check on Lucy, but I am half listening to the conversation. Out of the corner of my eye, I see Miles sling his arm over Melanie's shoulder. Then I overhear him say, "I guess I'll date Melanie since you wouldn't let me have Sophie."

My neck heats up and I look over at Liam who is very still. He appears to be caught off guard and now I know the best thing I can do is stay over here with the kids and pretend I have heard nothing.

"I guess I'm everyone's second choice then," Melanie snaps, but she doesn't move out of Miles' embrace. That's a relief.

"Sophie and I are just friends," I hear Liam say to Miles and Melanie, and then I feel the color drain from my face. *Just friends.* I'm sure Liam didn't know I was there. He was distracted by the grill, but the comment still stings a little. I try to be inconspicuous as I walk quickly back up the steps to the deck. I catch Claire's eye and hers widen in concern, but she doesn't follow me.

Liam comes barreling after me. He puts the plate of burgers and hot dogs on the table in front of our guests and tells them to help themselves. I rush into the powder room and lock the door. He's right outside the door, knocking softly. "Sophie," he says firmly. "Open the door, Sophie."

I turn on the water so I can muffle his voice and stare at myself in the mirror. I can't cry anymore. The only thing I can do is put on a happy face and try to enjoy myself. For all I know, Liam was playing it cool, just like I was by avoiding him all afternoon. *We both know we're not just friends.* I take a deep breath, splash some cold water on my face, and reach in the pocket of my jean shorts for my guava lip gloss. *I am okay.* I tell myself. But I know deep down, I'm not okay. Far from it. Good thing I have an appointment with Dr. Stevens tomorrow.

I'm about to open the door when I hear Claire approach from the other side. "You know there's an upstairs bathroom, too," she tells Liam, and he must retreat because a minute later she says, "Sophie, it's me. Open up."

I open the door and she wraps me in a hug.

Thank goodness for Claire.

CR

The party wraps up without Liam and I ever saying two words to each other. It's better that way. I parked myself next to Claire and Derek through dinner and dessert. The last of the guests leave by 8:30, Liam goes home to put Lucy to bed, and Ellie and Dr. Stevens go for a walk. Claire, Derek, and I are sitting on the deck, finishing the last of the wine when Liam saunters back over holding a baby monitor.

Derek nudges Claire. "I'm really tired babe. We've got a long drive tomorrow morning. Let's go to bed."

Claire looks at him suspiciously. "Go to bed? It's 9:30." He nudges her and she looks up to see Liam walking up the steps. "You know what? I'm tired too." She stands quickly and turns to give me a big hug. She whispers in my ear, "Wake me if you need me."

I smile and say goodnight. When I turn around, Liam is sitting in a chair at the table, his shoulders slumped and his brows furrowed. He looks forlorn.

"Sophie." The way he says my name is unlike anything I've ever heard. He says it as if it's the last word he will ever speak. "I don't know what you heard that upset you. Whatever it is, I'm sorry."

I sigh and plop down across from him. "You don't owe me any explanations, Liam. After all, we're just friends."

The recognition on his face turns to shame. "Sophie, I just played it cool. I didn't know what to say. We haven't even talked about what is going on here." He waves his hand back and forth between us. Then he leans closer to me, resting his elbows on his knees.

"Nothing's going on, Liam," I say, protecting my heart.

"Sophie. You know that's not true," he rasps. He reaches for my knee and rubs his thumb in tiny circles on the cap.

"Well, I don't know Liam. You said it yourself; you've never

done this before. My life is a mess. Maybe we should just forget it."
I get up out of my chair and walk down to the patio. I am feeling
very exposed having such a candid conversation on the deck.
Liam follows me, seemingly unwilling to let this go. I stop on the
cottage stoop, remembering that I never checked for anything I
may have left here.

"Sophie." He catches my arm from behind me. "Stop running
away from this." He whirls me around to face him and there is
pain in his expression, the cause of which I can't detect. I search
his face for a clue. "I haven't done this before because I haven't
wanted to take a chance, and I didn't think I deserved it. Until I
met you." He steps closer to me. "Sophie, I—"

I hold up my hand. "Stop, Liam. Don't say anything else."

And then his lips are on mine, kissing me hungrily, first my
mouth, then my jawline and my neck. Chills run up and down my
spine when he finds his way back to my mouth. I sigh into his kiss,
opening my lips for him. It's like nothing I have ever felt before.
His hands are moving from the back of my neck, up and down
my sides. His hand finds the hem of my T-shirt, revealing my bare
skin to stroke my hip bone. I wrap my arms around his back and
I do the same, wanting desperately to feel the heat of his skin on
my palms. He groans into my mouth and tries the handle to the
cottage door—it's locked. I take this as a sign and push away from
the kiss.

He looks like I feel—hungry for more. "Liam," I whimper.

He pulls me close again and buries his face in my neck.
"Sophie, we're so much more than friends."

Chapter Thirty

Liam

We're interrupted by Ellie and Doc's voices coming around back. Ellie clears her throat when she sees we're standing outside the guest house.

"Oh, it's just you two left?" she asks, raising her eyebrows in mock surprise.

"I forgot I left stuff in here, but it's locked," Sophie mutters awkwardly.

"Uh-huh." Ellie smirks and digs a house key out of her purse. "Here's the key." She jangles it before tossing it to me. A slight upward curve of her lips telling me she knows exactly what's going on here. She leans in and says, "We're going to get started cleaning up." She and Doc link arms and walk up the steps and into the house.

I hand the key to Sophie, and she unlocks the cottage door and walks in, flicking on the lights. I follow her like a lost puppy, hoping to continue our kiss. She turns to me, questions all over her face. "Liam, this isn't a good idea."

I pull her close so she can feel what she does to me. She wraps her arms around my back and lets me kiss her neck. "What's not a good idea?" I whisper into her soft skin. "You can't deny what's between us."

When she pulls back, her eyes are glistening and uncertain. "I know. I feel it too." She murmurs. "But..." She runs her hands up my back and under my shirt. I'm sweating and my skin instantly cools at her touch.

"Sophie, just let me kiss you." I pull her over to the teal sofa, knowing going to the bed is a bad idea. She sits with her legs up under her and faces me. I touch her face and pull her to me, kissing her softly, and then deeper. She doesn't stop me. She kisses me back. Then she's on my lap, straddling me and running her fingers through my hair. A groan escapes me and she counters it with a moan of her own. I know she can feel my dick hard for her between her warm thighs.

I kiss her neck and graze her skin beneath her shirt. I single-handedly lift my T-shirt over my head in one swift movement. She follows suit and then she leans back for me to kiss her chest and unclasp her bra. She slides her arms out of it, letting it fall to the floor and revealing her perfect breasts. Her nipples peak for me as I take one in my mouth and then the other. Sophie hisses in pleasure and directs my mouth back to hers.

I lift her off me and lay her down on the couch, towering over her with my hands on either side. My heart is hammering in my chest; I can't remember the last time I was this nervous with a woman. Neither of us are speaking but we can't stop looking at each other, searching each other's faces for something. "Sophie, you are so beautiful," I whisper. I lean down and kiss her again, she wraps her legs around my waist, trying to urge us closer together. We're a mess of limbs and lust and I'm reaching for the button of her shorts when she sits up, putting some space between us.

"Liam, this is too much too fast," she says, breathlessly. "I mean, I want it. Believe me, I want it. But we haven't talked about any of this."

"What's the problem if we both want it?" I smirk, trying to lighten the mood that has suddenly turned tentative.

Sophie is quiet for a moment, chewing on her bottom lip. "I'm scared, Liam. My heart is just starting to heal. I don't want to get hurt again." She swallows and looks down at her hands. I don't speak for a minute. She traces her fingertips around my collarbone.

"You think I don't know how to be monogamous and I'm

going to hurt you," I mutter, feeling ashamed.

Sophie winces as if my words sting, but she doesn't reply so I know I'm right. She reaches for her shirt and doesn't put it on but covers herself.

"I'm not a playboy, Soph. I just guard my heart." My voice is husky, brimming with emotion.

"Why, though? Why haven't you been open to love before? You're forty years old." She scoots backward and further away from me.

I grimace. I guess we're doing this, so I think about her question—one I have never been able to answer. Doc has asked me many times, especially lately, and I can't give him a different answer. I scrub my hands down my face and then look at them because if I meet her eyes, she'll undo me. "Because I don't deserve it," I say quietly.

Sophie narrows her eyes. "Who told you that? You don't deserve it?"

I'm growing impatient because talking about feelings is not my style and Sophie is pushing me. "Please, just drop it, Sophie. We can take things slower," I grumble, reaching for my own shirt and putting it on.

"No, Liam. I won't drop it. I want to know you," she presses. She moves to reach for me, but I get up and start pacing the room.

"Sophie, *this*. This is why I have never been in love. Because you can't know me. If you knew all of me, you'd hate me," I snarl. Sophie recoils at the brashness of my voice.

"Okay," she speaks slowly. "Then I don't know where that leaves us. I like you so much, Liam." Her voice wavers. "If I can't know all of you...then what?"

I shrug and drop my arms. I am suddenly exhausted and unexpectedly emotional. I don't know how to handle what I am feeling for this beautiful broken creature in front of me. I'm panicking because I have never been able to say my feelings for a woman out loud. Not even Cara when we were just kids, and I wasn't yet hardened from the world's anguish. Sophie scares the hell out of me. She is so fragile herself right now, and I am emotionally volatile. It's a terrible combination, and it won't lead anywhere good.

A lump forms in my throat as I look at Sophie's confused face. "I like you so much too, Soph. But I don't think I can be the man that you need me to be for you." I furrow my brow and look down at the floor because if I see her eyes fill up with tears, I will throw reason out the window. "I'm sorry, Sophie." I grab my shirt and then I selfishly turn and walk out the door, leaving her dumbfounded.

CR

I panicked. That's the only way to explain it. As soon as I get back inside my house, I know what a mistake I've made. Sophie's eyes were full of sadness and confusion and I hate myself for leaving her like that. Over the last eight weeks, Sophie has grown to be my best friend. Not because she has known me for years and knows everything about me, but because she doesn't know everything about me. She makes me forget who I am and how I've hurt people. When I am with Sophie, I feel like someone else. The worst part about all of this is that when she finds out about the accident, she's going to want nothing to do with me. It's too bad I had to go and fall completely in love with her.

When people who don't know me well hear that I don't do relationships, they think it's because I'm afraid of commitment or I don't like monogamy. It's the contrary. I would love to wake up to Sophie every day and build a life with her. I don't feel that I deserve to, because Cara will never fall in love and that's my fault. I am trying to redeem myself by taking care of Lucy and giving her a beautiful life. I know she deserves a mother but finding someone who will accept me for who I am is the hard part. I'm just not sure Sophie will. I also think she deserves someone so much better than me. She is brilliant and beautiful, caring, compassionate, loving. What am I? Broken and cynical. Grouchy. How could someone want to be with me?

Sophie does. A voice in my head keeps telling me, but I am just not sure. It's unfair for me to keep going back and forth with her. Logically, I know that. When I'm around her, I have no control of my emotions and all I want to do is get as physically close to her as possible. She should be curling up in bed with me right now and instead, she's probably crying alone in her bed. I am worried that I can't guarantee that I'll protect her heart, and she'll get hurt by both James and me. I think that's the part that is holding me back. I am a coward. I need to just sit down with her and tell her everything.

I climb into my bed and pick up my phone. No messages. I can't resist sending her one though.

Me: I'm so sorry, Sophie.

Sophie: Me too, Liam. I know we could be great if you would let yourself see what I see...

Sophie: But I have to protect my heart.

Me: I understand. You don't need my bullshit. Will you still be my friend?

She doesn't answer the last text message, and a dull ache settles in my chest that I am not prepared for. An unfamiliar pain sears through me. Is this what it feels like to have your heart broken?

ℭℜ

I am early for Doc the next morning. My chest hurts and I'm angry at myself and my heart is heavy with sorrow. But not because of anything we have ever discussed in therapy before. I'm afraid I have pushed Sophie completely away. Every mistake I've made is like a fresh wound that I keep pouring salt into.

I'm sitting on the stoop of Doc's office at 8:53 a.m. when he strolls up, whistling happily and looking jovial. He senses the anguish on my face and his smile falls. "Liam, are you okay, son?" he asks as I stand and move so he can unlock the door.

I cough and clear my throat, following him into the office. "I think I fucked everything up." My voice comes out hoarse.

"Come in, Liam. Let's talk through it." I must look really bad because Doc foregoes his usual tasks and walks right into his office, turning on the light and gesturing to the couch. "Have a seat." He walks over to the window and opens the shades. Then he walks over to his water cooler and fills us both a cup of water. He hands me the water and then sits near me in an armchair. "What's going on?"

I exhale loudly and slouch onto the couch. "It's Sophie."

"Ah," Doc replies. "You know, Ellie and I thought we interrupted something last night." He gives me a knowing smile.

"I think I'm in love with her," I admit, rubbing my beard that I didn't bother to clean up this morning. "Of *course*, I'm in love with her."

Doc almost laughs and holds his hands up in a confused gesture. "What's the problem, Liam? That's great. You have never gotten here before."

I groan. "It's not great. I put a stop to everything because I panicked. I am so stupid. Sophie doesn't know anything about me. I've let her tell me everything about herself and I've held back all the things that make me me. Once she finds out, she'll hate me. I don't deserve her."

Doc doesn't react because he's heard me say all these things about love before, but that was when the woman was some arbitrary possibility. Now, she's real. Sophie is a very real person with very real feelings. "Tell me, Liam. Why do you think you panicked? You are feeling these things which already means you've made so much progress."

I shrug and am quiet for a moment as I try to articulate what I want to say. "I don't know. I sometimes think I could take a chance and try it out. Be in a real relationship. But there are no guarantees, and I don't want to hurt Sophie more than she is already hurting." I lay back on the couch and squeeze my eyes closed. I have a headache from lack of sleep.

"See, this is progress, Liam. The very fact that you are thinking about Sophie in this scenario and not just yourself is progress. Progress is not linear. Some days you will make none and some days you may even go backwards. But you're consistently trying to improve. There is just one thing you have left to do." Doc pauses—he's waiting for me to fill it in.

"What?" I ask, impatiently. I need someone to give me a relationship guidebook.

"Forgive yourself, Liam," Doc says. "It's as simple as that. You were just a kid. You did the right thing. You stopped at your stop sign and then you drove through it. It is not your fault that someone else ran theirs. It's *not your fault*, son. It has taken you twenty-two years working with me to even admit that you want to be loved, and you still think you don't deserve it. You do. You just have to forgive yourself."

Hot tears prick my eyes and I sit up. I can count on one hand the number of times a session with Doc has made me cry. Angry? Yes. Rageful? Yes. Have I thrown things? Yes. Cried? Rarely. I sniffle and wipe my nose with the back of my hand and try to pretend it's not happening, but Doc knows me like a father knows his son. He tosses me the tissue box like a football, and I catch it giving him a woeful smile. I blow my nose and then meet his eyes. "I don't know how to do that."

Doc nods his head. "I know you don't but maybe if you allow yourself to fall in love, you'll see that it's okay for you to move forward with your life." He pauses before he says the next part. "This next thing I'd like to say, as a friend to you and not as your doctor, if that's okay?"

I shake my head and wait for him to continue.

"If you aren't going to allow yourself to get serious with Sophie, then put some distance between you. Hurt people *hurt* people. You say you think you messed it up. I am sure all is not lost, but if you aren't sure what you're doing or what you want, I want you to take a step back and think about it. Part of growing is recognizing what is good for the people you care about, too. So just take some time to figure it out." He reaches over and pats my knee in a fatherly way. "You're going to be okay, kid."

I hope he's right.

Chapter Thirty-One

Sophie

Claire and Derek left early this morning. After Liam left me, I went and woke up Claire. We stayed up late talking about everything and I think that's the reason I feel okay this morning.

I decide to walk to my appointment with Dr. Stevens. I think the fresh air will be good for me. I'm reflecting on the past eight weeks here in Cape May, and I am beginning to question if staying here is the best thing for me. I came here broken-hearted, and in some ways I still am. But I've taken the time I needed to just be. To just exist. And then I had to go and fall for someone else in a rapid amount of time. Liam's rejection last night hurt me so much, but I think I'm all out of tears.

This morning I am numb. Instead of feeling down, I am going to use his rejection as redirection. I want Liam. I really, really do. But I also deserve to show up for myself and set a healthy boundary. Liam doesn't know what he wants, obviously, and that's okay. I just have to do the best I can with what I know right now. I want to continue watching Lucy until I figure out where I am going and what I am doing. I know not all days will be good days, but I can find little pockets of joy in each day. Lucy is a pocket of joy for me. Maybe I came to Cape May to find that.

As I'm walking, my phone rings. It's Claire, even though I just said goodbye to her an hour ago. "Can't get enough of me?" I joke when I pick up the phone, instead of saying hello.

Claire laughs. "You know that's the truth, babe. But no. I have a reason for calling." She pauses for dramatic effect.

"Go on," I encourage. "Make it quick, I am almost to my appointment."

"Do you remember my intern Trevor that I had last year?" she asks, excitedly.

"I do, yeah." I stop to take a sip of water and glance at my watch. Maybe if I am a few minutes late, I won't run into Liam since his appointments have consistently been before mine.

"Well..." she drawls slowly. "He is opening his own practice in September! At home...in Scranton. He's looking for a few other therapists to work out of there with him. I told him you'd be perfect!" She is practically screeching in excitement. "And it's not until September so you can take your time moving home, finding a place, but then you can just slip right back into your old life."

I am so speechless I have to stop walking. "Wow. You told him about me?" Sometimes Claire gets ideas in her head and tries to run with them before she's thought all of it through.

"Of course I did! He said he would forward me over the info but would want to meet with you sometime in July or August. That works out nicely for you since you're summering!" Claire is giggling, she is so elated.

I don't know what to say. On the one hand, I appreciate her thinking of me. She is trying to show me that I have other options besides this place. Maybe Cape May really isn't the right place for me.

"That's great," I say, trying to sound optimistic. "Forward me the info. I promise to consider it." I mean that, especially given the events that have transpired with Liam. I may need a change...again. "I'm at my appointment now so I've got to go. But I appreciate you thinking of me, and tell Derek to drive carefully."

"I will," Claire says exuberantly. Then her voice turns softer. "Please, Sophie. Really consider it. I miss you so much."

I let out an exasperated breath. "I will. I promise."

I hang up and glance around at my surroundings, making sure Liam isn't anywhere to be seen. Feeling secure, I open the door to Dr. Stevens' office and almost get knocked over as Liam is coming out.

"Oh," is all I can manage to get out of my mouth.

"Sophie," he says hoarsely. There it is again, that way he says my name, like there are no other names in the world. "I was hoping to run into you."

I feel myself go cold. "Oh really, why is that, Liam?" I ask, folding my arms across my chest. I have sunglasses on or else he would see the frustration in my eyes.

"Yes, really," he says. He takes a step closer and reaches for my hand, but I am quicker. I put it in my back pocket. "Because..." His expression turns pained as he drops his hand. "Soph, listen. Can we find time to sit and talk? I want to explain everything to you."

I sigh. "Liam. Your moods change with the tides. I don't know what there is to talk about at this point." I frown, looking down at my feet.

Liam gets a pleading look on his face. "There's so much to talk about, Sophie. Please say you'll hear me out."

I almost cave but then I remember talking to Claire last night about boundaries and I decide to respect my own. "Liam, we're friends who have kissed a couple of times. Let's just leave it at that, okay?" I know I'm being stubborn but this time, I need to keep my guard up. I don't give him time to reply. "I'm going to be late."

Liam steps aside for me to enter, his shoulders slumped, and his lips pressed together. He can't hide his crestfallen expression.

Dr. Stevens is waiting for me in the waiting area when I walk in. He smiles warmly, like he didn't just see me for dinner last night. "How are you, Sophie?" He says as we walk back to his office.

"I'm okay. To be honest, I'm feeling a little bit lost." I plop down on his couch and feel my skin prick at the thought of Liam sitting here just ten minutes prior.

"Lost? How so?" He sits near me today, in an armchair. "Is it about Liam?"

"Oh...Liam told you about us?" I am caught off guard by this.

222

I guess in a town as small as this, not even Doc can stay quiet.

"He might have mentioned you. But if that's not what you want to talk about today, we can move on." He sips a cup of water.

"I mean...Liam is certainly part of it. I am trying to find my place here. I know I should be working and figuring out if I want to open a practice—that's always been a dream of mine. But I don't know what I'm doing here. If it is falling in love with Liam, then that makes deciding to stay here easier. But Liam is full of mixed signals, and he doesn't think he deserves to be happy, so I don't know where that leaves me. I'm sure he has PTSD from the accident but—" I'm rambling, and Dr. Stevens cuts me off.

"You know about the accident?" he asks, surprised.

"I do...but I don't think Liam knows that I know." I wince. "I sort of Googled him."

Dr. Stevens cracks a smile. "Well, I think that's reasonable. Most people Google their new love interests." His eyes crinkle with a grin.

"The thing is, this morning Claire told me about someone she knows opening a practice back home in Scranton. He will be looking for other therapists to work out of his office. I could move there and do that, but I guess I was sort of looking for a reason to stay here. Then again, staying here and seeing Liam every day may not be good for me either." I sigh. "Everything is so messed up."

Dr. Stevens is quiet for a few moments, seemingly lost in thought. I am biting my cuticles and mulling over possibly moving again when he speaks. "Sophie, how would you feel about working out of my practice, with me?"

"Like...you're offering me a job?" I ask in disbelief.

"Sort of. I have an extra office back there that I was planning to redo, and it could be yours, if you want it." He says this so sincerely I almost cry.

"But just last night you were talking about retiring!" I exclaim. Then I feel guilty. I can't be the reason he doesn't.

"Yes. And I still will...but you can rent the place from me and take on my clients who don't require the care of a psychiatrist, and you'll have the practice you've always dreamed of." He smiles. "You won't offend me if you say no. But I don't have any children to take it over and I know you love it here and I want to give you an opportunity to stay." He pats my hand, and I am so touched.

"If I say no, what will you do with it?" I ask, genuinely curious. Knowing his plans will help me decide what to do.

"Well, I own the building, so I suppose I'd just sell it," he says, leaning back in his chair and loosely crossing his arms. "I have to fix up the office space to sell it regardless, but if you want it, when you're ready to start your own practice, you can buy or lease it from me." He smiles and his eyes are so kind. I trust him.

"Wow, Dr. Stevens, that's...that's just so nice." I wipe a stray tear that has fallen from my eyes.

"You don't have to give me an answer now... Can you let me know by the Fourth of July?" He asks.

I nod my head vigorously. "Yes. Definitely yes. I promise to think about it." I stand up and walk over to hug him, taking him by surprise. I came to this appointment feeling so lost, with the fear that I'd have to leave Cape May and start over somewhere new again. I have been worried about my career options for weeks, and I don't have to anymore. Now I have two possibilities for moving forward and I can't help but feel hopeful for the future, with or without Liam.

❧

When I get home, I find Ellie cooking lunch for Lucy. Lucy is happy in the highchair watching a toddler show, and Ellie seems happier than I have ever seen her as she hums along and sashays around the kitchen.

"I'm back!" I call, coming through the front door.

"Oh good! You can have some lunch with me." She grins over her shoulder as she reaches for some plates. "How are you doing, dear?"

I walk to the fridge and get myself a cold water bottle and

then plop into a kitchen chair. "It's beautiful out there today," I say, breathlessly.

"And how was your appointment?" Ellie asks, setting a turkey sandwich in front of me.

"Thank you," I smile, picking it up and taking a bite. "It was good, I think. Dr. Stevens offered me a place to come and work with him."

"Ah," Ellie nods as if she already knew. "He told me he was going to do that." She reaches for my hand. "I want you to know, you can stay here as long as you like."

I meet her eyes and cover her hand with my own. "Thank you. I told him I need to think about it. I love it here but...Liam." I sigh. I find it difficult to finish the sentence and the emotion must be written all over my face.

"Oh...yes. I understand. You will figure it out. Things always work out in the end." She nods and scoots her chair up to the table to eat her sandwich.

"I don't know," I say quietly.

"You two looked pretty cozy last night," she teases. "Maybe there's hope."

I laugh and nudge her with my foot. "We looked cozy? I'd say you and Dr. Stevens looked pretty cozy yourselves," I tease.

Ellie's expression changes from coy to pure happiness, smiling so broadly her eyes crinkle. "You know what? We are. Robert has been my friend for years and that's all it's ever been. But lately, I don't know. We're both alone, and I think we're seeing that it is possible to have two great loves in your life. One in your youth and then maybe if you're lucky, you find it again."

"Oh, Ellie! I love this for you," I say, grabbing her hand and squeezing. "I hope I find love again one day too."

"You will, Sophie. Who could not love you?" She looks at me with such sincerity that I almost believe her but then doubt creeps back in.

"Well, I could think of a few people," I say wryly.

"The problem with Liam isn't that he doesn't love you. The

poor boy doesn't know how to love himself. He's an eighteen-year-old kid stuck in a forty-year-old's body." Ellie looks wistful. "I'm sure you have figured out by now that Liam has never gotten over losing Cara."

I blow out a breath. "Well, unfortunately, two broken people probably don't belong together," I say, moving to clear my plate and pick up Lucy.

"Or... they could heal each other," Ellie says.

I don't know what to say to that, so I change the subject. "I've got Lucy for a little bit if you want a break. I thought maybe we could take a walk downtown."

Ellie shoos me away with a smile. I get Lucy in the stroller and start a slow-paced walk under the shade of the trees across the street. I started this morning not knowing what was next for me, and I am going to end the day with a few different possibilities.

I try to imagine taking Liam out of the equation entirely. Where would I want to be? I still think that Cape May is the place for me. Then again, maybe I should go home. My family is there—Dad, Carol, Simon, Laura, and the twins. I miss them so much. My friends are there too, albeit, I haven't heard from them much. Maybe they feel stuck in the middle of my divorce. Claire immediately took my side, but I don't think the others knew what to do. Still, the idea of going home is comforting, even though I run the risk of running into James and Brittany. I would have a new job, one that would challenge me in different ways. Not my own business, but professional development just the same.

It's a lot to think about. I stop the stroller in front of a children's boutique, and Lucy and I peer in through the window at a cute dress. The door opens and two older women come out. They notice Lucy right away and start cooing at her. Lucy gives them her famous gummy grin, and I feel proud to be with her.

"She looks just like you," one of the women tells me. "She's just so cute."

They are so genuine, and it takes me by surprise. I should tell them that Lucy isn't mine, but in my heart, it sure feels like she is. For now, I decide to hold onto this feeling, to let myself savor the moment. Because deep down inside, I know it's unlikely that anyone will ever say something like that to me again.

I beam with pride. "Thank you!"

The women leave and I think it's time to head home. Lucy and I walk a couple of blocks over, and I decide to let myself look at our old house on Jackson Street. I pause in front of it. There is a Weekly Rentals sign in the front yard. I ache with loss knowing our family home is nothing more than a rental property now. A heaviness builds in my chest. This town holds so many memories for me. The only silver lining is that other families will come to Cape May and make memories in the same place I did.

I say goodbye to the house and turn up Perry Street toward Ellie's house. I'm just in time to catch the mail lady with a certified letter. "Are you Sophie Bennett?" she asks me, holding a pile of mail. On top is a yellow manila envelope with my name on it. I see the sender reads *The Law Offices of Evans and Moyer.*

"I am," I say, reaching for the pen and scribbling my signature. She thanks me and gets back in her vehicle.

I am paralyzed on the sidewalk with a pile of mail in my arms and Lucy in the stroller when Liam gets out of his truck and interrupts my thoughts. He plucks Lucy from the stroller and then turns his attention to me. "Whatcha got there?" he asks curiously.

I exhale and meet his gaze for the first time today. "I think... it's my divorce settlement."

Chapter Thirty-Two

Liam

It's been about two weeks since Sophie and I really talked. She hasn't come to yoga with me or even texted me about going. She's keeping her distance, and I guess I can understand that. From her perspective, I just toyed with her heart and her mind. She doesn't know my story because I've never taken the steps to talk to her about my past. I have been telling myself that I am open to love and a relationship, but if that were true, I think I would have let her see me. Now I have realized that time is passing, and the world is moving on without me. I have been going through the motions my entire adult life. I was sad and then I was spiraling, and then when I started to heal, I was merely existing. So now, I am doing the work.

Life can feel as if you're stuck in a rut and everything is moving slowly, or it can feel like it's moving too fast. The more I think about it, the saying "Time heals all wounds" isn't actually true. I've had twenty-two years to heal, and I have only just made the choice to start. Doc has got me thinking about time and forgiveness, and I realize now that if I don't allow myself to heal and forgive, then hurt and trauma will continue living inside me forever. I won't be able to move forward or have a fulfilling life until I take these steps. I'm trying to learn to let go and forgive myself, maybe even love myself. At forty, I can honestly say that I'm still a work in progress.

I see Doc twice a week. I try to give Sophie the space she

needs from me, even though I desperately want to be near her. I've realized, a big part of forgiving myself is letting go of the fear of something going right. If I don't forgive myself, I never have to be vulnerable. I never learned how to embrace something good because I always expected it to go wrong, or I told myself I didn't deserve things to go right. Doc says that I need to leave the past in the past because I can't change it. I need to focus my energies on the life that I want to live now. I think I want a life with Sophie. No, I know I do. I just have to figure out how to bring her back to me.

So while I have been doing the work with Doc, I've also picked up some new clients who are looking for custom coastal-inspired furniture in their new beach homes. I've been busying myself with those projects at night after working with Danny during the day. It's been so helpful to have those things to work on because if I didn't, I think I would be obsessing more over how I left things with Sophie. She told me my mood shifts like the tides and that stayed with me. I was allowing my insecurity to control me and giving her mixed signals. Not anymore. I know what I want and it's her.

Now we're in the middle of June. Ellie has been spending a lot of extra time with Doc, and I suspect something is going on there. The weather channel is calling for a massive storm tomorrow. We don't usually get a lot of rain in June, but they say it's coming. Ellie and Doc are taking a trip, and even though I know Ellie will prepare Sophie before she leaves, I am worried about her. I'm in the grocery store, picking up some items Lucy and I need to hunker down and ride it out when I find myself wondering again if Sophie has what she needs. Since we're not exactly talking, I decide to approach it first via text. I pull my shopping cart off to the side and hand Lucy a couple of Cheerios while I figure out what to say. I am not sure she even wants to talk to me. I take a breath and open the message, grimacing when I see our last exchange and how hurtful it was.

> **Me: Hey Sophie... I know Ellie is going away tomorrow. I just want to make sure you have everything you need for this weather coming our way. It's supposed to be a doozy.**

I force myself to keep walking around the store instead of staring at my phone. A few moments pass and I'm in the cereal aisle when I see the three dots indicating she is typing. It remains that way for a solid minute, and I get my hopes up that maybe she's typing a lot. Wrong.

> **Sophie: Yep. I'm good. Thanks.**

I force out the breath I was holding. Well, I can't push her. There's nothing else to do but wait until the storm comes and then check in with her.

☙

The rain comes in with a vengeance early the next morning. It's coming down hard but so far, that's all it is. Part of me thinks that the weatherman hyped it up and it won't be anything major, which is a good thing. I decide it's a good day to start working on Lucy's room, since she's with me and I can't take her in my workshop. We head upstairs and I'm planning to prep the walls for painting. Eventually, I will replace the carpet, but I figure it's best to paint first. I settle Lucy down on the floor and I start mixing the spackle. Maggie follows us upstairs and is pacing around the room. She sniffs Lucy and Lucy giggles. I smile over at the two of them and turn back to my work, only to be startled by a large crack of thunder.

Maggie runs to my side. Another crack of thunder and a whine from Maggie. Then the lights flicker, and I am getting worried they will go out. It's dark enough in this room without losing power. I seal up the spackle and abandon ship.

"Come on, girls, let's settle downstairs." I pick up Lucy and we're walking down the steps when another loud crack of thunder comes overhead. My mind goes immediately to Sophie. Sure, she's a grown woman and it's just a thunderstorm. But she's alone. No one wants to be alone during a storm. What fun is that?

I place Lucy in her playpen and tell Maggie I'll be right back. I run out the front door and sheets of rain are coming down sideways. It feels like needles the way it's pelting me. I didn't think this through. I'm wearing a white T-shirt, jeans, and no shoes and I am drenched in a matter of thirty seconds. I run up Ellie's front steps and bang on the door at the same time a crack of thunder hits. "Sophie!" I yell and knock simultaneously.

She comes to the door in another one of those lounge outfits she likes so much. She has her hair down and wildly curly. She's not wearing makeup except for that lip balm and she is beautiful as ever. Upon seeing me she looks alarmed, "Liam! Is everything ok?" A loud crack of thunder and a streak of lightning lights up the sky.

"It's fine. We're fine. I just wanted to tell you to come over and ride out the storm with us." I wipe water from my face that's dripping down from my hair. "It's not supposed to stop until tomorrow."

Sophie bites her lip. *Oh my god.* "Liam, that's nice but I'm really fine over here. I'm binging a show and I have plenty of snacks," she smiles, hesitating. "You know... It's probably better if I stay here."

Before I can try to convince her, another loud crack of thunder and lightning sizzles the pole right outside our two houses. All the lights and sounds in Ellie's house go off. We've lost power. "Are you sure? Sophie, come with me, please," I urge.

She hesitates for another moment and then relents. "Okay. Let me just throw some stuff in a bag." She jogs up the steps and leaves me standing on the porch. It's drafty in the house and I'm soaked. I have a little shiver happening when she comes back down. She's holding an umbrella and has her feet in rain boots. "I just noticed you're barefoot!" She half laughs, half scolds.

"Well, this was supposed to be quicker," I retort. "Come on!"

Sophie opens the umbrella and I put my arm around her and lead us over to my house. The cracks of thunder won't stop and when I walk inside, Lucy is crying. Maggie is sitting next to the pack-and-play with her head on the side and whimpering. "Oh girls, I'm sorry." I run over and pick up Lucy, but she is reaching for Sophie.

"Let me take her," Sophie says, grabbing Lucy from me. "It's okay, baby girl." She gives her a kiss on the head and my heart explodes.

I stand by watching the woman I love but can't have, nurture my baby girl and I don't know what to do with myself. "I think I should try to get Maggie to go outside before I change out of these wet clothes. Come on, Maggie." I call her and for once she comes the first time.

"Be careful," Sophie warns. She sits down on the floor with Lucy to play. Lucy is happy with Sophie, and I know I can't take for granted that she'll always be here. *Unless I can get her to stay.*

I know she won't stay out there if I'm not with her, so I put Maggie on the leash and take her outside. We walk down the slippery deck steps and through the sloshy grass. She's taking her sweet time because every time there's a crack of thunder she spooks and runs over to me. "Come on Maggie, do your business," I say impatiently. Finally, she squats to pee, and I am waiting for her to finish when the sliding glass door opens.

"Liam! Liam, come quick!" Sophie is shouting but I am having trouble hearing her over the rain. I grab Maggie's leash firmly and pull her up the steps, running to Sophie.

"What is it?" I ask breathlessly.

Sophie's eyes are glistening, she looks...proud? "She walked!"

Sophie shouts, tapping my wet chest excitedly.

I push past her and inside the kitchen. I whip off my wet T-shirt and throw it in the sink, hurrying to Lucy.

I think I catch Sophie eyeing my bare chest. I feel desire creep up the back of my neck watching her check me out. She bites her lip and shakes her head as if she's trying to clear it. "She decided she wanted a toy from across the room and she pulled herself up on my arm and walked over to get it." Sophie clasps her hands together and holds them over her chest, bursting with pride.

"That's so amazing!" I grin at Sophie, I want to pick her up and spin her around, but I know it's best if I don't. Instead, I run over to Lucy and pick her up, kissing her all over. "Yay, Lucy girl! Will you do it again for Dada?" I don't even try to stop myself anymore. I am her dad, and she is my little girl.

❦

I get Lucy to take a nap later in the day. Sophie and I are sitting next to each other on the couch now, neither of us saying much. We played with Lucy on the floor in the dark all morning and I couldn't help but envision us as a little family. There's a lot that needs to be said and I'm not sure where to begin.

I clear my throat. "Do you want some food?"

She smiles half-heartedly. "Sure. I'm starving."

"I'll cook us something good." I stand up and head for the kitchen. Maybe some time alone in here will help me get my head on straight. If we're going to have the conversation, I am the one who needs to start it. I know that. I just don't know how.

"Can I help?" she asks at my back.

I turn around and her face looks so hopeful I can't say no.

"Sure," I grin. "I'd love your help."

I'm thankful the gas stove works with a lighter. We're standing at the counter chopping vegetables for a stir fry and it's comfortably quiet. I'm lost in my own thoughts about where we go from here. I take the cutting board I'm chopping on and scrape its contents into a sizzling pan. "I love stir fry," I tell her.

She breathes in the scent of the onions sauteing and moans in agreement. "Me too. I love to cook."

Of course she does. "It's nice to cook with you," I tell her genuinely.

She doesn't say anything but that's okay. I am working up the courage to tell her everything. I throw the rest of the vegetables and the chicken into the pan and toss with sesame sauce. I have my back to her when she speaks.

"Liam."

The way she says my name comes out rapt with emotion. I turn around and see a look on her face that is a mix of pain and desire. Her eyes are glassy but her cheeks are rosy. She takes a few steps in my direction. I don't say anything, but I put the spatula down and take a step closer to her.

"I miss you," she finally says.

I breathe a sigh of relief. "I miss you, too, Sophie." I step closer and wrap her in a tight hug. "I have missed you so much. I have no one to do yoga with." I say into her hair.

"You've been going to yoga without me?" She pulls away and swats my shoulder, feigning annoyance.

"Hey, I'm trying to keep my stress levels down," I tell her and pull her close again. "But I have been really sad about the way we left things."

"Me too," she says into my chest.

My timer beeps and I pull away. "Let's eat."

Chapter Thirty-Three

Sophie

Even though I was hesitant at first, I am happy that Liam came and got me. I have been wanting to talk to him since I received my divorce settlement. In a few more weeks, my divorce will be finalized and I will be officially single again. I don't know what else we are going to talk about today, but I had to start the conversation. The only way I could think to start it was with the truth.

I miss him. I miss him so much it aches, like I have been missing him my entire life. I miss him like there was no life before him and without him, I am not completely whole. The few weeks of space between us really showed me how much he means to me. Even if he can never commit to a relationship with me, even if I end up moving back home, I want to know Liam. He has become everything to me.

We're almost finished eating, then Liam pushes his cleared plate away from him and I stand up to take our dishes to the sink. He is sitting at the table with his head in his hands and he isn't talking. Rather than push him, I pack up the leftover food and wash the skillet we cooked in. It doesn't feel awkward. It feels okay, just to be here in his presence.

Liam got out of his seat so stealthily that I don't even know he is behind me until I turn around and he startles me. His brows are furrowed, his lips pressed together in a tight line. The focus of his gaze on me feels like he can see right through me. He lets out a shaky breath. "Sophie, I think I am ready to let you in now," he rasps. "You have been so open with me in sharing about yourself. And I have held a lot of myself back from you. I haven't given you the chance to know or understand me," he pauses and licks his lips. "There are some things I want to share with you, if you want to listen. Can I show you something?"

He holds out his hand for me to take and I do. He leads me upstairs to a closed bedroom door, different from the room I know he sleeps in now—we're in a teenage boy's room. The double bed is made with a navy-blue comforter and various pillows. The wall has a Rookie of the Year poster of a Phillies player that I don't recognize. Another poster of what looks like the whole 1999 Phillies lineup hangs above his bed. On the opposite wall, a desk with an old desktop computer and a bulletin board above it with a smattering of pictures of teenage Liam and friends. There's a Duke Baseball flag pinned to the board and some Duke University pamphlets. An SAT prep schedule is pinned up next to a varsity letter. I turn around and see a varsity jacket and various baseball hats hanging up on the back of the bedroom door.

The room looks as if it's been untouched for quite some time. The dresser and the fan both have a layer of dust coating their surface. I step toward the desk and squint at the photos. I focus on a group shot of Liam and the guys I have met in baseball uniforms. Then I see a picture of Liam in the middle of two pretty, young girls, one I recognize as Melanie. The other is clearly Cara, the girl I saw in the articles. There's a prom picture of Liam with the same pretty girl that has Junior Prom 99' in gold on the bottom corner. And lastly a close-up of Liam with his arm around another girl whose face looks familiar to me but that could be because she is so obviously Liam's sister. I turn to Liam in confusion.

"This is your room," I say, waiting for him to fill in the rest.

He nods and coughs. "Yes. Well, it was when I was young. I haven't turned it into anything else yet." He sits down on the floor and leans against the bed.

"Why are we in your room?" I ask him, sitting down next to him so our legs are touching.

He's quiet for a moment and then reaches under the bed and pulls out an overstuffed shoebox that is coming apart at the corners. He takes the taped-together lid off and exhales deeply. There are newspaper clippings with the headlines I saw in my Google search. There are a ton of pictures of Liam with the girl on the bulletin board. He picks one up that shows him with his arm around the same girl at the beach. He's looking down at it and fiddling with it, not meeting my eyes.

"The reason..." He pauses and wipes his eyes that I didn't realize were tearing. He coughs before continuing. "Sorry. The reason I haven't been able to fall in love before is because when I was eighteen, I was in a tragic car wreck that killed my girlfriend. I was driving. And I've spent every day of my life since then punishing myself." The words spill out quickly and then he looks at me with torment.

I reach for his hand and give it a squeeze to let him know I'm listening.

"Cara was...so smart. And beautiful. I know when people die, everyone says they lit up a room, but Cara really did. She could make you like her within seconds of meeting her. She could convince me to do anything, no matter how much I didn't want to. She was full of wild ideas and just radiated happiness. I thought I was going to marry her." He bites his lip. I shift closer to him, not letting go of his hand. "When she died, I spiraled. I blamed myself even though we were hit by a drunk driver. I got kicked off the baseball team. I lost my scholarship. I went to school under the influence like three out of five days a week. I was fucked up."

I let out a breath. "Oh, Liam. I'm so sorry."

"I was such a disappointment to my parents. I don't know if they couldn't see that I had PTSD or if they just didn't know what to do. They sent me to Dr. Stevens, and he has been helping me ever since. At first, our sessions only involved me being resistant, but eventually, it felt like he was the only one who was really listening. I graduated high school by the skin of my teeth. Probably because half of my sessions with Doc were us doing my homework together.

When Leah graduated two years later, my parents said we could stay in the house, but they were moving to Florida. I think they were tired of looking at me." He looks down at his hands and his shoulders shake with a soft sob.

"I wondered where your parents were," I admit, softly.

"I thought maybe when Leah died, they would come back, maybe be with me and Lucy. But I think I have caused them too much pain, and they couldn't stand to see Lucy without Leah." He holds back a sob, and I stroke his knee, giving him the courage to continue. "As time went on, I just got worse and worse. It's amazing I still have the friends I do. Melanie...she was in the car with us. She became my ally. She's the only person who understood what it was like to be in that car and suffer that loss... At least that was the way I saw it for years. There were some very dark times for me when Melanie helped pick me up. I would say the reason I am here today is because Melanie's friendship saved my life."

A twinge of unnecessary jealousy tugs at my chest when I hear this. It would make sense for Liam to be with Melanie, she knows him inside and out. I could never know him like that.

Liam is looking down at the floor, twiddling his thumbs while he speaks. "Melanie shouldered my pain when I no longer had the strength to endure it. Over time, it grew into a sexual relationship. But I could never see Melanie without seeing Cara. I felt so guilty that I was driving the car and I got to live, Melanie got to live, and Cara had to die. I let it eat me up inside until I destroyed every relationship I had except that one. I didn't start getting better until Ellie and her late husband Eddie took me under their wing. Ellie saw how tired my parents were. In some ways I think she judged them for abandoning me and moving away," he pauses. "Ellie is like a second mother to me. Eddie is the reason I am a carpenter. And Doc never gave up on me." He sniffles and then rests his head against the side of the bed, closing his eyes.

"Wow, Liam. That's...just wow. Thank you for telling me all of that. It must be so hard to talk about." I squeeze his knee. For the first time since he started talking, he brings his gaze up to meet mine. I feel a chill shoot down my spine.

"A few weeks ago, you asked me why I have never had a serious relationship, and I couldn't give you an answer. I thought if you knew everything about me, you'd hate me. You'd think I was responsible for Cara's death." He grabs my hand and pulls it to his chest. "The thing is...up until a few weeks ago, I hadn't forgiven myself for it. I thought I couldn't be happy, and I didn't deserve love, that I should be punished. And I didn't want to forgive myself, truly, I didn't. I thought I could be okay my entire life without ever falling in love, so I didn't really do the work in therapy to forgive myself and move forward. I just didn't want to." He meets my gaze and brushes his free hand along my jawline, and I think my heart might explode out of my chest. "Until I met you."

We hold each other's gaze for a split second and then he pulls me into his chest, kissing me hungrily. It's as if the past few weeks without each other has left us both deprived. I climb into his lap, straddling him and running my fingers through his hair, cupping his face. I feel him grow hard and desire runs through me. He runs his hands up my back and buries his face in my neck. The roughness of his beard gives me goosebumps and I let out a moan. He kisses up my neck and along my ear lobe and jaw until he's finally back to my mouth, kissing me slower and softer this time. The tenderness will be my undoing. I press my forehead to his and our noses brush.

"How could you ever think I would hate you?" I whisper, then grab the back of his neck and kiss him deeply. He hoists up to a stand, holding me with my legs wrapped around his waist before laying me on his teenage bed. With one hand, he pulls his T-shirt over his head. I sit up on my elbows so he can help me remove mine. Our eyes are locked as he unclasps my bra and gingerly lays me back on the pillow. I let out a soft moan when his mouth finds my pert nipple and devours it before moving onto the other. He kisses down my side to my belly button and then back up to my neck, finding my mouth again.

I find the button on his jeans and undo it, helping him kick them all the way off. Reaching around, I use his ass to pull him closer to my heat. Running my fingernails up and down his spine, I lift my hips as he anxiously tugs down my pants. He looks down at the lacy red thong I am wearing, and he must remember catching me with it while I was unpacking because he lets out a lusty growl and buries his face in my neck.

"Oh my god, Sophie." Finding his way to my mouth, he kisses me deeply, teasing and biting. "You're gorgeous."

I find the waistband of his boxer briefs, and tug them down, freeing his perfect erection. Grasping his thickness tightly, I slowly move my hand up and down, eliciting a moan from him that heightens my own arousal. Liam returns the favor by gingerly pulling off my panties and running his index finger between my wet folds until he finds the sweet spot that makes me moan his name.

He eagerly moves his mouth from my own, kissing down my body until I feel his hot breath between my thighs. He's gentle at first, tentative in the way he kisses my most delicate area. I pull his hair and then he is hungrier, gently sucking until I cry out his name. With his free hand, he reaches inside me, stroking and licking simultaneously until I am completely undone, trembling on his strong hand with my release. The world goes black as a jolt of pleasure radiates throughout my body, leaving my legs shaking.

With my undoing, he moves his body up to face me and kisses my mouth. I taste myself on his tongue and I crave more. I cup the back of his neck, deepening the kiss and biting his lower lip. Reaching down, I rub him over my entrance and his eyes roll back.

"Sophie," he whispers. "Are you sure?" I nod and grip him tighter, a devilish grin on my face. "Are you on the pill?" he asks.

I bite my lip and look down at his impressive body, trying not to let his question kill the mood. "I don't think pregnancy is something we'll have to worry about...and I've only been with one person in the last thirteen years. I'm good if you are." I pull him close and kiss him softly. "I've been waiting for this."

And with that, he's inside me, filling me to my core. His

movements are slow and tender at first, while he kisses my neck and my breasts, gently sucking. I make a noise that comes out as a half moan, half sigh. Liam is beautiful as he moves over me, never taking his eyes off me, to be sure I'm enjoying it as much as he is. More than that though, there are emotions between us that heighten every sensation. Liam sees through me and when we connect it feels as if we were always this way.

As he's closer to his own release, his thrusts become urgent. He holds one of my legs to go deeper and we both yell out in pleasure. Our eyes lock, every ounce of emotion we've held back bubbling to the surface as we find our release together, collapsing in each other's arms.

"I've been wanting to do that for a long time," he whispers in my ear, lightly kissing the lobe.

"Me too." I snuggle into his big spoon and sigh. "It was... everything."

"Want to do it again?" he jokes, nipping at my neck.

I laugh. "Eventually."

We stay like that until Lucy wakes up from her nap.

Chapter Thirty-Four

Liam

Bringing Sophie into my childhood bedroom was not to try and get her to sleep with me. I felt like she couldn't possibly grasp the gravity of my story unless she could get a glimpse into who I used to be. Now, as we're lying here wrapped in each other's arms, I know it was a fundamental step toward moving forward together.

Lucy is talking to herself in her crib, and I sigh into Sophie's neck, not wanting to tear myself away from her. There is still no power, but I can no longer hear the pelting rain so maybe it is letting up. I give Sophie a tight squeeze from behind and sit up to throw on some clothes. I turn around to look at her lying there naked on my bed and she's smiling up at me. "What?" I ask, feeling shy. I reach for her hand, unwilling to stop touching her.

"I'm just admiring." She traces her fingers up my forearm.

I growl and lean down to kiss her again. "I gotta get Lulu. Take your time and meet me downstairs." I leave the room feeling lighter than I have in years. Being with Sophie has awakened something inside me that I didn't know was there. I can't exactly say what but maybe it's...hope?

❡

The hours pass slowly when you have no power. Sophie and I play as many games as we can with Lucy to pass the time, but now it's getting dark. "I should find some flashlights," I tell her. "I know where I have one for sure." I guess I wasn't as prepared for this storm as I thought.

"Do you have any candles? I think Ellie left some for me. I could run over and get them," Sophie offers.

I purse my lips and think for a minute. "You're going to think this is nuts but I'm pretty sure there are a bunch of candles in one of Leah's boxes." I grimace. "If you feel like rooting through them."

Sophie shrugs. "If you don't mind, I'll have a look." She pulls her phone out of her pocket and turns on the flashlight.

"I'll make us some dinner," I shout, walking to the pantry to grab the pancake mix. Then I pick up Lucy and put her in the highchair. I am trying not to open the refrigerator and let out the cold, but I reach in and grab yogurt for Lucy, milk, eggs, and butter. Everything still feels pretty cold. "How do you feel about breakfast for dinner?" I call to Sophie. She doesn't answer me immediately, so I walk to the front room. She's sitting on the floor with a wooden box of Leah's, engrossed in what she has found.

"Did you find any candles?" I ask, raising my eyebrows.

Sophie is caught off guard. "Oh...yeah. Sorry. I got distracted. Breakfast sounds good." She puts the wooden box back in the larger box she found it in, grabs the candles, and stands up. "I'll help you." She walks past me and into the kitchen.

I walk over to the box she was sitting by and peer in. I recognize the wooden box as Leah's treasure box. When we used to go to Sunset Beach, she would put all the treasures she found in there, special shells, Cape May diamonds, that sort of thing. I feel a twinge inside my chest that Sophie was looking at it. Maybe now is as good a time as any to start going through them. Sophie could be my support. She's already seen me cry more than any grown man would like. I will ask her after dinner.

When I get back in the kitchen, Sophie is whisking the pancake batter and humming happily. She already has the pan heating up on the stove. My heart swells watching her, and I'm frozen in the doorway.

"Do you mind if we put chocolate chips in them?" she asks hopefully. "If you don't have any, I think Ellie does. They were my favorite when I was a kid," she beams.

I walk over to the pantry and open it, reaching to the top shelf where I keep the bag. I turn back to her grinning and shaking the bag in my hand. "Mine too."

❧

We eat and talk about growing up in Cape May, our families, memories from our youth. We make silly faces at Lucy and before I know it, I'm singing her the ABCs. *Who am I?* Lucy is so happy because I am happy, and I can't imagine going back to the way things were before. The rain has let up considerably, but Sophie hasn't said she wants to leave. We have Leah's candles lit all over the downstairs and we're overwhelmed by multiple fragrances. I don't care because Sophie looks beautiful in the glow of their light.

I find myself fumbling for words now that we've cleared the air. I haven't kissed Sophie again since we were in bed earlier, but I really want to. I hope she'll stay the night, but I also don't want to get ahead of myself. I know when I put Lucy to bed, it'll go one of two ways... She'll either excuse herself to head home or she'll snuggle into me and stay.

Sophie gets up to clear the dishes, and I clear my throat.

She turns and eyes me, squinting at me curiously. "Did you want to say something?" She giggles. "You always clear your throat before you say something important."

I laugh nervously. "I do not."

She shakes her head and teases, "Yes you do." She grins. "It's okay, I kind of like it." She opens the dishwasher and puts our plates inside. I can't help but admire her as she moves so easily around my home. She is gorgeous. I want her to be all mine.

"Well, I was just wondering if...after I put Lucy to bed...would you want to help me start looking at Leah's stuff? Deciding what to keep and what to donate?"

Sophie meets my gaze and smiles. "I would love to help you, Liam. Thank you for trusting me with that."

I cough to fight off more emotion bubbling out of me and walk over to her, putting my arms around her and pulling her close. "You make hard things feel easy, Sophie," I whisper in her ear. She looks up at me with so much desire I think I'll carry her right back to bed, but Lucy interrupts us with an impatient screech to get out of the highchair. I plant a soft kiss on Sophie's lips and stroke her cheek.

Then I turn away to wet a paper towel and clean up the toddler. "Okay, Lucy, let's get you cleaned up for bedtime." I busy myself wiping her face and hair, which is covered in yogurt. If we had hot water she would need a bath, but our water heater is electric.

When I look up, Sophie is watching me, almost as if she doesn't believe what she is seeing. "If you want, you can pour us some wine while I put her to sleep," I suggest. We're both doing a lot of giddy grinning at each other. For me, it's about being alone with Sophie again. I can't wait.

"Liam?" She interrupts my thoughts. When I look up, she wears a hopeful expression on her face. "Can I put Lucy to bed?"

My heart fills with something I can't explain. "Of course you can. She'd love that."

♔

Sophie is upstairs with Lucy and I can't wait for her to come back down. As much as I want us to go back into the bedroom, I also am looking forward to going through Leah's things with Sophie's support. I pour two glasses of pinot noir and wait in the front room, tapping my foot and fidgeting in an armchair.

There are a lot of boxes in front of me. My parents packed most of them. I know some of them have her clothes and shoes because when I cleaned out her closet, I just threw them in boxes. I probably should have donated them right then but truthfully, I couldn't imagine parting with her things that soon.

Sophie comes down the stairs so quietly she sneaks up on me. I jolt out of the chair, grinning like a fool, and hand her a glass of wine. We clink our glasses together and sip, eyeing each other. I notice a blush creeping up her neck. "You make me nervous," she finally admits.

I set my glass on an end table and put my arms around her. "I'm sorry. I don't mean to." I kiss her forehead. "Why are you nervous?"

She pulls back to look at me. "I don't think I have ever felt this way before," she admits. "It's alarming."

I nod my head. "For me too." We are quiet, looking at each other for a moment more. It would be easy to scoop her up and carry her to my real *current* bed but I also want her to help me with Leah's things and for her to get a glimpse of who my sister was. I kiss her softly on the lips and smile. "Shall we get started?"

Sophie nods and crouches down to her knees next to an unopened box. "Okay, so how do you want to do this? Do you want to do it quickly by making donate and keep piles or do you want to examine each thing?"

I press my lips together in thought. "I think some things we'll be able to make quick decisions on, like clothing and shoes," I pause. "But her special things, her photos, and things that meant something to her... I think I need to save those for Lucy," I say, walking over to a few boxes that I know have clothing in them.

I open one up and right on top is a bunch of bathing suits. I awkwardly hold up a hot pink bikini top that is very stringy. "Like this."

Sophie bursts out laughing.

"See, we can donate this stuff," I say, rooting through the box a bit more to see it is clothes, socks, and bathing suits. I'm grateful there isn't any underwear in there—my mom must have taken care of those items. I shudder at the thought. It continues like that for a bit before I push all of the clothing and shoe boxes to one corner of the room, and we can move on.

I can see the couch now, so I sit on the edge of it and open the box in front of me. It's full of photographs—I swear she has three shoeboxes of loose photos and several photo albums here. Leah was sentimental. "This girl took so many pictures. She used to carry around those little plastic cameras you got at CVS and take photos of everything. I know I need to keep some pictures for Lucy, but this is a ton." I give a half-hearted laugh. "How do you even decide what ones to keep and what ones can be tossed?"

"I bet there are a lot of duplicates too," Sophie ponders. "You know, pre-digital camera when you couldn't tell if you got the shot." She purses her lips in thought. "You know, there are a lot of services online that you can send your photos to, and they put them on a jump drive or a website for you to save digitally and then I think they send them back to you. That's an option." She opens a photo album and flips through it.

"That sounds great but, I'm not sure I can handle the heartbreak that will come with that," I murmur, putting the photo album I am holding back in the box.

"I'll do it for you," Sophie offers. "I have lots of time right now and it won't be emotional for me like it might be for you." She reaches for my hand and squeezes. "Let me help you, Liam. It'll take my mind off the fact that I have no idea what the hell I'm doing with my life."

I give her a half-hearted laugh. "Do any of us really know what we're doing with our lives?"

She only shrugs in response, and I worry I've hit a nerve.

"Okay. If you don't mind, I'll carry them over to your house when the rain stops and you can do it. Please let me know what it costs though. I don't want you paying for it."

"I will," she grins. "I'll root out duplicates and bad photos before I send it off too, to minimize the cost." She scoots closer to me and climbs in my lap, giving me a soft peck on the lips.

I smile into her mouth. "Thank you." I wrap her in a squeeze. "This means a lot to me."

She pulls back and cups my face in her hand. "I know," she

whispers. "Now, let's get moving." She hops off my lap and moves to the box she had been looking at before dinner. She reaches in and pulls out the wooden box.

I clear my throat to push back the sadness that is enveloping me. "That's Leah's treasure box," I tell her, with a nostalgic smile that doesn't meet my eyes. "She used to collect shells and Cape May diamonds and other treasures she found and keep them in that box."

Sophie runs her fingers over the top of the box. The wood has a fine seashell border engraved on it and if I remember correctly, Eddie made it for her. "May I?" Sophie asks, treading lightly.

I nod my head but stay where I'm sitting. I am not sure if I can stand to look inside. Sophie gingerly opens the lid and rakes her fingers through the box's artifacts. She smiles holding up a mini conch shell to me and then holds it to her ear. "I hear the ocean," she says with a giggle. She holds up to her eye a larger Cape May diamond that is almost clear and peers through it. "I see you," she teases. She continues going through the box and showing me what she finds for a few moments and then she gasps, holding up a necklace on a chain that is either made of black rope or is just so tarnished it looks black. The stone is held by a metal charm that is in the shape of a mermaid tail. "I swear I had one just like this," she smiles. "You have to save this whole box for Lucy. She will love having her mom's treasures."

I nod in agreement, flashing back to that day in my mind. I remember the necklace well because my dad didn't want to buy it. He said she had enough Cape May diamonds; she didn't need one on a necklace. But we were with a few friends and their kids, and the other kids were all buying something in the gift shop. My parents used to tell us that gift shop purchases were for vacationers to remember the beach. But we were locals, so we didn't need to buy anything because we'd always have the beach. Leah somehow got the pouty puppy dog lip and convinced him in a matter of minutes. I didn't get anything that day, but I didn't mind. I was happy just wrestling and throwing the football on the beach with my friends.

"Liam?" Sophie interrupts my thoughts. "You okay?"

I shake my head and give her a nostalgic smile. "I was just lost in a memory."

Sophie nods. Just then, as if the heavens wanted to bring us back to the present, the lights and appliances turn back on and the house goes from nearly silent to loud enough to wake Lucy. We run around the house shutting off lights and the TV and blowing out an excessive amount of candles before she wakes up, meeting back at the bottom of the steps.

"Well, that's probably my cue to go," she says regretfully, gesturing to the front door.

I furrow my brow and step closer to her. "I don't want you to go," I rasp, embracing her and nuzzling her neck. "Stay with me tonight."

She takes no convincing.

Chapter Thirty-Five

Sophie

I've been in Cape May for ten weeks and I know this is where I'm meant to be. I came here broken and afraid of what was next for me. I feared I would never have a family and as it turns out, I have found family right here in a place that has meant so much to me my whole life. I was lost but I'm not anymore. If I were my own patient, I would have told myself to trust the unfolding of my life. To take the time to just exist and when the dust settles, you'll find you aren't broken, you are expanding, growing into who you are meant to be.

Liam and I have been seeing each other every day for the past three weeks. Yoga is back on! I won't be cliche and call it a love like I've never known before, but it might be. We haven't said those three words yet and I don't expect Liam to be able to say them any time soon. Every time I feel it, I have to stop myself from blurting it out to him. Sometimes I catch him looking at me and I think, *he definitely loves me.* But you don't go forty years unable to say I love you to someone and then magically you can. The chemistry between us is magnetic. When we're together, I feel like we are two people combining to become a single soul. That is cliche, but I can't help believing it. Things are really good. So good that when James is calling me this morning, no lump forms in my throat. I don't have any anxiety, and I don't wish him ill will. I do notice that I need to change his photo on my contact list because we are so not married anymore.

Liam is sitting next to me. We're drinking smoothies at a little cafe table outside our favorite spot. Lucy is in the stroller sharing sips of Liam's when my phone starts buzzing. We both look at James' name for a moment. I don't move to answer it until Liam nudges me with his foot.

"Are you going to answer that?" He tips his chin toward my phone, his blue eyes insistent. *God he is handsome.*

"Okay. If you're sure you don't mind." I pick up my phone just before it goes to voice mail. "Hey, James," I say coolly.

"Put it on speaker," Liam mouths to me and I roll my eyes, but I do it because he asked.

"Hey, Sophie," James says tentatively. "I have some news."

"Okay..." I trail off, waiting for him to fill in the blank.

"We got an offer on the house. Ten thousand dollars over the asking price. I sent it to your inbox. If you like the stipulations, we can close really soon." He sounds hopeful.

I meet Liam's gaze and he silently claps his hands and mouths, "Yay!"

"How soon?" I ask. "I mean, the usual closing is like thirty days, isn't it?"

James exhales. "That's the thing. I'm not living there. The house has been empty and the buyers are asking if we could do it sooner."

"Wow. *Well,* how soon?" I ask. "Let me open the email, hold on."

I swipe out of the phone call and open my email app. In a PDF attachment is an official offer from the buyer's agent. I scroll to the bottom and see James has already signed his portion. It's all dependent on me to sign the agreement. I almost want to just completely wash my hands of it. Whenever they want to close, great, let's do it. I hold the phone up to Liam for him to skim. James is rustling around on the other end. Lucy is babbling loud enough for James to hear.

"Who is that?" James asks curiously.

"Oh, that's Lucy." I don't offer any more detail than that.

"This looks good. I'm in," I say, smiling at Liam.

"Great. Any chance we can make this a two-week closing?"

"Do whatever you have to do," I tell him. "I'll make the drive back."

James is obviously excited that the phone call went as well as it did. I hang up the phone and audibly exhale, as if a weight has been lifted off my shoulders.

"Are you happy?" Liam asks, reaching for my hand.

I don't know what I feel. Happy that I can move on, yes. Sad that this part of my life is officially over? Yes. I can't deny that. My marriage to James was my life for thirteen years. Now I am in a new state and a new town that makes me feel nostalgic and hopeful all at the same time. And I'm falling in love with someone else. I don't want to say all of that to Liam so I give him a warm smile instead.

"Yes," I say emphatically. "Will you come to the closing with me? You know, for moral support."

"I wouldn't miss it for the world." Liam grasps my hand and I know he means it.

❦

The closing is set for the last Friday in June. Liam and I decide over coffee the next morning that the best option is to drive up the night before and drive home right after.

"There are plenty of hotels close by." I purse my lips trying to remember which ones.

"Why don't we just stay with your family?" Liam frowns, cocking his head at me.

"Oh," I pause. "I guess we could do that." I chew on my lip, hesitating.

"If you aren't ready for me to meet them, that's fine." He looks like a wounded animal.

"No, no, that's not it. I just haven't really told them I'm seeing someone." I wince.

"Is that what this is?" Liam teases, pulling me close and kissing me softly.

I pull back and swat his arm playfully. "You know what I mean. They aren't expecting me to be serious with anyone so close to my divorce."

Liam nods in understanding and I think maybe it'll be dropped. Then again, I don't want to hurt his feelings. My dad has always been approachable when I have something I have to talk about. This would be no exception.

"Okay. I'll call my dad." I say, reaching for Liam's arm. "No sense putting it off since I can't get rid of you anyway."

Now it's his turn to playfully nudge me. We're going to be grossing out everyone around us with our affection for each other.

Needless to say, my dad is thrilled when I call him. He is excited to hear all about Liam, and I am careful with how much information I divulge. I want Liam to share what he is comfortable with. My dad is so happy to have us. He says he's inviting the family over Thursday night for a barbecue, so I should prepare Liam to meet them all.

We left Lucy with Ellie and Doc for the night and made the four-hour trek to Scranton. It's nearly 4 p.m. by the time we get there. I didn't realize "the family" included Carol's sons and their wives too so I am surprised when we pull Liam's truck up to my dad's house and there are three additional cars parked out front. They must've cut out of work early on a Thursday for this. "You ready?" I ask him.

He grins. "Parents love me, I'll be fine." He hops out of the truck and saunters around the front to open my door and help me down. Then he reaches into the bed of the truck to grab our overnight bags. We cut across the grass to the front door and it swings open before we even get on the stoop.

"Aunt Sophie!" Sammy and Sarah come barreling out and throw their arms around my legs. It's been too long since I've seen them, and they look a few inches taller than they were in April.

My brother comes to the front door and wraps me in a Simon

hug. "Oh, I've missed these hugs," I say into his chest. I pull away from him. "This is Liam. His hugs rival yours." I laugh.

Liam holds out his hand and Simon shakes it. "Hey, how are ya?" He grins.

Simon cocks his head and eyes Liam while he shakes his hand. "Simon." They spend a couple of seconds sizing each other up before Simon says, "You look so familiar to me." He scratches his chin.

"Well, he's not from here so you wouldn't know him." I push Simon inside and take Liam's hand, leading him into the foyer.

"Hey! There they are." My dad bellows, getting up from his recliner where he's watching the Phillies to greet us. He holds out his hand to Liam. "I'm Bill, Sophie's dad." Dad's eyes are sparkling with excitement. *Maybe he has been worried about me.*

"Liam." Liam shakes my dad's hand and Dad pulls him in for a hug.

"Oh, a nice firm grip." My dad practically shouts. "That's a good sign, Sophie."

Liam stifles a grin and looks my way. He's clearly caught off guard by how enthusiastic my dad is.

"Okay, come on in. I'll introduce you to everyone else." My dad ushers us inside. Liam follows my dad into the living room where he introduces him to Carol's family and offers him a beer. Simon and I watch from the foyer.

Simon side-eyes me with a smirk playing on his lips. "Didn't take you long."

I swat him in the chest. "Shut up," I laugh.

"He still looks so familiar to me though. He must just have one of those faces." Simon shrugs and we move to join the family.

All things considered, the dinner goes well. Liam is at ease and personable.

Carol catches me getting another glass of wine and whispers in my ear, "I really like him, Sophie." She pulls me into a hug.

I really like him too. He seems to fit with my family and to be honest, James never did. I know everyone overlooked it because they saw us in love and they thought I was happy, but this is so different. I take a sip of my wine and walk over to the picture window in the kitchen. Out back I see Simon, Liam, and Sammy playing catch. Sammy just started Little League. Watching Liam jump right in with my family is a little bit of an epochal moment for me. It feels like a different lifetime and yet exactly where I am meant to be all at the same time.

Ӏʘ

The look on James' face when Liam walks into the closing with me is something I won't soon forget. I actually feel a little bad for him. I fully expected him to show up with Brittany, which is why I wanted Liam there for support. James is caught off guard.

"Hi," James says, eyeing me cautiously.

"Hey, James." I suck in a breath. "You remember Liam." I gesture toward him.

"Hey." Liam holds out his hand and James shakes it. "I'm going to sit out there if you need me, Soph." He gestures to some chairs outside the conference room. "You good?"

"Yeah, thanks." I stand on my tiptoes to peck him on the lips before he goes. When we pull apart, he gives me a pleasantly surprised grin.

All-in-all, both men were cordial, and the closing goes off without a hitch. James and I sign the papers and congratulate the new owners who look to be happy and naive newlyweds. Liam hangs back but I know he's there if I need him. The realtor hands us each a separate check and for the first time since all of this started, I know I'm okay.

When we leave, we pause outside the office building and James and Liam shake hands.

"Take care of her," James says, eyeing Liam carefully.

Liam grins, stepping back to be at my side and draping his arm around me. "It's my pleasure."

James and I hug goodbye.

"Good luck, Sophie," James murmurs in my ear as we embrace.

"You too." I pull away. "With everything." I surprise myself because I actually mean it.

I think it's time to have a conversation with Liam about us and where he thinks this is going. I realize that to a guy like Liam, that might mean pressure he isn't ready for but seeing him with my family has made my feelings for him grow deeper. I want to know if he's in it for the long haul with me. Plus, I haven't told him about the possibility of moving back here and I need to talk to Claire's friend. We climb in the truck to head out and Claire's ears must have been ringing because suddenly my phone is.

"Hey stranger!" I say, answering FaceTime.

"Where are you?" Claire makes an impatient face.

"On our way to see you!" I grin. When I found out about the closing, I called Claire that night and we planned to meet her and Derek for lunch before driving back to Cape May.

"Yay! Okay. We'll meet you at La Azteca in...twenty?"

"Sounds great." I hang up and smile over at Liam who is punching the address in his GPS. I grab his thigh and give it a squeeze. Everything feels right.

He glances over at me, a mischievous look in his eyes. "Should I find somewhere to pull over?"

"No!" I laugh. "We'll be late. There will be plenty of lovin' when we get home." I lean in for a kiss. Home. That sounds right.

◯&

Lunch is perfect. The conversation is good, and the margaritas hit the spot. I am so happy that this little trip worked out for Liam to meet my family and for me to see Claire. I think I actually can have the best of both worlds.

We're standing outside of the restaurant and the guys are talking about the Phillies lineup while Claire and I hug goodbye.

"Before I forget," she says, pulling back, "please call Trevor.

He needs to know if you're interested and if you want to meet with him. I don't care what you decide, but just call him so I don't look like a jerk."

"I promise, I will." I give her one last squeeze. "Come down and visit soon!" I say as I climb in the truck. "The beach misses you."

We're quiet for the first few minutes of the drive, I'm humming happily to the radio, and Liam is focused on the road. I glance over at him and notice he is a little tense, so I reach for his leg and rub it. He doesn't look my way.

"Everything okay?" I ask him.

"Yeah. I'm fine." His reply is curt.

"Really? Because you don't seem fine." I press, pulling my hand back. "Your body language changed completely."

Liam ignores that and sighs. "Who is Trevor?" he asks brusquely.

"I didn't think you heard that," I mutter under my breath.

"What was that?" he asks, glancing at me and then back to the road.

Okay so we're doing this now.

"Trevor is Claire's old intern. He is opening a practice back here in Scranton, and he asked if I would be interested in working out of it." I sigh. I glance over at him waiting for his response.

"You told him no though..." It's a statement, not a question. Followed by, "Right?"

I don't like Liam's implication that I should have definitely told him no or the direction this conversation is going. We haven't had any sort of conversation about a serious commitment since the night we first got together. "I haven't told him anything yet," I admit with a shrug. "I haven't even called him."

Liam exhales like he might be relieved to hear this.

"But I have to call him," I say, like he should already know that.

"To tell him you aren't interested?" Liam glances over at me. I'm quiet for a minute thinking about what I should say. Liam seems bothered by my hesitation. "Sophie, you aren't interested in moving back here, right? I thought you were staying in Cape May." His voice wavers.

"I don't know, Liam. I don't even know the details of the job yet." I lean my head back against the seat. This is not how I saw this conversation going.

"What about Lucy?" he asks warily. But what he really means is 'what about us?'

"I have to take the call, Liam. I promised Claire I would. And we haven't even had a conversation about where we stand." There, I answered both the spoken and unspoken questions.

"Where we stand?" Liam scoffs.

"There is plenty of time for us to discuss this," I say calmly. "I wasn't even sure if we are a we. That's why I didn't bring it up yet." I pause and wait for him to reply.

Liam swallows and pulls the car over to the shoulder. He puts the car in park and turns to me. "Sophie, I'm not good at confessing feelings, as you have probably figured out by now." He licks his lips and reaches for my hands. "I've spent every free moment I've had with you so maybe I just thought it was obvious but Sophie, I'm totally gone for you."

My breath hitches in my throat. "You are?" I whisper.

Liam's lips curl up lightly and he kisses my knuckles. "I am. I'm sorry if I scared you. It scares me to think of you leaving."

How could I leave this man? But it's fast and putting all my eggs in one basket is scary too. I swallow the lump forming in my throat. Traffic is whizzing by and I'm anxious to get on the road. "Liam, I care about you—and Lucy—so much," I murmur. "This is just something I have to decide for myself. Can you just give me some time to figure things out?"

Liam sighs. "I don't want to, but I will," he grumbles.

"Thank you." I reach forward and pull his mouth to mine by his T-shirt and plant a kiss on his mouth.

He pulls back onto the road, and we head for home.

Chapter Thirty-Six

Liam

I am relatively quiet the rest of the drive back to Cape May and so is Sophie. We discuss music choices briefly, Sophie points out a couple of shortcuts, but otherwise, we don't have much to say. I'm internally panicking but I'm also a little mad that she is thinking about leaving and hasn't said anything to me about it.

Logically, I don't know why I am even upset with her. She has dealt with a lot the last few months. She doesn't need me making things harder on her. Realistically, why wouldn't she want to move home? I just assumed that spending every waking moment together and sharing a bed most nights meant we *are* together. I haven't brought it up though. There has been no conversation because, as I have told her multiple times, I haven't done this before. I didn't realize I had to formally ask her to be my girlfriend.

The fact that she is considering moving away from me, Lucy, and Ellie and *this place* kills me. I can't believe she didn't even tell me. I don't know if I can let myself get closer to her now. All this time I have been thinking I am falling in love with her and maybe she hasn't felt the same. She's been in love. She's been *married*. I haven't. I don't know what this is supposed to feel like or what the rules are.

I pull in my driveway and hop out of the car, making my way around to open her door like I usually do. She beats me to it and closes the door before I get to her. She looks a little glum as she starts walking.

I catch her hand. "Soph," I rasp. "I'm sorry. I got scared. I don't want you to move."

At this, she softens but doesn't relent. "Okay, well. I have to have the conversation, Liam. I might stay, but if it's a good opportunity for me, then I might not." She crosses her arms over her chest, closing off her heart from mine.

I nod. Ellie is at my house with Lucy because it's late, but Sophie doesn't move to follow me. "You coming?" I ask hopefully.

"I think I'm just going to stay here tonight," she says without looking at me.

I don't know what to do so I stand there helplessly. This is the first night we won't have slept together in weeks, and I'm frozen at the foot of the driveway watching her walk away from me.

Okay. It's okay. Maybe some space is good. Distance from a complicated situation never hurt anyone. I try to convince myself.

It's not working. My chest tightens and I feel the familiar sensation of panic rising in my throat. *I really hope I didn't fuck this up.*

❧

Sunday comes and I haven't heard much from Sophie besides a few text messages. I asked her yesterday if she wanted to hang out and she told me she was doing some work and starting Leah's picture project. I tried to tell myself it's okay, I saw her yesterday. We don't need to spend every waking minute together.

When I still haven't heard from her Sunday morning, I send her a text.

> **Me: Soph, I know you're busy but…did you want to go to yoga tonight? I just need to ask Ellie if you do…**

She writes back fairly quickly.

Sophie: Sure. I'd like that.

Okay, maybe she's coming around. We agree to meet out front and walk since the air isn't too sticky. We fall in step together and she lets me hold her hand while we walk. This is giving me reason to hope that we're okay.

"Sophie, I'm sorry if I upset you with my assumptions the other day. Are you ok?" I glance over at her, willing her to look my way.

"It's okay," she says sincerely. She squeezes my hand. "I'm still not sure what I'm doing though, so please be patient with me." She gives me a faint smile that I think is meant to comfort me, but all it does is tear me up inside.

"I'll try," I say, and I mean it. I chew on my lip, mulling over my next question. "Besides, moving home, do you have any other options you want to share with me?" I have never been good with the unknown and it will be truly hard for me to wait to hear her plans. It's been years since I've let someone in and now, I feel exposed. If Sophie leaves, it'll break me. I want us to be as upfront as possible about this.

Sophie looks sideways at me. "Actually, there is another option," she hesitates.

I slow my pace and look her way, waiting for her to continue.

"Doc asked if I wanted to rent his extra office space and see patients out of there." She stops walking and I whirl around to face her.

"Sophie! This is great." I wrap her in a hug.

When I pull back she closes her eyes and takes a deep breath, as if she's summoning the gods of patience. "It is, Liam. It would be a great opportunity." She pauses and reaches for my hand. "The thing is, I have to make sure I would be saying yes to him for the right reasons. Can you understand that? This is my *life* we're talking about. I can't be impulsive here."

I know I'm coming on strong, it's just that I'm crazy about this girl. I meet her earnest gaze and nod, dropping her hand. "Yeah. Okay. I'll do my best."

Be cool, man.

☙

Yoga class is smooth sailing. I am getting more limber, so I am better able to keep up. The downside for me is that Russ is teaching tonight, and he is paying too much attention to Sophie. He is walking around, fixing her form, and in my opinion, finding any excuse he can to touch her. I guess I'm not giving off enough boyfriend vibes because he waits for us at the desk when it's over.

"Did you enjoy class, Sophie?" he asks her, eyes bright. He's completely ignoring me.

Sophie moans, a noise that should be reserved for me in my bedroom, and rolls her shoulders back. "It was excellent. Thanks, Russ." She smiles. She doesn't give him any indication that she likes him, but she also isn't insinuating that she's with me and I hate it.

I touch her lower back as we walk out the front door. She doesn't move away but she seems a little uncomfortable. "Do you want a smoothie?" I ask, hoping to steal a few more minutes with her.

"I'm pretty tired," she says apologetically. "I think I'll just go home tonight." She gives me a regretful look and I can't take it anymore. I stop walking and catch her hand, pulling her off to the side so we're not in the way of other pedestrians.

"Sophie. Talk to me. What did I do? This cold shoulder is killing me," I beg, plopping down on the bench. "I don't want to smother you; I'm trying to give you your space, but I have to know." I drag my palm down my face.

Sophie's expression softens and she sits down next to me. "Liam, I'm sorry," she touches my chest, and I feel a spark shoot up my spine. "I just think... I'm just taking time to think about what I really want. Can you give me that?"

I sigh. "Of course, I can. But it's hard because I let my guard down and now, I feel like I better put it back up or you're going to break my heart." I take her hand and hold it to my chest. Then I bring it to my mouth and kiss it.

Sophie exhales as if she is exasperated. "I promise I won't break your heart, Liam." It should be reassuring but it leaves me feeling empty. We walk home in silence.

☙

Monday morning, I am at Doc's office before he is, leaning against the cold white stucco and sipping an iced coffee. He whistles when he walks up, his happy mood is a stark contrast to mine. I find it annoying even though I shouldn't. He is surprised to see me.

"Liam. Did we have an appointment?" he asks, pulling out his phone to, I presume, check his calendar.

"No. I'm sorry. I just—do you have any time?" I must look rundown because Doc doesn't hesitate.

"Of course. I have just twenty minutes though, so talk to me while I do my opening chores." He unlocks the door and ushers me in. I plop in a waiting room chair and wait for him to come out of the bathroom with his watering can. "What's going on?" He asks, concerned.

"Well, I met Sophie's family last week," I start. Doc's ears perk up in surprise, but he doesn't speak. "It was great. Everything clicked."

"That's wonderful, Liam. Why don't you look like you think it's wonderful?" He stops what he's doing and looks warily at me. "You were making such progress."

"It is wonderful," I growl. "It is. It's just on the way home I found out she might be taking a job in Scranton and moving back there. And she didn't talk to me about it at all. I found out by accident." I sulk. I wait for him to be as outraged as I am by this turn of events, but he remains stoic. "If she leaves, it'll crush me," I mutter, putting my head in my hands.

I look up at Doc; he's watching me carefully. "She told me you asked her to come work here. It seems like a no-brainer. Why wouldn't she just accept your offer?"

"I did offer her the other office here. She could see patients out of it and work alongside me. I asked her to give me an answer by the Fourth of July," he says. "She has three days but really it doesn't matter when she tells me. I had to fix the room up anyway to sell the place." He stands back up and walks behind the counter to turn on the phones. He glances at his watch. "Look, Liam. I've got to get ready for my patient. My doctor advice to you is to communicate with Sophie. If you love her, you need to *talk* to each other and come to an understanding. My advice as your friend? If you want Sophie to pick you, to pick Cape May, don't get mad at her. Don't push her away. Make her *want* to stay."

I tap the top of the desk and turn to go. "Thanks, Doc," I call, waving over my shoulder.

I walk around town for a long time thinking about ways I could make Sophie want to stay. I mean... I love her. I know I love her. I could try telling her that. That would probably be a good start. If she'll even talk to me. We texted but we didn't hang out this past weekend besides yoga. And the texts are short answers that leave me feeling worse. I am wracking my brain trying to think of things she likes or ways to show her what she means to me. Doc's office would be a dream come true for her. She loves it here; she's been so happy. I know she misses her work or she wouldn't be looking for other options. I turn up Lafayette Street and I'm walking past the stores, peering in windows. I pass a coastal furniture store that I've contributed to in the past. One of my raw edge tables is in the window.

Then it hits me... Sophie loves my work. Doc is fixing up an office in hopes she will take it. What if I build her a desk? Like the teakwood end tables in the waiting room that she said she liked. That might not make her stay but it's a gesture. I plop down on the bench outside the store to mull it over. I would need to get my hands on some more of that teakwood. I think my supplier could help me out, but it would need to be like yesterday and he's two and a half hours away.

I pull out my phone and shoot him a text. It takes him a few minutes, but he thinks he has a slab of teakwood I can have. I try to stress the urgency to him and he says I can either wait until tomorrow and he'll meet me halfway or I could drive up today and meet him at the barn this afternoon. I'm going with today.

I literally run home to talk to Ellie. Sure, it would've been easier to just text her, but I can't help but hope I'll run into Sophie. I jog up the steps and I'm huffing and puffing with my hands on my knees on the front porch when the door opens. Sophie is standing there, holding Lucy and snickering at me.

"What are you doing? Sprints again?" she teases.

I stand up and put my hands behind my head, pacing back and forth. "Oh good. You're here." That's all I can get out.

"I'm here." She smiles. "We're here." She bounces Lucy and she giggles. "Where's the fire drill?"

"I have to drive a few hours to get something for work," I tell her, hurriedly. The longer it takes me to get on the road, the later I'll be back. "Can you stay with Lucy? You or Ellie if you're busy."

"I've got her," she says. "Go, go. Do what you have to do." She gives me a wry smile.

"Thank you!" I kiss Lucy's head and Sophie's cheek and jog back down the steps. Thinking better of it, I turn around and bound back up them. "Sophie," I breathe, tipping up her chin so she can look me in the eye. "I want you to take all the time you need to make the best decision for yourself. I'm sorry if I made you feel like you can't do that." My voice comes out husky.

Sophie's eyes are glittery when she says, "Thank you." She stands on her tiptoes and kisses me; Lucy reaches for me and grabs my earlobe, giggling.

"Ouch, Lulu!" I yelp, laughing.

Sophie looks much more at ease than she did yesterday. She

grins at me and waves her hand away. "Go on, get out of here."

"Okay. Bye!" I plant one more peck on her lips and rub the top of Lucy's head before I'm off.

I've never built anything in three days but I'm damn sure going to try.

Chapter Thirty-Seven

Sophie

It's a total lie that relationships are supposed to be easy. Even with the right person, it takes work. It takes a constant commitment to show up every day for that person and for yourself. I made that commitment with James, and I honored it. He's the one who didn't. He's the one who broke us. I made the decision to try to work things out until he dropped the bomb that he was going to be a father, but I would surely not be the mother. All I have ever wanted was to create a family like the one I grew up in. It wasn't always easy, but we knew we were loved. We knew we could depend on each other and when things got hard, we leaned on each other. James couldn't give me that.

Liam can and I am pretty sure he wants to. Sometimes, when I let myself really imagine what it might be like to be a family with Liam and Lucy, I think nothing would make me happier. Fear of making the wrong choice is what is holding me back. I am newly divorced, on my own, the world is at my feet. I could take the job back at home and continue to heal surrounded by people who know and love me. I could also stay here and try things out with Liam, who may just be the greatest man I have ever met. He's so broken and raw and yet, he let me in. What if I try things with him and it fizzles out? It's only been a few weeks. That would break him...and probably me too. I have no idea what the right choice is.

On Monday, I kept Lucy all day. It was late by the time Liam returned and he didn't seem like he wanted to talk. He said he needed to get some stuff done in his workshop. It felt like a brush off but I'm telling myself it's because he is giving me the space I need to think.

On Tuesday morning, I meet him outside when he drops off Lucy.

"Can I see you tonight?" I ask, reaching for his hand before he can walk away.

"Can I let you know how the day goes?" He grimaces, biting his lip.

My disappointment must betray my face because he pauses, raking his fingers through his hair. "I'm sorry, Soph. This project is huge, and it is just taking up every free moment right now."

"Okay, I understand. I'll see you later." I force a smile as I wave him off.

He waves as he hops in his truck.

I groan and close the front door after he leaves. I carry Lucy into the other room and find Ellie, her brow knit together in concern. "You ok, Sophie?" She reaches to take Lucy from me.

I sigh. "I want to say yes, but...not really. I feel like everything with Liam got all messed up." I shrug and drop my arms at my sides.

"It didn't, sweetheart. You just have to find your footing again." She soothes, reaching to push some hair behind my ear. She's so nurturing, it's no wonder Dr. Stevens is crazy about her.

"It hasn't even been long enough for me to be this upset. It would be easy to walk away," I murmur.

Ellie makes a noise that sounds like hmm. She waits for me to continue.

"It might be the realization that I'm about to be officially on my own for the first time in a long time coupled with not seeing eye to eye with Liam, but I feel a bit lost again."

Ellie gives me a reassuring smile. "I promise, you'll figure things out, sweet girl."

I sigh deeply again. "Would you mind keeping Lucy for a bit? I've got to make some calls."

Ellie agrees and I head upstairs to call Trevor.

ରେ

Trevor answers right away and he is happy to hear from me. He tells me his practice will be on the south side of Scranton, and it will be a nonprofit counseling center for low-income community members suffering through marital and family problems, addiction, and grief. It sounds amazing, and I am excited for Trevor. Trevor tells me a few others he is hiring will be looking for roommates if I'm interested.

The job would be different than anything I have done before. I haven't ever worked for a non-profit. I don't want to pass up a great professional development opportunity for me. Being closer to my dad and brother, two of the most important men in my life is also a great selling point. And Claire, oh how I've missed my best friend. But no Liam, Lucy, or Ellie who have become family to me—my heart constricts at just the thought of losing them. I've grown to love them all so much.

Moving home has plenty of drawbacks but I know working for a non-profit would allow for professional growth that I might not otherwise have the opportunity for. Of course, that would mean owning my own practice is out the window again for a while. I will need to think really hard over the next few days. I wish I had some kind of sign. Something telling me *this is what you need to do.*

I lean back against my bed and eye my box of personal items from Dad's house. I have no idea what is in there, but I have to imagine copies of my certificates for counseling are.

I hop off the bed and kneel next to the box. When I open it, the first thing on top is some picture collages from my early elementary years. *How embarrassing.* I laugh, putting them aside. I see my high school yearbook from my senior year, and my middle school yearbooks too. There's a picture frame with a picture of Claire and I in front of a flowering pink tree in our prom dresses. I look at it for a moment, remembering that day. My mom had recently passed, and I didn't want to go to the prom at all. Dad was a mess. I felt like I couldn't leave him to go out and have fun. Simon and Claire convinced me that I would regret it if I didn't. Simon took me to pick out a dress and said if I didn't find one that I liked, he'd let it go, but he strongly felt I shouldn't miss it. I ended up picking the first dress I tried on.

When the day of prom came, Simon took me to get my hair and makeup done. I felt so beautiful. He went with me to take prom pictures with all our friends. He probably took this photo. When I look back, I think how lucky I am to have had both Simon and Claire as constants in my life. There aren't many people who have seen me at my best and my worst and stuck around for the long haul. They will still be there even if I decide to stay in Cape May. I look at the picture one more time and smile. Then I put it out on my bedside table, it deserves to be seen.

I pull out some other photo albums before coming to a shoebox full of seashells and Cape May diamonds. I remember collecting them almost every weekend that we visited here. *There are so many. I wonder if I should take them to the gift shop and donate them to be sold.* I dismiss that thought almost immediately. I put the lid back on the box and then pull out my childhood jewelry box. It's pink and purple with a unicorn on the top, and when you open the top, a unicorn spins playing the song "Thank Heaven for Little Girls."

I did not expect to find this here but inside it is some of my mom's old jewelry that my dad gave me after she passed. Dad must've thought to stick it in this box. I move the costume jewelry aside and I'm immediately shook to my core. At the very bottom of the jewelry box is the very same necklace I found in Leah's treasure box. I *knew* I had a similar necklace. I pull it out and examine the tarnished chain with the tarnished mermaid tail holding a still clear and shiny Cape May diamond.

"Huh," I say, considering it closely. I honestly cannot remember the day I got it. I don't remember many specific instances of my time here as a child. I remember what we did and the places we went but I don't remember the exact details. My therapist brain knows this is because my last memories here were clouded with the loss of my mom. Sometimes trauma causes someone to repress memories. I put the necklace back in the box and toss it aside.

A little bit more digging and I find what I'm looking for. A big manila envelope stuffed with my high school diploma, college and graduate school diplomas, and photocopies of my certificates allowing me to be a practicing therapist in the state of Pennsylvania. I sift through, pulling out what I need, and then snap some photos of them. I drop them in an email to Trevor with the promise to let him know as soon as I do what my plans are.

My thoughts are interrupted by the front door opening and closing loudly.

"Ellie? Sophie?" It's Liam and I am embarrassed at how quickly I jog down the steps. He is surprised to see me without Lucy and raises his eyebrows. "Where's Lucy?"

I pause and look at him leaning on the stair post. His presence fills the room. He's wearing a tight blue T-shirt and gray shorts. He has a backwards hat on, and his clear blue eyes are making my belly do somersaults. But he looks tired, weary even with dark circles under his eyes and a slump to his shoulders. "I asked Ellie to keep an eye on her so I could make some phone calls." Something flashes in his eyes when I say this. I see his jaw tick. He's restraining himself. When he doesn't say anything, I step closer to him and touch his hand. "Maybe Ellie took her on a walk," I offer.

"It's fine, I'll just call her." He pulls his hand away and steps back.

I suck in a breath. "Liam," I urge. My voice is wavering. He looks up but doesn't say anything. This is agony. "Can we hang out tonight? Can we talk? Please. I want to talk to you. About my plans." I sound desperate but I can't find it in myself to care.

Liam shakes his head and closes his eyes like he is fighting an internal battle. "I can't, Sophie," he says.

"O-okay..." I stutter. "So is this it then? We're done?" I can't believe this is happening.

Liam shuffles his feet and looks down uncomfortably before speaking. He pushes his lips together like he's thinking about what to say. "No, no. This isn't it," he pauses. "I had a very urgent side job come up that I have to work on every free moment."

"Oh," is all I can say. I feel wounded anyway. *A side job is more important than talking to me about where we stand?*

Liam reaches out and touches my face, giving me a small half smile. "We'll talk in a few days, okay?"

He doesn't wait for my response. He pecks me on the lips and he's out the door before I can reply.

◯◿

I spent Wednesday in a major funk. Ellie can tell because she has offered to entertain Lucy for me. I don't have it in me to put on a show for anyone. I'm pretty much hiding in my room alternating between mulling over my options and making pro-con lists. How am I supposed to decide what I'm doing with my future if I haven't even seen Liam? I need to see him to know that I am loved and cherished and that he cannot imagine life without me. My pro-con list is split fifty-fifty and that is making it even harder.

Now it's Thursday morning, the Fourth of July. I'm not in any kind of mood to celebrate even though Ellie is cooking up a feast and there are fireworks tonight. I owe an answer to Dr. Stevens and Trevor and I'm no closer to deciding anything. I want to ask for an extension like I would have for a college paper. I know Dr. Stevens would give it to me, but Trevor is a lot like Claire. He'll want to know what I've decided. I plop down on my bed, holding my phone, my fingers hovering over a text to Liam.

> **Me: Hey... can we talk today?**
> **Please.**

He doesn't answer immediately, and I toss my phone aside in frustration. I could clean this room up. There are still boxes in different corners that I need to unpack if I stay. Then there's Leah's boxes of photos behind the door. Leah's box. I groan out loud. *I totally dropped the ball on that.* I get off the bed and walk over to them. Sorting photos would take my mind off the crap swirling around in my head. I lift the first one down off the stack and sit in the middle of the fluffy area rug with it.

I open the box and right on top is a bunch of childhood photos. Leah and Liam at the beach, Leah and Liam playing soccer. Leah with her soccer team, and Leah with her parents holding a trophy. *Okay, this will be easy. And I love old family photos.* I pick up a big pile of loose photos that are in a box within the box and spread them out on the carpet. There are so many. Some are duplicates so I quickly choose the best option of the similar photos and separate them into piles. Then I grab another handful of loose photos and add them to the spread. This is a selection of pictures from a day they were at Sunset Beach. I am sorting and separating when one photo catches my eye and takes my breath away.

I pick it up and examine it closely. It was taken during the golden hour. The subject in the foreground of the photo is Leah looking to be about eight years old with missing front teeth and her arms around a girl of the same age with brown hair and emerald eyes who looks an awful lot like...me. Their lips are purple, and their hair is wet but their missing tooth smiles are big. Around their necks are two identical Cape May diamond necklaces with a mermaid tail charm.

Then something else catches my eye. Playing football behind the two girls are Liam and my brother Simon. The photo background is blurry, as if it were taken in portrait mode today, but it's definitely Simon. My pulse quickens and I feel a chill run through my entire body. I know I had beach friends. We were here every weekend. My parents and their parents drank beers on the beach while we boogie-boarded until dusk. I couldn't remember the names of those friends today if you promised me a million dollars. I just couldn't. Because, eventually we stopped coming and in the end, they were beach friends. There was no easy way to stay in touch back then. I flip the photo over to confirm what I already know. Written on the back of the photo is:

Beach Besties Leah & Sophie

Sunset Beach

1994

I drop the photo and run to the bathroom to splash cold water on my face. We were friends. Liam, Leah, Simon and me... We were friends. I run for my phone and see Liam still hasn't texted me back. I call him. No answer. I call him again. No answer. I need to talk to him. I hammer out a text message.

> **Me: Liam, please call me. It's urgent.**

But I don't have time to wait. I grab the picture and my matching necklace and I run down the steps and into the kitchen where Ellie is cooking food for the party tonight. She turns around and cocks her head with concern.

"Sophie, dear. What's the matter?" She puts the spatula down and comes closer.

"I need to find Liam." I blurt out. "He's not answering my calls. I have to talk to him." I'm almost panicking.

"Okay, okay. Calm down. He's at Robert's office." Ellie says, rubbing my arm.

"But it's the Fourth of July!" I wail, running for the front door and slipping on my sneakers. "I have to go!" I yell. And I run.

Chapter Thirty-Eight

Liam

"Maybe if you turn it vertical and angle it back toward you as you go in backward," Jack suggests. He's standing off to the side while Danny and I struggle to move Sophie's brand new live edge desk into what will hopefully be her new office. I stained the teakwood a light sand color and filled in the center and cracks with blue resin that looks like the ocean. I hope she will love it. I have never built something so quickly.

I told Danny on Monday that I couldn't work all week because I was trying to finish this project, and he actually came over and helped me work on it last night. I have avoided Sophie all week and I saw that she texted that she wants to talk today. I have to get this set up and then call her to come down here.

"Why don't you stop making suggestions and help us, jackass?" Danny snaps at Jack. Jack steps forward and lifts from the side. The table has black steel legs, so it is heavy as shit. It took four of us to get it on my truck and then I had to hope Sophie didn't see me pulling out of the driveway.

"Okay, we're in," I say when we've crossed the threshold. Doc had the office painted a pale gray-blue color that I think resembles the sky just before sunrise over the ocean. He got her a plush tufted gray armchair and a matching chaise lounge for her patients to sit on. There are dark sea blue window sheers on the two windows that look out to the back alleyway and freshly painted white plantation shutters. He hung some local art on the wall and Ellie managed to snag her framed credentials from a box in her room last week when she was over at my house. My favorite is a canvas photograph of Sunset Beach at dusk with sparkling diamonds amongst the pebbles on the shoreline.

I hope the office is enough to make her want to stay. If she doesn't stay, I don't know what I'll do. Maybe Lucy and I could move to Scranton with her, but it would be hard. I have a hard enough time working and managing childcare for her. I have clients here who come back to me for my work again and again. I would be starting completely over, but I would do it for Sophie.

My phone buzzes in my pocket. "She's calling me," I tell them.

"Don't answer it. We're not ready," Danny says, sliding his end of the desk into place so it's even with my end. Jack comes behind it with the armchair.

I hit decline. It rings again a moment later, this time I let it go all the way to voicemail. Sophie follows up that call with a text asking me to call her, it's urgent.

"I think we're good, boys," I say anxiously. "I can't thank you enough for helping," I tell them, walking back out into the waiting room. They get the hint and follow me out.

"Go call your girl," Danny says, slapping me on the back.

I grin. "Wish me luck," and I close the front door behind them.

I walk back into the office that will hopefully be Sophie's and take a final look around. It looks great. If all goes well, I will show her the desk, tell her I love her and that I want her to stay. Then we can go to Ellie's party and tell everyone else. She can tell Doc she's accepting his offer and all will be okay. I take a deep breath and dial her number.

It rings about six times before going to voicemail. I try again and the same thing happens. I try a third time and fire off a text that I'm trying to reach her. She asked me to call her and said it was urgent. What if something happened to Lucy? I rub my hands down my face and crack my knuckles. I'm pacing the room when I hear the front door jingle.

"Liam!" Sophie's voice is frantic. "Liam? Are you here?" Her voice is moving toward the hallway.

I look out the door of her office. Relief fills me when I see her. I can tell by her face that she feels the same. She runs to me and we meet in the hallway.

"Sophie," I rasp, cupping her face. "I have been calling you. You said it was urgent?" I'm searching her face for answers.

"I ran out of the house so fast I must've left my phone." She is breathing heavily. I stroke her jawline, and she gives me the most genuine smile I've seen from her all week. "I have to talk to you."

"I have to talk to you too," I say, grabbing her hand in mine and letting them hang between us.

"You first," She says, biting her lip.

"Come on." I take her hand and walk backwards toward her office. "Close your eyes."

"Okay..." She does as she's asked and lets me lead her the few steps into the room.

"Open them," I tell her excitedly.

Sophie gasps when she sees what we've done with the room. She walks around and looks at every detail, stopping when she gets to the frames with her certificates and awards. Her jaw drops. "How did you—"

"Ellie," I grin.

"That sneak," she giggles.

She walks over to the photo of Sunset Beach and strokes the edge with her fingertips. Then she turns back to me and smiles. "Wow." She walks over to where I am standing in front of the desk. I step aside so she can get a proper look. She walks the length of the desk, running her fingers along the live edge until she's in front of me. She meets my gaze with tears brimming in her green eyes. "You made this for me?" She whispers.

I move to take her hands in mine, prepared to spill my guts, but I then realize she has something in her hand. "What are you holding?" I ask curiously.

She blinks and a tear rolls down her cheek as she hands

me one of the items in her hand. I hold it up, examining it. It's a necklace, almost exactly like Leah's. "I told you I have one just like it," she whispers, batting at another stray tear.

I finger the stone on the mermaid charm and look at it closely. It's the same all right. "And what's the other thing?" I whisper but I think I already know. I swallow a lump forming in my throat.

"It's a picture from the day I got it." She hands it to me, and I look down at it. Suddenly, the memories of that day come rushing back.

We just had dinner at the point and the girls were looking for Cape May diamonds while the boys and the dads threw the football around. The moms took the girls to the gift shop after. Leah wanted the necklace because Sophie was getting it, and she really wanted one too. My mom must've told her to go ask her dad because she ran out in the middle of the football game stomping her feet and crying for it. My dad was mostly ignoring her. A moment later, little Sophie came running out holding two necklaces.

"I bought it for you," she had said and Leah grinned at her. "Friends forever," Sophie said, hugging my sister.

"Okay girls, let me get a picture!" Sophie's mom had called out. "Put on your necklaces and get close together."

A moment frozen in time. Leah and Sophie were beach friends. Simon and I were too.

"Oh my god," I breathe. "We've always known each other."
Sophie was meant for me.

"Simon did say you look familiar," she giggles.

I step closer to her, resting my hand on the back of her neck. "Sophie," I whisper her name, pressing my forehead to hers. "I am so in love with you." And then I kiss her and it's like the first time all over again. Without hesitation, I hastily drop to one knee and take her hands in mine.

I don't have a ring, I didn't think this through, but knowing what I know now, how could I waste any more time? Sophie's face is surprised but not unwilling. I clear my throat, and my voice still comes out hoarse. "Sophie, clearly we were meant to find each other. My life hasn't been the same since you walked into it and left a mark on my heart. I know it will never be the same again, it'll be better than I have ever imagined." Improvising, I reach for the necklace again. "I know it's not a ring, but Sophie, I love you so much. Will you please do me the honor of being my wife?"

She is openly crying now as she puts her hands on my cheeks and strokes my beard. "I love you too." She pulls me up to a stand and kisses me softly, sending warmth through my entire body. "Yes, Liam. I will marry you."

I pull away from the kiss and hold her close to my chest. I close my eyes and breathe her in. "So does this mean you're staying?"

She looks up at me and barks out a laugh. "How could I not?"

Epilogue

Sophie

"Sometimes, good things fall apart, so better things can fall together."

One Year and Some Days Later

I fluff the skirt of my yellow sundress and slide my feet into my brown leather sandals. I give myself one last once over in the mirror, apply my guava lip balm, and toss my hair over my shoulder. It's Ellie's surprise seventieth birthday party today, and I am so excited.

I jog down the steps of my husband's childhood home that I now share with him, to join my little family waiting in the foyer. I already knew I was going to stay when Liam told me he loved me. I knew I was going to stay the second I found the photograph. I wanted a sign and there it was, right there in Leah's box of photographs. It made perfect sense to me at that moment why things with James didn't work out. I was meant to find my way back to Liam. It sounds corny but I believe Leah was looking down and helping us find each other.

Liam and I got married just six months after I moved to Cape May on a rainy Saturday in October. What can I say? When you know, you know. I was worried about the rain because we were having a beach wedding but just before I walked down the aisle, the clouds parted, and a rainbow appeared overhead. Leah...I'm sure of it.

Lucy was our flower girl, and she wore a pale pink halter dress with rosettes on the top and a tulle skirt. I wore a simple lace V-neck gown that dropped low in the back. Liam wore a tan suit with a white shirt and an open collar. Claire stood by my side joined by Ellie. Liam had Doc as his best man because he said Doc never stopped believing in Liam's ability to forgive himself. Danny, Jack, and Miles joined him.

Of course, my family came. Simon was elated and to this day won't stop talking about how he knew who Liam was "the whole time." Liam's parents flew up from Florida and stayed in the house with us. I loved getting to know them. I fully believe seeing Liam heal and fall in love helped to heal them too.

When I reached the huppah, finally standing at Liam's side, I glanced over at his mom, and she was crying. She blew us a kiss and mouthed "thank you" to me. She told me later she was thanking me for saving her son. I don't think I saved him; I think we saved each other. Our wedding was a beautiful day that I will remember forever but our life? Our life is magic.

"Mama!" Lucy shrieks when she sees me. She tries to wiggle out of Liam's arms. She is almost two and a half and is becoming a little spitfire. I take her from Liam, and she puts her hands on my face. "Mama, you look pretty." She strokes my face. Turns out, I did get to be someone's mama after all.

Ellie is still our neighborhood grandma. She and Robert are enjoying retirement together and traveling all over the place. When they're home though, they're babysitting Lucy for us so we can work. Shortly after I told Liam I was staying, we went to Ellie's house where we shared the news with everyone else. I asked Robert if he would be willing to sell his office space to me and he said yes. He still saw patients part-time for the last six months, but now he's fully retired. I'm trying to convince Claire to move down here and work with me. I think I'm getting closer.

Today is a beautiful August day. It's hot but there is a cool morning breeze that is bringing with it the salty smell of the ocean.

We're gathering at a breakfast place downtown that Liam and I bought out for the morning, and Robert will convince her to go out for breakfast for her birthday. We get there early to make sure everything is set up, there are balloon arches and a photo-op area. There is a buffet and a mimosa bar, and everything is decorated in yellow, cream, and champagne colors. It looks beautiful. We're expecting all the Perry Street neighbors, Ellie's church friends and book club and my family even made the trip. As our guests arrive and mingle, I get a text that says they just parked.

"Everybody, they're almost here! Find a hiding spot," I shout. Everyone finds a less than obvious spot to stand or crouch down and the room becomes hushed.

The moment Ellie walks in, the room erupts in chaos as everyone yells, "Surprise!"

Ellie shrieks and her eyes search the room for Liam and me. When she finds us, she points and says, "You got me good!" We laugh and walk over to hug her and Robert. She gives us a big squeeze.

"You have to give Ellie her gift now," Liam nudges me, hoisting Lucy up higher in his arms. As it turns out, Liam and I have been keeping a secret from everyone. I found out earlier this summer that I am pregnant. It was the shock of my life and the last thing I expected but as it turns out, sometimes things really do work out for a reason. I was meant to become a mama... with Liam. Today, I am thirteen weeks along—further than I have ever made it—and we are so excited to share the news.

"What! No gifts," Ellie swats him. "This party is my gift."

I reach into my handbag and pull out a small gold box with a cream-colored ribbon and hand it to her. "Don't worry. I think you'll want this one," I grin.

Ellie gasps as she opens the box to find a square black and white ultrasound photo. The ultrasound tech typed on the photo, "Hi Grandma!" and we just knew we had to save it for Ellie's birthday present. "You? You're pregnant?" she asks, and I see her eyes fill with tears immediately.

My eyes prick with tears as well and then we hug, rocking back and forth. I pull apart from her, sniffle, and wipe my eyes. "That was *the hardest* secret to keep," I exhale.

Liam chimes in, "We know you already act like a grandma to Lucy, but we'd love it if you would officially be grandma to her and this little girl too." He is beaming.

"Girl?" Ellie shrieks, covering her mouth.

I nod through my tears and wipe my eyes.

"We're going to call her Leah Eleanor." Liam wraps his arms around all of us in a triple hug and I know we're making a scene now.

"Now *that's* something to celebrate!" Ellie shouts, pulling away from us. "Everyone! Forget my birthday, Sophie is pregnant!"

The room erupts into cheers and congratulations, and I think I have never been happier.

છૈ

I've learned a lot in the last year. I've learned that you can love someone hard and have them never love you back the way you love them. I've learned that sometimes you have to pick yourself up and carry on even when it's the hardest thing you've ever had to do. I've learned to trust the timing of my life and to believe in fate. Things can fall to pieces, but sometimes you have to let them fall apart so better things can fall together. The tides may change but one morning you will wake up and just know it's going to be a good day, without having prayed for it the night before. That's worth waiting for, even if it takes thirty years to find it.

Acknowledgements

I have always been a writer and if you ask my best friend, I told her the day we met seven years ago that I would write a book someday. Growing up, I was the introverted girl, hiding out in my room, writing short stories in spiral notebooks and then forcing my parents to listen while I read them aloud. In middle school, I graduated to a computer, using up all of the ink to print out my stories.

In the seventh grade, my English teacher told me I should consider being a writer when I grew up. Whether she knew it or not, her words stuck with me, prompting me to earn a degree in literature. But writing the book fell by the wayside until my 39th year. Feeling lost in the throes of motherhood and familial responsibilities and searching for personal fulfillment, I asked the universe to give me a sign. *What should I be doing with my life?*

The answer came quickly when one morning I woke up, sat down at my computer and *Changing Tides* version one was born. It was a realization of a dream that lay dormant inside me for years. There are so many people who helped make this dream a reality. First, my agent, Katie Monson. Thank you for taking a chance on me and seeing through the murk of that first version. You saw the story through the words, and I'll forever be grateful for your partnership and friendship. You changed my life. To everyone else at SBR Media, you are all are rockstars! I'm so grateful to be a part of this agency.

Meredith Wild, my amazing editor, this book would not be what it is without your guidance and expertise. You made it shine, and your vision for the book and for Liam's character turned this book into something far better than I could have done myself. I count myself lucky to have found a home with Page & Vine. To the rest of the team, Haley Boudreaux, Kelly Kramer, Amber Renee, Victoria Cardoso, and Jordyn Wentworth – you are all so awesome! Each of your contributions made this book what it is, and I couldn't be more thrilled to work with this wonderful group of professional book lovers.

To Erica Ouimet – my soul sister. Thank you for reminding me to write a book! Thank you for reading the very first chapter of the very first version and every chapter after that. Our evening walks to talk through plot lines, your constant reassurance, and belief in me and this seemingly impossible dream have kept me going. I will forever be grateful for you, your friendship, and your sisterhood. I don't know what I did to deserve you in my life, but I will never take you for granted and I love you so much.

To Oana Bell, from our chance meeting on the place that used to be Twitter, to becoming critique partners and friends, you are my writing soulmate. Thank you for talking me through tough plot points, imposter syndrome, and the querying trenches. I'm forever grateful for that first DM and everything that came after. When you first read *Changing Tides*, you called it a *soul book*. That belief you had in the book and in me got me through some very tough months, as I questioned everything I was doing. It's an honor to be your critique partner and friend. Thank you for your feedback and encouragement throughout the past year and beyond. It was invaluable to me, and I will always be grateful.

To my other early readers who are all great friends—Christen Nascimento, Nicole Dingler, Kristin Seymour, Mom, Sara Lawless, Pina Friedman—thank you for reading the earliest, messiest version of this book and loving it anyway. You all gave me the confidence to keep going. And to my later readers and author friends, Rosie Potter, Megan Anderson, and Lily Parker, I am so grateful for your encouragement, feedback, and suggestions, but most importantly, your friendship.

Christy Schillig, your guidance throughout the querying and

publishing process has been invaluable to me. You only knew me as a friend of a friend, and you still took me under your wing. I'm honored to call you a mentor and a friend. Thank you for everything.

To my family: my parents who believed I could do this and still read it despite my warning about the spicy chapters. To my mom, who babysat for endless hours so I could meet my deadlines–eight hours with Gemma Rose is no easy feat! To my dad, for telling everyone he knows that I wrote a book and it's going to be published. You taught me so much about life and you molded me to be the person I am. I love you both so much.

To my three amazing kiddos, who have often said they wished I was still a stay-at-home mom because "you're so busy now!" Thank you for putting up with mommy working so much and for being proud enough of me to tell anyone who would listen that your mom is an author. I'm so proud of you, too.

To my husband, Kevin, who thought writing a book was a fun little hobby for me, until it wasn't. Your selfless, unconditional love is a daily inspiration to me. You are my rock, my everything. I wouldn't be the person I am without you today, and I still can't believe you're mine. Thank you for seeing me. Thank you for loving me at my worst and celebrating with me at my best. Thank you for the beautiful life you have given us and for picking up the slack when I was holed up in the office working endlessly to refine this manuscript. There's a little piece of you in every book-boyfriend I write, and I am lucky enough to call the OG my husband. I will love you until the end of time.

And lastly, to you Dear Reader, for picking up this book by an unknown debut author and giving it a chance. I never thought I'd be so lucky to have people holding my book in their hands and reading my words.

I had a dream to hold my book by my 40th year and here I am. From the bottom of my heart, thank you, thank you, thank you, to every single one of you who believed in me when I didn't always believe in myself. You have all changed my life for the better.

About the Author

Linny Mack grew up a voracious reader and writer. She spent her days of adolescence up in her room writing her own stories and cutting her characters out of the Delia's catalog. Now, Linny is a debut author of contemporary romance. When she isn't writing your next book boyfriend, she is spending time with her real-life romantic hero and their three children in New Jersey.

To learn more, visit: www.linnymack.com

LINNY MACK

Chasing Stars

A CAPE MAY NOVEL

Chasing Stars
Available September 16, 2025

Miles Corbin lives his life on his own terms. A successful real estate agent by day, and a surfer Casanova by night, Miles lives every day like it's his last. Scarred by his recent divorce, Miles prefers to keep love at arm's length. He'd much rather chase thrills in the ocean over risking love again. That is until Jenna Rossi walks into his life.

When Jenna Rossi inherits her family's neglected beach house in Cape May, New Jersey, she plans to sell it quickly and move on with her life. But charming property manager Miles Corbin has other ideas. As he helps her navigate necessary repairs, he also becomes her personal tour guide through the tranquil beach town's romantic charm, determined to give her even more reasons to stay.

As their new friendship blossoms, deeper feelings begin to take root. Miles hasn't opened his heart again since his divorce, but something about Jenna makes him want to take a chance. Jenna swears she doesn't need a white knight, nor does she want one, but Miles' thoughtfulness and guidance has her dropping her guard and falling hard.

But just when they're settling into the idea of forever, a secret from the past threatens to tear them apart for good—one that connects them in ways neither could have imagined.

STORIES WITH IMPACT